I0606493

HORROR CARNIVAL

EDITED BY
ANTHONY GIANGREGORIO

**NOW AVAILABLE AND COMING SOON
FROM
OPEN CASKET PRESS**

RATS
ZOMBIE BUFFET
BIGFOOT TALES
DECAY: A ZOMBIE STORY
CREATURE FEATURE
DEAD CHRISTMAS
HORROR TALES AND TERRIFYING STORIES
2012 ZOMBIE WALL CALENDAR
HOLLOW POINT: A ZOMBIE NOVEL
WARRIORS OF THE APOCALYPSE: BOOK 1

HORROR CARNIVAL

Copyright © 2011 Open Casket Press
ISBN Softcover ISBN 13: 978-1-61199-038-6   ISBN 10: 1-611990-38-6
All stories contained in this book have been published with permission from the authors. All rights reserved.
Open Casket Press is an imprint of Living Dead Press.
ww.livingdeadpress.com
No part of this book may be reproduced or transmitted in any form or by any means, electronic or mechanical, including photocopying, recording, or by any information storage and retrieval system, without permission in writing from the copyright owner.
This is a work of fiction. Names, characters, places and incidents either are the product of the author's imagination or are used fictitiously, and any resemblance to any actual persons, living or dead, events, or locales is entirely coincidental. This book was printed in the United States of America.
For more info on obtaining additional copies of this book, contact:
www.opencasketpress.com   Cover art by Jason Bailey

Table of Contents

THE MAD HATTER

JONATHAN TEMPLAR

DJ had given Ryan and Alise the keys to the apartment, and had told them they could stay for as long as they wanted, but there were certain rules he needed them to follow — *to the letter*.

If they were going to do any business of their own, they had to do it elsewhere, away from the apartment. DJ had worked hard to cover all his bases, he owned half a dozen properties dotted around the city and none of them were in his name, no one would ever know they were his unless they had reason to look very closely at the deeds and the complicated chain of ownership he'd constructed. And he was very keen that *no one* looked too closely.

Ryan and Alise were strictly small time, a little bit of opportunist thieving, some dealing now and then, but nothing that had gotten them noticed. They were small fry, not even twenty years old, with no future to look forward to and a past to forget.

Ryan knew DJ liked them though—liked Alise more, Ryan reckoned—and he was happy to give them a roof over their heads with no rent required on the understanding that he might ask them for the odd favor now and again.

The apartment was on the fourth floor of seven, forty odd apartments in total on the block, maybe a dozen still occupied. The others were empty and boarded with steel shutters or had been burnt out years ago by vandals for the sake of something to do on a Saturday night.

It had a balcony that flooded when it rained with a view over the rest of the estate. There was no central heating but there was an electric fire, and DJ had rigged it so that they bypassed the electricity meter, stealing their power from someone else. There were no beds, just a couple of mattresses on the floor, and some plastic garden furniture was in front of the old analogue TV that was only good for watching DVDs on.

It was as fine a home as Ryan or Alise had ever lived in.

They hadn't seen DJ in over a week, since they'd first moved in. He was all over the city doing business. They had eaten dinner from Styrofoam containers, mostly pizza and burgers from the takeaway van on the corner. Money was running a bit low but Alise would give the man who owned the van a blow job in exchange for a meal. The guy had suggested that maybe if she did a little extra, he might be able to throw a few more things their way. Alise wasn't too keen; he smelt of grease and said weird things when he orgasmed. Ryan felt bad enough about the transaction already and he didn't think he could handle it if there was worse, but they knew they had the option. It was *always* an option, for Ryan as well as Alise.

When there was nothing else left to sell, they always had themselves.

"It's what DJ's gonna tell us anyway," Alise had said as they lay on a mattress in the dark, the lights of the estate giving the room a yellow hue that seemed as though the air itself was sick.

Ryan inhaled his joint, thinking, not thinking.

"You've seen the stuff he's got on DVD over there," she waved her hand at the pile of discs surrounding the old TV, a tottering pile of Steven Seagal, Ultimate Wrestling and porn. Some of the porn was wrapped in homemade sleeves, stuff that had been run off on a PC or photocopied. They both knew what DJ sold in the market or through the seedy little sex shops that hid themselves away behind black-painted windows somewhere off Main Street. He used this apartment to film most of it.

"It doesn't have to come to that, 'Lise. I've got some other projects."

"You've got nothing," she said, but without any cruelty. It was just a fact.

"I have too. Ronnie's coming around later. We've got some things to work out. He might give us some easy money. We could get out of this dump, go back over the river."

"You mean you're gonna go thieving again?"

"Well, I'm not going to be doing any investment banking in the near future, am I?"

Ronnie was with them within the hour.

Alise hated Ronnie. He had a face like an acne-splattered rat; thin with a long nose and a mouth that always seemed to be giving a sly half smile. She thought maybe his teeth were too big to keep his lips closed over them. He only talked to Ryan; never acknowledged her.

"So I got a thing, if you're interested."

"Tell me about the 'thing.' I'll tell you if I'm interested."

"It'll piss DJ off."

"DJ's been good to us," Alise said.

Ronnie ignored her as usual and just leered at Ryan. "You know why DJ's being nice to you, don't you? He'll let you stay here for as long as you like, but he'll be back soon with a few requests, and he can be very persuasive. And you won't want to end up back on the street now, eh?"

"I'll deal with that if it happens."

"Don't be an idiot, Ryan. He's let you stay here so you'll get nice and cozy, get used to having a roof over your head with winter coming. He knows you don't want to go back home, knows your brother will kill you if you go anywhere near your mom after what you did. So he'll tell you that you can stay here for as long as you want, might even get you a bit of furniture, make the place comfortable. Only then he'll turn up one day with half a dozen of his 'special' mates, and your girlfriend here will be the one paying the rent."

Now Ronnie did turn to Alise, turning an imaginary camera on her. "Smile for the camera, sweetheart," he said with a grin.

"Piss off," Alise hissed.

"That isn't gonna happen, Ronnie," Ryan said. "I'm not gonna let it."

"Then why don't I tell you what I've got in mind."

And he did.

The apartment next door was occupied and it was secure in a way that few on the block were or ever had been. There was no glass panel on the front door, just sheer reinforced wood. There were at least three deadbolts securing it. They could be heard being pulled back when the man who lived there went out, as he very occasionally did. There was no access from the balcony; there was a nest of barbed wire lining the balcony railing and the wall on the side that adjoined DJ's apartment.

Ronnie didn't know who lived there; said that he'd asked DJ once and DJ didn't seem to know either, or didn't care. Ronnie figured if it was someone worth knowing, then DJ would.

But Ronnie also figured that some people liked to stay under the radar, liked to keep their business quiet. He'd seen the man who lived there, and he looked wealthy. He wore quality gear: a long leather coat that nearly reached his ankles and a wide brimmed hat that hid his entire head. He looked like a Don from a mafia movie. Someone who dressed like that but lived somewhere like this, someone who made sure his apartment was secured like a safe house, they had to be dealing something worth taking.

"You want to rob the next door neighbor?" Ronnie nodded his head with enthusiasm to make his point.

"DJ would kill you," Ryan said. "The first thing he said to us was not to do anything that would bring the law within half a mile of this place, and you want them on his doorstep? You're mental."

"Oh come on, screw DJ!" Ronnie said. "He just pretends like he's your best mate, like he'd do anything for you, but the only person DJ has any interest in is DJ. Him and the cash in his pocket."

"Shit!" Ryan rubbed his head in the hope that the idea would go away.

"Come on, Ryan, you know it makes sense. If you stay here, your girl's gonna be screwing every gorilla DJ can line up. You'll be lucky if she can still walk to the toilet when they're done with her. You want that?"

"No," Ryan said quietly. "Look, tell me what your plan is and I'll think about it."

"No thinking about it, Ryan. We go today. DJ's up north on a job and he won't be back for days. No messin' around. We go in as soon as the creepy bastard next door goes out."

"*How* do we get in?"

Ronnie slapped a palm against the wall, and it shook with the impact. "We go though here."

Of course Ryan didn't really have any choice.

Ronnie had a couple of heavy duty mallets in his car that he'd 'borrowed' from his brother who worked in construction. The same mallets would probably be tearing down all the walls in this hell hole of an estate once the last few tenants had been relocated and DJ and his kind had pocketed some astronomical fee for the property they'd somehow managed to acquire.

The mallets were heavy, the kind of heavy that felt good in Ryan's hands, gave him the confidence that he could unleash some serious damage.

So they waited, and smoked the apartment into a yellow haze of tobacco fumes until they heard the sound of the neighbor leaving. After bolting the three locks on his door, his footsteps faded.

Ryan and Ronnie were suddenly a flurry of action, eager to get at the wall. Ronnie was cooked, had been since he'd arrived. He had a twitchy edginess that was always close to exploding into violence. Ryan had been dwelling on Ronnie's little talk about DJ, had chewed over his festering resentment, the anger he'd become adept at hiding as he tried to accept the inevitable consequences of DJ's friendship.

Ronnie was pumped up when he started at the wall, but Ryan was summoning months of repressed rage.

Their side of the wall gave easily. It was hollow between the apartments; no insulation required for property built as cheaply as the estate had been. The air was thick with the dust. Ryan and Ronnie breathed in dry plaster, coughing it up. They pulled as much away from the wall as they could, making a large hole, then started on the neighbor's wall, keeping their blows low so they could make a chasm easy to crawl through rather than having to climb up and over, just in case they had to get out in a hurry.

They broke through quickly, pulling old plaster and wood slats away in chunks. Minutes later, they were through.

Ronnie dropped his mallet and rubbed his bony hands. "Let's go shopping," he grinned. He crawled through the gap first, pushing aside dangling flaps of wallpaper and plaster. Ryan followed.

"I'm coming with you," Alise said.

"No you're not," Ronnie called back.

"I'm not staying in here. If DJ comes back I'd rather be in there with you two than have to deal with him."

"Fair enough. Another pair of hands will be good. We can get the stuff out more quickly that way," Ryan agreed.

Ronnie hissed through his teeth, something he'd seen tougher, more intimidating people do to great effect but it made him look like as if he'd just failed to whistle. Alise followed Ryan through the hole; all three of them coated in a layer of dust that made them appear like underfed ghosts.

"Cold in here," Alise said, hugging her shoulders. Her arms were exposed and had broken out in goosebumps.

It was. It was quiet, too, or perhaps that wasn't the right word. It was *still*. There was no noticeable breeze, but the air was far colder than it had been on the other side of the wall. The corridor was dark, and the walls were painted a deep blue or a black that was a stark contrast to the light pastel wallpaper in DJ's apartment. It made the walls look closer together, the ceiling lower. There was no carpet on the floor and the surface was smooth, as if it was tiled. It was hard to tell. A long strip of fluorescent lighting ran along the center of the ceiling, giving off a dull light that the walls seemed to swallow. A section further down the corridor flickered erratically and buzzed.

Ryan shivered. "He can't have a factory in here, it'd be hotter than this, wouldn't it?"

Ronnie scratched his head. "Dunno. Weird, though Look, you two go down that way to the bedrooms, see what's there. I'm gonna go the kitchen. Grab anything you think might be worth selling and dump it back through the hole."

They went their separate ways. It was odd, Ryan thought. He watched Ronnie heading up the short corridor, then he realized that it wasn't short, not as short as it should be, surely. It was next door to DJs and these apartments were all built the same, but this corridor looked longer. The front door looked further away than it should. For a brief moment, he was tempted to put his head back into the hole and look through to the more familiar environment of DJ's place, then compare the two just to put his mind at ease. But he figured it was just the decor, the different coloring made it unfamiliar.

He led Alise to their left; the turn in the corridor that should lead to two recessed doors, what should have been two double bedrooms. There were no doors. Instead there was another corridor, the same dark color as the one they'd just left, but longer, stretching to a bare wall perhaps thirty feet away.

"That's weird," Alise said, biting her lip.

"It's more than weird, 'Lise, it's messed up. What's this guy been up to in here? He must have built into the apartment at the back."

"Let's have a look," Alise said, and strode confidently down the corridor. There were no doors on either side, no windows, and no pictures. Just bare walls.

They reached the end of the corridor, turned the corner, and another corridor faced them, as long and featureless as the one they had just traversed.

"This isn't right," Alise said.

"He must have bought the apartment behind, too. *Must have.* Knocked into it, taken down the walls."

"Let's go back." Alise pushed past him. Ryan had the impulse to go on, to find out what was at the end of this corridor, to find a marker that would allow this apartment to make some kind of sense. But Alise's instincts were right, it was better to leave.

They turned back to the corridor into which they had first walked. Only it wasn't. It was another long empty run of blue walls and cold tiles. The hole in the wall wasn't there, just smooth surface all the way along.

"What the hell's going on?"

"I don't like this Ryan. Where's the hole?"

"Ronnie?" Ryan bellowed. There was no answer. "Ronnie!" he called even louder.

"Where's he gone? Is he putting us on? Is this something him and DJ have set up?" Alise asked, a heartbeat away from panic.

That was a good idea, Ryan thought. Perhaps this was a set up. It would explain why Ronnie was so happy to just screw DJ over. DJ must have been worth a lot to Ronnie, the income he helped provide and the drugs he peddled to his dealers. For Ronnie to betray him, well, Ryan had put it down to the coke, the edgy fidgeting that Ronnie couldn't hide, the tell tale signs of someone whose addiction was starting to take control of them.

But this would make sense as well, if Ronnie had put some cameras in here somewhere, had made some sort of weird set that they would unknowingly 'perform' on. Were a bunch of DJs friends going to jump at them from around a corner, had they found themselves plunging head first into some sick porno set up just when they thought they were avoiding it?

If DJ thought they had betrayed him, he would be *pissed*.

Ryan's fists were clenched. He was ready for it. He took Alise's hand and led her roughly to the next corner. When they turned it, he was ready for them, ready to be pounced on, had convinced himself they'd be there waiting for him. They weren't. It was just another corridor.

"Ronnie!" he shouted, angry now, near panic.

Alise clutched him. "Where do you think he went?"

Ryan shrugged. "There must be a door here somewhere." He hurried down the corridor, Alise scampering after him. Another empty corridor led away to the right. They ran down that one, and it led to another, then another to their left.

They stopped.

"This can't be happening," Alise said. "We've come too far along; we'd be past the front door by now. There's nothing out there, just the walkway and the balcony. There's no way this is possible, Ryan." She was really biting her lips now, and had started twirling her dark hair with nervous fingers.

"They want us to panic," Ryan said.

"Who does?"

"DJ and Ronnie; who do you think? This is a set up, something they've planned." He looked up at the ceiling. "You think I don't see it, you pair of assholes?" He was shouting now, although his voice seemed to go nowhere. "You think we're stupid? That we're going to just fall for it. Well, screw you, both of you. I'm gonna find you and I'm gonna mess you up."

From somewhere that might have been the other side of the wall or the other side of the world, a door banged closed.

"There they are!" Ryan yelled with triumph and ran down the corridor. Alise went after him, calling his name. He weaved through what was now a maze, to the left then the right, all the corridors identical, all featureless. There was no further sound.

Ryan finally stopped. "Come on, I know what you're up to, just give it up," he said to no one.

Alise caught up, her breath still a long way behind. "Ryan, stop it, you aren't helping."

"I heard them, 'Lise. They're down here somewhere. I'm gonna break their fucking heads in when I find them."

"No, Ryan, this isn't right. Wherever we are, it isn't right. What if that bang was the guy who lives here coming home?"

"There is no guy living here, you stupid cow. Nobody lives here."

Alise grabbed his arm. "But what if someone does live here, Ryan? *What if they do?*"

Ryan was trying hard to focus on DJ and Ronnie, telling himself that they were to blame for this trap or whatever it was. He was trying hard not to listen to the other voices whispering in his ear, the ones that told him differently.

"Shut up," he hissed at Alise.

And then Ronnie screamed. It was from ahead, around the next corner, somewhere close. It was a scream that would be impossible to fake.

"That was Ronnie!" Ryan headed off. Alise tried to stop him but failed.

They turned the corner, Ryan first. Ronnie was at the other end, staring to his left, down another corridor they couldn't see. He was holding one arm at the elbow and his mouth was open and drooling in fear.

"Ronnie!" Ryan shouted.

Ronnie's head snapped around, his eyes alight with hope at the sight of them.

"Help me!" he screamed in idiot terror. "Keep him the hell away from me!" He cast a glance back down the other corridor, gave a little whimper at what he saw, then rushed toward Ryan and Alise.

Halfway down the corridor, Ronnie simply…*exploded.*

He burst like a balloon of flesh popped with a pin, his blood spraying the walls and the dark tiles. Pieces of him, none bigger than a tennis ball, slapped the floor as if it were raining meat. In an instant, Ronnie transformed from a human being into organic carnage, a fleshy, gristle-spiked mess that coated the corridor and dripped from the ceiling.

Ryan and Alise stood with open-mouthed, shock-frozen faces that were splattered with the gore of the man who had led them into this place. It was only then, with the mist of Ronnie's blood in the air, that Ryan could see what Ronnie had run into, the mesh of wire so thin it was almost transparent, like a sharp spider's web designed not to catch prey but to slice it. It had been invisible before Ronnie had hit it and it was only his blood that made the wire mesh appear.

This wasn't a game. And if it was a trap, it was not one that DJ or Ronnie had conceived.

Alise made some noise, an attempt to articulate something, but her brain was still estranged from her mouth, still trying in vain to process what it had just experienced.

At the end of the corridor from which Ronnie had run, *someone* appeared, darker than the walls around him, colder than the chill air.

Ryan grabbed Alise and pulled her back the other way, around the corner, down the way they had come.

"Don't run, Ryan, don't run," she whimpered. But it was all right, he thought but couldn't say, we've been this way already, there wasn't any wire.

He turned to his left at the end of the hall, and then he knew it was wrong, that it should be the other way, that it wasn't the way they had come. The corridors were changing around them, left became right and right become left and nothing was certain; everything changed as soon as he stopped looking at it.

And then there was a door. The first he'd seen since crawling into this nightmare. Ryan didn't hesitate; he ran to it and pulled it open, using a metal handle like on a great big freezer. The door opened slowly, with difficulty, it was heavy and thick. Ryan pushed Alise inside and slammed it closed behind him. There was no lock, but he put his back against it, hoping his weight would be a strong enough barrier.

Alise just stood there, with blood dotting over her face and her clothes, her hands at her side.

"We're going to get out of here," Ryan said.

She shook her head. "No, we're not."

"Yes we are. We're gonna get back to the apartment. The hole in the wall is around here somewhere; we've just got to find it."

"We went down the rabbit hole," Alise said and giggled. The giggle worried Ryan. It wasn't a noise he'd ever heard her make before. "We went down the rabbit hole and there's no way back up, no way back up, no way back up, no way…"

He slapped her.

Her head snapped back and her hair flew out and she stopped talking. Then she was silent, and that was even worse.

"Get a grip, will you?" he said. "We're gonna die if we can't get out of here. Whoever owns this place is a freaking lunatic, Alise, and he's in here somewhere."

Alise sobbed. "Did you see him?"

"No. No I ran before I could. I just got a glimpse of him. Did you?"

She chewed her lip again.

"Did you see him, 'Lise?"

"He's the Mad Hatter, Ryan. We're lost down the rabbit hole and he's the Mad Hatter."

"For God's sake!" Ryan shouted and hit himself this time, slapped his forehead as hard as he could, hard enough that his vision swam.

Ryan moved away from the door. The room they were in was empty, but there was another door facing him. He opened it. Beyond was an identical room and another identical door. He opened that one as well. There were three more rooms after that and they carried on through. Then there was a different door, a wooden one.

Then they were finally somewhere different.

Ryan had once spent two Saturday afternoons working in a butcher's shop. He'd quit shortly after that. He always quit a job sooner or later, but the memory of those miserable afternoons rushed back to the forefront of his mind as soon as he went into the room.

It was the smell, the underlying scent of blood spilled and meat sliced; a smell that got under your fingers and wouldn't go away. Not the smell of meat cooking, one that could make his mouth water and his stomach call out for feeding, this was the smell of meat *spoiling*, of the decay and purification that came with death. It was the smell of blood spilt and left to fester as a sticky pool of maggot food, the smell of flies feasting on dead flesh.

They both recoiled. Alise retched and almost vomited. Ryan just held his hand over his mouth and tried not to breathe in.

There were tables in the middle of the room, three of them, metallic but dulled with age. The flat surfaces were dirty, stained with what could have been rust, what Ryan hoped was rust, but was almost certainly dried blood. Underneath were wire trays, and on the trays lay instruments, as ill-maintained as the table itself and just as gore-splattered. The instruments were like nothing Ryan had seen even at the butcher's shop; jagged edges and sharp blades intended for obscene purposes. On the frame of each of the tables were shackles that would have been used to secure people to the tables.

Ryan took Alise by the hand and led her past the tables. He saw that there were shelves on the far wall, wooden shelves from ceiling to floor, and on them were bottles, or jars. They were all full of a grim yellow liquid. Things floated inside them. Pieces of things.

"What is this place, Ryan?"

"Don't look," Ryan told her. She didn't need telling, and put her face into his shoulder as they approached yet another door. Its handle was black and round, old fashioned. They passed through into another empty room, but this time there were two doors, one opposite and one on the wall to their left.

"Which way?" Alise asked.

"What do you reckon; shall we keep going this way?" He pointed to the one ahead. Alise shrugged, it didn't matter either way. Ryan made the choice, reached out to the door, and put his hand on the knob.

The other door flung open suddenly and a dark figure, tall, just a shadow, reached through, and with arms too long for his body, snatched Alise. She was pulled through before she had time to scream. The door slammed closed behind them.

"Alise!" Ryan leapt at the door and pulled it back open. Beyond was just another empty room, another door facing him, but no sign of Alise.

He ran to the next door, adrenaline pumping. There was no time to be scared yet. It opened into another empty room. He opened the next door, another empty room. And another, and another.

From somewhere distant, he heard a shrill scream. The scream broke into a moaning, sobbing wail that slowly faded away to nothing.

"Alise!" he howled. But of course she didn't answer.

Ryan kept going, losing count of the doorways, the same loose black doorknob each time. Finally, he found himself back in the abattoir. The metal tables were in front of him again, but he saw that the one closest to him had moved away from the other two since he'd last been in here, that the clasps had moved down. He could see the surface on one of the tables was slick with newly spilt blood, smeared across it like black paint in the cold light.

Ryan staggered to it and ran a finger through the blood. Wet. Fresh. *Warm*. His attention was caught by a jar that now faced him on a shelf, directly before him as if placed there so it would be the first thing he saw when his eyes shifted to the shelves. A large jar with frothing liquid inside it, and on the front of the glass was a label stuck haphazardly across, the word *ALISE* written upon it by a finger that had been dipped in blood.

Ryan went back through the door he'd just passed through. He had to leave the room, feeling sick, a kind of sickness that was new to him, a sickness of grief perhaps, or more likely despair.

"Alise," he whispered, his back to the wall. He realized he was back in a corridor, not the endless parade of doorways and empty rooms. It felt almost like a relief. The hole in the wall was in a corridor somewhere… *Somewhere.* He let out a bark laughter at that, then staggered off, aimlessly. He turned the first corner and Alise was on the floor in front of him, propped up against a plain wall, her arms hugging her belly.

"'Lise?" he whispered cautiously.

She turned to him. Her eyes were full of hideous knowledge, as though she had lived ten years since he'd last seen her five minutes ago, and in those years they had seen things he could barely contemplate.

"Ryan," she said in a cracked and broken voice. She was shaking fitfully.

"I'm here, 'Lise, I'm here." He took hold of her, and she was cold, icy cold. And wet. He lifted up a hand and saw it was coated with her blood.

"Oh, he hurt me, Ryan. He hurt me so much. He did things to me. He made me watch while he took bits out of me. So many bits. All gone now. All gone."

"It's all right now, 'Lise. I've got you." Ryan knew that he was stepping away from her even if his words insisted otherwise.

"He did things to me," she croaked and curled up into a ball, warmed by a puddle of her own blood.

Ryan stood up and saw the man who owned the apartment standing halfway down the corridor. He *was* the Mad Hatter; he understood what Alise meant now. He had a hat on his head that had the widest brim he'd ever seen. It seemed to touch both sides of the corridor. He was wearing a dark coat, long, down to his feet. He was almost as Ronnie had described him, but Ronnie had only got glimpses, Ronnie hadn't seen him for what he really was. Ryan felt shivers of recognition dancing through him.

It wasn't a hat after all. It wasn't a coat.

Hands that weren't hands stretched out, both of them gripping sharp things that dripped with remnants of Alise.

Ryan turned and ran in terror, no thought for spiderweb traps or if there was anything left saving of his girlfriend. He just ran down corridor after corridor, turning whichever way the corners led him, and all he could hear above the blood pumping through his body was the harsh scrape of the Mad Hatter's sharp things as he dragged them along the walls in pursuit.

And then miraculously, Ryan found the hole. It was there in the wall where it had always been, plaster and wood scattered over the floor in front of it, a puddle of dust and debris on the tiles. Ryan whimpered in his throat like a child on Christmas morning who had found just what he wanted under the tree. He fell to his knees, and scampered through the hole desperately, expecting at each second to feel the grip of the Mad Hatter's not-quite-hands on him, pulling him back into the maze and a slow lingering death.

But the Mad Hatter didn't reach him. He was back in DJs apartment, back in the world of pastel wallpaper and dirty mattresses, DVDs and fast food containers left scattered on the floor. Ryan blubbered and nearly wet himself with a sense of aching relief that nothing in his life had ever come close to matching. He had gotten home, he had escaped. In those few moments, he didn't spare a thought for Ronnie or Alise. He was overcome with his own survival.

Ryan needed to get out of the apartment, needed to see the sky, to remind himself that there was still civilization out there, that he had escaped from whatever terrible world he'd stumbled into.

He needed to keep moving, keep running away.

He rushed to the door, flung it open to let the world in.

The Mad Hatter stood on the doorstep with his arms spread wide.

He enveloped Ryan before he could struggle, and inside that long coat there was a darkness that ran deep, a darkness full of the screaming faces of a thousand victims.

They pulled Ryan down to be with them, to share their suffering. Alise was there, and Ronnie. They welcomed him home.

The last sound Ryan heard were the deadbolts being pulled shut on the Mad Hatter's door.

Then there was only pain.

THE AUCTION

MATT KURTZ

Mr. Black, the auctioneer, stood onstage in front of the audience of nearly a dozen, all seated on cushioned chairs and dressed in what the local bumpkins might refer to as 'their Sunday best.'

The crowd consisted of people from all over the country, with lots of money and a particularly acquired taste.

Over Black's shoulder, a white canvas curtain stretched the width of the barn, making the place look more like a makeshift community theater than a private auction house. A photograph of the lot currently on the block—an industrial kitchen set containing state-of-the-art blenders, ovens, meat smokers, stoves, pots, pans, Crock pots, and chest freezers—was projected on the thick canvas.

Standing behind a wood podium, Black clutched a gavel in one hand and a stack of index cards in the other. The setting was so intimate there was no need for a microphone to amplify his voice. His eyes shifted between a portly, elderly gentleman wearing thick, coke-bottle glasses and a young, thin fellow with a crooked, hooked nose. The two remaining bidders were locked in battle over the kitchen lot.

The younger fellow—currently—held the highest bid.

"Do I hear twenty-five?" Black asked the crowd, but might as well have been pointing directly at the spectacled gentleman.

Specs was still debating whether to counter-bid. He had already paid a small fortune on the previous lot—gently pre-owned items from a slaughterhouse—but it was money well spent. He'd put to good use his newly acquired instruments, replacing his existing ones, and in turn, become a much more efficient butcher.

Beak, his hooked nose competitor, wanted the kitchen stuff. He yielded to the older gentleman's final bid on the slaughterhouse lot, granting him victory. Out of all its cutlery, meat hooks, pulley systems, bleeding bins, and sledgehammers, the only thing of any interest to Beak was the cartridge-fired captive bolt pistol—a brutal tool used to stun cattle before their eventual slaughter. But even that wasn't much of a loss, considering Beak had a custom-built contraption that probably worked better than the decades-old pistol. His current instruments used for livestock butchery were fine as they were. He had only been interested in winning the lot to resell it for a tidy profit, since not all in his industry were privy to such untraceable items sold at the auction.

"Then twenty it is," Mr. Black said. "Going once…"

Specs glanced up at the picture projected on the canvas behind the auctioneer's head…at all those heavy duty industrial kitchen appliances. It was good quality stuff and would undoubtedly compliment his slaughterhouse winnings. If he could score the highest bid, then all he would need was some quality livestock and he'd be back in business, doing what he did best.

"Going twice…"

Specs raised his pudgy hand high in the air.

"Twenty-five," Black said, pointing at Specs.

Beak bit into his lower lip and tasted the blood that ran over his tongue.

"Do I hear thirty?"

Beak stared at the projected photograph. A win on the culinary lot was essential. Unlike the slaughtering lot, he *really* needed to replace his kitchen items, and what was currently on the block was perfect for his intended remodeling job.

"Then twenty-five it is, folks. Going once…"

Beak ran the numbers in his head to make sure he'd brought enough cash for the counter bid.

"Going twice…"

Beak inhaled sharply and held his hand high.

"Thirty," Black pointed at him. "Thirty thousand."

Specs grimaced from the loss.

"Do I hear thirty-five?"

The canvas curtain onstage rustled, stealing the crowd's attention from the auction. All on the floor focused on the wall of cloth behind Mr. Black. The simple swaying of the canvas seemed to bring the reserved crowd to life. Some rose slightly from their seats in anticipation of the next item on the block: the livestock.

"Then thirty it is. Thirty going once…"

Hoping to get a glimpse at the quality of meat being herded onstage behind the curtain, the crowd ignored Black. After all, most only came for the final lot of the evening. They knew it would be exquisite and would allow a much welcome break from having to hunt the US Prime themselves.

"Going twice…"

Beak's focus returned to the man onstage. Had he already won the lot? Was the kitchen lot his?

Mr. Black cleared his throat, hoping the gesture would regain the crowd's attention. "And…"

Beak noticed Specs' distraction and smiled. He knew the old man's thoughts had already moved on to the next lot. "C'mon…c'mon…ya stupid bastard. Say it!" Beak hissed at the auctioneer under his breath.

"And…" Black tapped the gavel on the wood podium and pointed at Beak. "Sold to the young gentleman for thirty thousand dollars!"

"Yes!" Beak yelled, clenching his fist in the air. The victory was bittersweet since no one else noticed that the particular auction had ended. Not even his fiercest competitor of the evening: the fat man with the glasses.

The auctioneer turned and nodded to someone backstage. He cleared his throat again and shuffled through the index cards, quickly scanning them.

"And now, ladies and gentlemen, the final auction of the evening."

The audience shifted back to the podium with baited breath. The room fell to complete silence. Mr. Black puffed up from all the attention he was now receiving.

"Collected from the southwest region of this glorious country of ours, we've selected the very best, the crème de la crème, as tonight's offering." Being a true showman, he stepped aside, pointed at the curtain, and curtsied.

The canvas ripped back, revealing a terrified man, woman, and little girl, all stripped naked and bound in shackles. Trembling uncontrollably, they winced from the blinding spotlight that blasted their eyes.

The crowd rose to its feet for a better look at the petrified family.

"Yes, for the right price, this family of three can be yours. Take them home. Do to them whatever your dark heart desires."

Through the crowd, Beak looked over at Specs to find the man already staring at him, smiling. They nodded to one another out of respect, knowing that, out of the potential bidders surrounding them, they would once again be the last two standing before the gavel fell.

And when it did, one of them would be the victor, bringing home the small herd of livestock needed to christen their newly acquired lots.

PLAY IT AGAIN, SAM

VINCENZO BILOF

Now, I see some folks using all kinds of strange things for weapons. And a wrinkled old prune of a man like myself ain't lookin' to make no art form out of poppin' them heads off, but I've seen some strangers come through town with swords. Fact, the first man who came through here after all the townsfolk left had a sword *and* a dog.

I remember saying to him, "What you figure to do with that?"

"You can't be taking the time to shoot when you should be running," he said. "If they get close to you, you need to have a weapon you can use close up."

It made sense to me. He sat at the bar eating up the grits and gravy I made, and he had this mangy mutt lying on the floor; it was missing half an ear, and the poor bastard's ribs were sticking out through its dirty-black fur. I asked what the dog's name was.

The good ol' boy shrugged. "It started following me a few miles back. Old mutt just kinda crawled outta the dust. Can't feed him none."

Then I asked him a question that I would ask everyone coming through town, and each time I asked it, I got a different answer. "Any idea what caused it?"

He raised his eyebrows and pursed his lips. He thought about it for a minute. "The dead have come back to life," he said.

It was the simplest answer I ever got, and probably the best.

Now he was a young fella, with big black circles under his eyes and dirt under his fingernails, and he ate like he ain't had nothin' in weeks, which I reckon was the truth. He just sat there chewing, and I think he wanted me to ask him what he saw, what he's been through, and where he might be goin'. None of it makes a difference to me, so I stood there wiping down a mug that was already clean. I remember he kept on chewing and staring at the wall of booze behind me, and I kind of figured what was runnin' through his head.

"What you want in trade for a fifth of Jack?" he asked.

Funny he didn't ask about food.

"You ain't got nothin' I want," I said.

"You want the dog?" The dog looked up at me with his tongue hanging.

I shook my head. "Can't feed him, can't watch him."

"I can just kill you and take it all. I can take all your food."

"Well," I said, "if you were goin' to do that, then maybe we wouldn't be talkin' about it too much. I'm an old man and I ain't got a care in the world if you want to run off with it. You can have every bottle you can take, and if you've a mind to, you can take my life and all the food in the joint."

He thought about it for a moment "Someone else will do it, but I won't."

I shrugged. His eyebrows got all heavy. "Give me a bottle, and you keep the damn dog," he said.

I never asked him what his name was. The dog still ain't got a name, and he comes and goes as he pleases. There haven't been too many travelers passin' through here, but most of them got swords or somethin' else.

I did see one guy luggin' a shovel. No one else has ever threatened me, and mostly I think it's because they expect to see *Turner's*, my bar; a little joint that's just off the highway, a place where a man can get a brew and listen to an old black man play the piano.

I get guests who come through here like they're ghosts, and they think that I'm a ghost, too. Maybe they think that my bar's sitting on the crossroads, right between Heaven and Hell.

I ain't really figured it all out.

When the woman first showed up, I thought she was an illusion, considering that I was drunk as all get-out, standing behind my bar and wiping it down. I should have been over at the well to get more water, or I should have been checking the generator that kept the freezer in the old grocery store running, or I should have been up on the roof of the courthouse looking over the slow desert for more stragglers, both dead and alive.

The truth of it was, I had me another hard night of drinking and carried it over to the following day, cause at the time, I couldn't deal with the nightmares when they came to me. I don't like to close my eyes and see Tom's old Ford spilling dirt and rocks in the street, or the Friday-night lights over the football field at the high school, or the church bells ringing on Sunday.

When I close my eyes, I see my dead wife. My two boys, my grandkids, and my own parents. I see the townsfolk gathered in front of Turner's on that last day, their faces solemn, pleading with me to go with them.

She stood in the doorway like most of them do when they first show up; she stood there blinking at me. She had her fists all balled up. The sunlight came in at the wrong angle, throwing shadows across the doorway. She took two steps in and I got a look at her: she wore long boots with jangling spurs, long leggings, and a shirt that was too big for her. Then I saw she had a sword. There was a gun in a holster on her other hip, with bandoliers crossed over her chest.

"Welcome to *Turner's*," I said.

She dropped her pack to the floor. She had long brown hair, and the lines in her face were as deep as mine, with big black caves for eyes, the corners of her lips twitching like she was about to snarl.

My guest looked around, inspecting the place "This is it? You stay here, without any kind of barricade, with your door wide open like this?" she said.

"That's right," I nodded.

"There are thousands of them, coming this way. They're all coming out west because winter's about to set in. They can feel it in their bones. You plan on just sitting here?"

"Ain't got nowhere to go," I replied.

"Do you think you're safe?" she asked, still walking around the bar, checking corners, looking for something. "They're going to come through here and rip you to pieces. They're going to eat you alive."

I just shrugged. "You hungry?"

She stared at my piano for a long time before replying. "What makes you think that you're better than them? They're slow and boring, but they've managed to kill nearly everybody. You're hiding in a little dream world here. I don't think you know if you're alive or dead."

"This here's my place," I said. "My grandfather built and ran it, and my father owned it after him. My name's Samuel Turner—people around these parts call me Sam. This is my home, and I ain't got no other place to go. I don't really understand what's goin' on in the world, and I ain't gonna trouble myself by tryin' to solve the mystery. I'm gonna do the best I can to get by, and my door's always open. If the Devil was in town, he could come in and have himself a glass of whiskey."

She struck a couple of well-tuned piano keys. I could hear the dog barking far away, outside. I wanted another drink. I thought maybe the crazy woman was going to blow my head off, because she had this wild look in her eyes, like she'd just realized the bank vault was wide open.

"I've heard the metal screaming of burning skyscrapers falling down into piles of dust," the stranger said. "I saw the living destroy the living. We're the ones who rioted and robbed, killing each other. The zombies are nothing more than a sick joke. And yet, you sit here in your little hole, like you live in a separate universe. It's like the nature of man could never touch you."

I started to think again that maybe she was all in my head. My head was throbbing, and the damn dog wouldn't stop barking.

She looked at me and whispered, "Why's the dog barking, Sam?"

"You know why," I said.

She had this sly smile on her face, and she turned and walked out slowly. Like a damn fool I followed her out into the empty town. I stumbled into the street, and I didn't bring a weapon with me. The sun was white and hazy, and the old town was bright.

A lot of people that come through are driving trucks, and they'd already siphoned all the gas that was left in the town. I could tell that the woman traveled on foot, mostly because she didn't look with a curious eye at any of the cars that were left behind.

We found a car parked in the middle of town, and a man was driving. The woman come up and pointed her gun at him, and he sat there with his hands over his head, begging her not to shoot.

"Get out of the car! Get out of the car, now!" she yelled, her voice echoing through the empty town.

The white boy stepped out of the car and she told him to get down on his knees.

He got down in the dust.

I heard him whimpering. "Please, I'm not one of them and I haven't been bitten or anything...we're hungry and we just want to stop somewhere... and we're so glad we've found someone else...please, just let me talk."

I didn't know what was happening, because I figured if the man was alive, why not leave him alone? He could come on by the bar and have a drink. I wanted to stop her, but the sun was in my eyes.

The dog kept on barking, but I didn't see him.

One of them *things* stepped out of the hardware store in front of me. It had on a red flannel shirt and dusty jeans, and I figured it used to be one of the strangers that had come through a week or so ago. When it turned to face me, I could see the skin hanging low off its face, and there was a big black hole through one of its cheeks. The side of its head was burnt, and its eyes were cold and wet, its hands limp like they belonged to a puppet. That mouth opened, and I just knew that the former man had tried to blow his own head off. The front teeth were shattered and broken, and the dried blood around the lips was black and crusted.

I hadn't swept through the town for any of them for a couple days because I'd done some hard drinking, and I was about to pay for it now.

I heard the woman screaming at the crying man who still knelt in the dirt. "Are you bitten?" she asked.

The man said no.

"Are you bitten, you son-of-a-bitch?" she asked again.

He shook his head, and she still had her gun pointed at him. She put it in his mouth. "What the hell are you doing with that dead woman in the passenger seat?" she asked.

He shook his head and closed his eyes.

More of them things came out, and soon they were all around me. I was drunk and my head was spinning. The dog was still barking somewhere, and I knelt down into the dirt and started to weep into my hands like a boy.

What a shame. An old man crying in the street. I didn't even cry when my wife finally died of the cancer years ago.

When I saw the woman standing over the man, holding the gun in his mouth, they were still arguing. Then his head jerked back and a red cloud came out of the back of his head, and he just collapsed right onto the ground, and folded right up.

Then I could feel *their* hands on me, cold and stiff. I looked from out of my fingers over my eyes and saw them all standing around me, the sun above making it hard for me to see their faces. I pushed their hands off me, and I heard a kneecap snap as one of them sank down into the dust next to me. It reached out and touched my face, and I could see the shrunken, wrinkled skin along the tips of its fingers. I pushed the weak hands away, and I could feel brittle bone like my own. The hot breath of a demon was on my neck, all rotten and sour, a smell so strong I had to cover my face; my eyes watered while my stomach threatened to erupt. I looked into the pale face of a dead old man and saw toothless gums, and his bald head had a long, jagged line in it like a cracked egg.

Then that big head exploded, and rancid brains splashed my face. There was another explosion above me, and I was too confused to know what was going on.

The woman who'd killed the living man in the street stood over me. "I'm defending the human race from itself," she said. "It isn't the survival of the fittest, or the strongest, but it's about the survival of the most alive. Are you alive, Sam Turner?"

I passed out cold.

I woke up on the hard billiards table at Turner's.

"My name's Evelyn," the woman said.

I sat up and found her sitting on a bar stool, cleaning her gun. Her sword was on the bar, next to a bottle of whiskey. She'd taken her shirt off, and sat there in a black bra over her bony body, her ribs exposed through long, horizontal scars and dirt. I kept thinking that I really needed to get the girl some food.

She didn't look up at me, but I heard her say, "In the desert I saw a child."

I tried to clear the cobwebs out of my head by standing up. The wind outside was howling fierce, and for a moment I thought that maybe there were a thousand of those dead things outside. Sure enough, the sun had gone down, and a naked bulb swinging above Evelyn's head was the only light on in the place.

"How long has it been since you've seen a woman, Sam?" she asked. "You're old but you're not dead. I know you get lonely, like everyone else. You want to touch another person to know that you're alive?"

"Haven't been thinkin' about it too much, tell you the truth," I said.

"You should've been more amazed to see me. As for me, well, I can't believe you're real. I almost *won't* believe it. The women were sacrificed first, you know." She took a long drink of Whiskey, letting it spill over her bottom lip and down her dirty body. She slammed the bottle on the bar and kept talking. "No laws, no morals, just plain savagery. The human beast. Like we needed or wanted an apocalypse all along. Like we've been waiting for it. An excuse to be ourselves. The women were the first to die. The women were dragged into the streets of Chicago by the living. They were made to pay for everything. The children were next, because they were vulnerable. You see, Sam, no one really cares about the undead." She never looked at me, her eyes only on her gun as she cleaned it.

"The child I saw in the desert wasn't dead, not yet anyway. It was a little girl. She wouldn't talk to me. Her face was covered in dried blood and she didn't even seem to know that she was alive at all. Her mouth hung open, and when I found her, I felt nothing but pity for her. I wanted to feed her, but I had nothing to give. I was starving, and thirsty. I'd convinced myself she was real, that she wasn't a mirage. I needed her to be real. I needed to be needed."

Evelyn looked up at me. "You can play the piano? Why don't you play while I talk? Play something a little slow for me, Sam. Play a song for the girl in the desert."

I saw the dangerous look in her eyes so I went and sat down on the stool. I cracked my fingers and looked at my old, black hands, thinking. I tapped at the keys a little.

She kept on talking loudly over the howling wind, and I strained to listen to her while my fingers moved slowly over the keys.

"The girl didn't have a name or a home," Evelyn said. "Together, we went from town to town, scrounging for food, trying to stay alive. We found nothing. Everything's gone, and everyone's left. It's almost like no one ever lived in any of those places, like no one ever had anything to say to anybody about the future. You know, about why we spent most of our waking moments working for it all to end this way, eaten up by our own dead. The girl and I drifted around, carried by the wind. I did nothing to reassure her, because I knew she would see right through my lies. We tried our best to hide, but there are so many of them. All of them look at you with hungry, hateful eyes. It's almost like they worship your flesh. The dead envy the living. Out there in the wasteland, you can't sleep, because they never sleep." She leaned back against the bar.

"We met an old man. We found him in one of the nameless towns, driving through in his pickup truck. He insisted that the girl was already dead. I told him he was wrong. He shared a couple cans of dog food with us over a fire, and told us there wasn't anything, anywhere. He said everything was empty. He said that everyone went west, and kept on going that way, through California and straight into the ocean. He said the dead coming up from Mexico are legion. I didn't understand how the dead could want anything, or how they could have any sense of self-preservation. He kept on telling me these things, and when I looked over at the girl, I noticed she wasn't eating her dog food. She just was staring, and listening. I whispered something in her ear. I think it may have been the only time I ever told her that everything would be okay." She rubbed her face with her hands, as if she was exhausted.

"The next morning, the girl didn't wake up right away, and I didn't try to wake her," she said. "The old man and I left our little campsite by the truck to scrounge around. When we returned, the girl was awake, staring like she always did. He told her to get into the truck, but she didn't move. He bent down to pick her up, and she leaned in and bit into his neck. I remember the blood, and the old man on the ground holding his neck, kicking and screaming as blood shot out through his fingers. The girl just stood there, a mouthful of flesh in her teeth, blood all over her lips. I ran away. I ran as far and as fast as I could. I left the old man there, screaming and bleeding. I left whatever supplies he had left, and his truck. I couldn't think about anything else, because at that moment, everything in the world seemed to have been destroyed. I felt like I could run forever and never find civilization again. That is, until I found you, Sam."

I stopped playing and looked up at her. "Earth is the real Purgatory, and here we are neither living nor dead," She said.

I was still wondering about the white boy I saw her kill. "Why'd you kill that man back there?"

She shrugged. "I like to know how it feels to kill, before I know how it feels to die," Evelyn answered. "I know what awaits me, Sam. I know what awaits you, too. When you watch a man rip out another man's stomach and take a bite out of it, you realize that we really can find a new low. Being able to kill is the only thing that makes me feel real."

"What about me?" I had to ask.

She stood up, and in the swinging light, the dark circles under her eyes swallowed her face. "I haven't decided yet if you're real."

"I'm as real as that sword you've got," I told her.

"Why don't you let me kill you with it? You can watch yourself die for a moment. You can watch the blood spill through your fingers after I rip the sword out of your stomach. It's a good death, I think."

She stopped talking and looked over at the doorway. A tall man was standing there, and with the wind outside kicking up so much dust and dirt, it made the night look red, and the sky had this funny orange tint to it, like the sun had never fully gone down. Evelyn picked up the Whiskey bottle and took a long swig, spilling some of it on her chest. She got up and walked over to the billiards table, and laid down on it.

"Take me away," she said to the man in the doorway.

The tall man stepped inside. He wore a leather motorcycle jacket. His lips were missing and he had big, white teeth. He walked in and three more followed him. They moved slowly like the dead, but they weren't all jerky, making me think for a moment that they were all still alive. They didn't look at me, but walked right over to Evelyn. I saw the name of their gang on the backs of their jackets, and it wasn't any motorcycle gang I've ever heard of. They were the 'Angels of Death.'

"Play it again, Sam!" Evelyn said. "Play that music for me one more time, while they worship my flesh!"

I turned back to the piano and started to hammer out a tune. My heart was pounding in my chest, but I didn't protest. I paused and glanced over my shoulder and saw them closing in on her, moving patiently.

The single light bulb overhead was swinging back and forth because of the wind blowing into the place, casting shadows in every direction.

My heart stopped for a moment, and I leaned over the piano. The wind howled. I wasn't sure if I was breathing.

"Come and get it, boys!" Evelyn yelled. "Love me, need me, want me! Put your hands all over me. Slide those hands up and down every inch of me!"

She writhed on the billiards table like a snake, throwing her hair back. They touched her with their hands, moving over her ribs, over her face and hair.

She closed her eyes and moaned. She arched her back and her lips parted. They lifted her off the table and carried her outside.

Her laughter cracked over the terrible wind, then I heard her choke like she was swallowing her own tears.

The tall man looked back at me, the one that had nothing but teeth, and I felt frozen solid.

I didn't make a move to get a weapon, I just stared right back.

They left with Evelyn, and her madness followed her into the strange red night.

I waited all night for them to come back for me, but they never did. I didn't sleep a wink. The next morning was bright and sunny, and only a gentle wind remained from the storm.

I looked around town, and I found the dog, sure enough, that mangy mutt was still alive.

I found the car and the headless corpses, including the white boy who'd had his head taken off by Evelyn.

Inside the car there was blood all over the passenger seat. It made me feel good to know that I hadn't dreamed up the whole thing.

I remembered Evelyn asking him about a dead girl in the passenger seat, but if there had been one, the girl was long gone now.

I found a sword shining in the dust, and when I picked it up I saw my reflection in the blade. It was a face I'd seen before. The weapon was useless to me, but it might make for good trade.

The dog started growling fierce, and I looked up and saw a woman hanging against the doorframe of the hardware store.

Her skin still had a little color to it, but her lips were curled back over her teeth, and there was hole in her neck that made her head tilt oddly.

I figured she was the girl that had rode into town with the white boy, and the reason Evelyn had killed him.

I listened to the slow silence of the desert, and I knew that I'd never felt so lonely in my life. Evelyn made me realize how the world had truly ended. I held the sword for a while and listened to the dog growl at the dead woman.

I decided it was about time I give the dog a name.

Travelers come and go; they meet me at *Turner's* like they expect it to be there, and they share a story and move on. Evelyn moved on. But that ain't for me.

The bar has been in my family for generations, and there's nowhere else for an old man like me to go. So let the living and the dead meet me here, and I'll serve them all.

It's what I do.

BORGO PASS
A Gothic Tone Poem

MIKE SHEA

The sun began its last day.

Solemn eyes fixed forward, thinking of the troops the captain led. A captain without a crew is only one thing, *Alone*. Virility is a simple word. An evolution fits much better here. That tenacity led the captain to this very cold, steel chair aboard the enemy's ship. Earth had grown past the trivialities of land squabbles to now look beyond. Looking into the blackness of space, though no distress call pulled us courageously or heroic embellishments of Man's curiosity.

The fact became clear. We simply outgrew our small island. We were turning into the wind now. We were leaving our home.

Being the last P.O.W. taken from the holding cells came as no surprise. Being unshackled was odd though. Most experiences with interrogation had been necessary. If this was a cruel joke, the false sense of freedom equaled nudity, as the embellishment of autonomy a swift darkness enveloped the room resting in disillusionment. Symmetrical measurements were impossible. The room was dark when it was entered, but now it was black. An unconscious, nervous laugh was stifled as a funny thought hit the captain. Saying the words seemed fake and predictable. Like they were staged.

"Is anyone there?" she called.

She realized that any thought process would be futile, his memories orphaned and unobtainable. The tension was broken with a striking shutter as a voice filled the captain's head. The words had a haunting sense of comfort for her, like mother's milk they began.

"May I ask you a question, Mrs. Harker?"

Her queerly cocked head bobbed so frantically that the black room spun. Looking everywhere for the source, she quipped at the voice.

"Do you disregard my rank out of ignorance or just a simple lack of respect?"

"It was not meant to offend you, only to convey envy," she said.

The voice bordering on kind and curtly began again. "Where is your home, dear Captain?"

Thoughts of home were strange to her. To some people the scurry and rustle of autumn leaves hold the word in the highest regard. To others it is the unmeasured scamp of a rat-filled head. Some revel in a home that others greet with sardonic coldness. All of these could describe home along with a million other feelings. To Captain Harker, home wasn't a place, though it did have a name.

She refused to even think her husband's name. To speak it only reinforced the idea that he had been dead for ten years. The words blew past her lips so softly that the slight tingle of passion only hurt more as they left her. She was unable to stop them as they came out. "Oh Jonathan."

Her stomach flipped and her complexion had gone white as a very real and unsettling fear filled her. She may never see him again. She sat and shook wishing she had been killed aboard the Argo with most of her crew. Surviving the beating the ship took, it could have easily been done. The scariest moment was the silence that took the place of the explosions, then the gentle rapping. Poe would have been proud, as it does describe fear. She wanted to vomit and burst into tears. The voice catching its cue from the silence began again. "Let me describe my own, when you came from the bottoms it rose before you like a titan. Cliffs chiseled by master hands."

A pause sounded, strategically placed so the audience of one could formulate a mental picture. A sudden operatic hysteria pushed on.

"The river Arges roared," the voice said. "Running water had such a distinct sound but this river created symphonies, making one long for its eternal music. Then to look upon Talmets and Amales is looking at a lover in such a seductive manner. The only equivalent is a pauper long for the princess. The dawn would soon sever the very vein of night spilling its life upon all below. The sun…"

The speech ceased so abruptly that she was caught off guard. She had actually become caught up in the reveille, forgetting her position, forgetting about Jonathan. She had even forgotten about the sun. Her words came out vehemently and filled with opposition. She wished to have nothing in common with these animals.

"The sun. The sun is dying. Our way of life is dying. You bastards knew that. Then you sat waiting for time to do its own dirty work. Cowards," she said.

"You have never seen a sun viewed as I have viewed it, Mrs. Harker. Memories of dawns rising like an awakening Goliath. Splitting the cursed embrace of dusk and dawn. To the night days are hindrances of solitude. To them, night is reserved for occasions where words are spoken only in the darkest of rooms, but warmest of places."

The words began to bombard her fragile psyche. Again she wished she had died aboard the Argo. She should not be in this situation. Some thoughts hurt too much to think about. The row that sadness splits, seeds of anger prosper. Realizing this, she spoke up. "Your blessed night and lover's words. How do you paint such a picture of beauty with such a dirty brush? You and your kind attacked us as we tried perilously to find a place to go. To find a home. You knew our chaotic situation with the sun. Do you think we would accept extinction? No shred of remorse can breech filling the ravine of disgust I have for your kind. What about my troops' memories? Are they to be so pompously reflective? Are their final memories to be a gasp for any semblance of hope or its place here? Whatever this place is, only a word could fill it. Hell is where we are and you might be a flunky henchman. I only know this one fact though. You do not have the courage to be a leader."

Unknowingly, she had risen to an invisible podium to address her impassive audience. Even the repetition of adjectives in her mind seemed justified. Frustratingly the room was still black. With no applause, she sat.

No sense of pride was reinforced when the voice clearly stated. "Mrs. Harker, this ship holds many bad memories," the voice said.

Vehemently, her rapture turned to despair. Her understanding that she was a dead woman only felt reinforced by a sense of dread. The coldness of the room only cemented it in place further. While contemplating her demise, things in the room seemed changed. Slow in nature, forcibly in presence. All sound from the room vanished. The voice a faint memory. The emptiness languished on insanity. The darkness became so dense, the captain gripping at reality blindly; her larynx froze. Like drowning in a place where the water runs black. The fear hit her with a dull thud. She was not running out of air, the room was. Her muscles contracted, and her skin recoiled into a trapped animal pinned down and filled with frenzy. Tendons pulled and stretched to a point that would never return to their athletic shape. Bordering on catalepsy, the worst came. Her mouth, a place from which she said "I love you" so many times, now turned on her. Withdrawing to a scared cave dweller, unable to fight, her teeth forced her mouth open. The sides opened first to form a horrific grimace. The air was being pulled from the room as she let out a scream. She needed the air. The dead don't breathe. Then within a moment's notice, it ceased. The orchestra of anguish paused for intermission.

"Do you know, Captain, I admire your planet's brashness to venture into the dark halls and passageways of space? Swiping your swords into the night. Searching for a golden fleece, eh? My dear, not all sentinels lead to evolution. Soon you will have no need for air. The darkness will embrace you."

As the words rained down on the captain, they had a foul, rancid smell to them—likened to an unearthed grave. Then the mental rainstorm worsened and the odor grew stronger; she winced.

"The ones I represent have fought similar quandaries and equal paradoxes," the voice said from within the darkness. "They are to reveille in battle, carnage and mostly victory. They heard the screams climb above the crests of Tatra. You see, for they are the things from beyond the blackness of space. Where you and I do not dare venture but where they lurk with eyes very wide."

"Then what are you, Ambassador or General?" she asked.

"Does it matter? Each fall short of saint, do they not?"

"It separates rank and command. It gives an order to those who need to be led."

"Did class at one time not separate us as well?" The voice seemed to tense while concluding with, "Catapults and arrows are now replaced with ambitions that young boys dream about while looking into space. The wizard's protective spell on man has been broken. With the sun gone you will not even be able to carve a stake for defense. Death places its own set of restrictions."

The phrases echoed through her. There had been speculation and whispers of exactly what the opposition had been from the leaders of Earth. It seemed the day they were informed of the sun's imminent extinction, the problems arose. Carriers were missing, many never heard from again. Messages were sent filled with banter and gibberish of people who recited prayers so old that they were almost unrecognizable. Prayers had no place for the betterment of mankind.

"Equality begins with a clean slate," the motto rang. Though the sounds from the logbooks clearly stated that many beliefs were still being practiced outside of the realms of law. Now wishing she had those words and prayers to help, her heart raced. Thumping inside, below her uniform, it seemed to raise proudly and then rescind tepidly.

Trying not to let her words have any intonation of her sense of dread, she said,

"You and your leaders studied our planet. It is so simple that now you feed on dead carcasses like vultures."

"You are still alive, Captain Harker. Your people are merely provisions. Your planet is another matter."

Reinforced with a stench, the words filled the room. How could humans be provisions for a race…stumbling to get the word out, a calmness hit her. Now the word came out with a simple begotten ease. "Monster!"

The echo from her voice was worse than the word. It hung painfully, unable to find a place to rest. Hollow and barren, like the hull of a ship awaiting a new crew. She then realized the plot of her tale. Her hand cupped her chest above her stomach to feel her heart. The beat was unbelievable. She clung tighter, her uniform stretching. One of her buttons snapped, and expecting to hear it hit the floor, she waited. No sound came. Time and her words held a precise moment.

Mounting and staging a strike-filled precision, the moment continued. Nothing but the sound of her heart filled the room. Pulsing and bloating it beat. Then in a single snap, a flutter of lush red light filled the room. Wild and gregarious. Blustery and wind-swept. The color held the surroundings in a garnet grasp, making any focal point elusive. Blinking, she was unable to see an army of crimson light forming on her right. She only caught the tail of it as it perched on the ceiling above her.

With unnatural grace, it crept down towards her from out of the darkness, seeming to be transfixed on its feet and the floor below them. The mass of color seemed to stop to steady itself, then began anew.

She could feel her heart begin to increase in its rhythm. She knew it was near her though its steps were too large to measure. It reached her feet first, holding them gently, coaxing relaxation into a dull ache, then slowly up her calves, slipping like a silken grasp around her knees.

Methodically, it rubbed her legs, knowing exactly where to touch and each response it would receive. It had such a confident quality that only comes with time. Her spine tingled with a cleanliness she had forgotten. Stirring something within, she thought she was dead. In her mind, she had been buried with Jonathan.

Scarlet fingers roamed up her chest and pulled her hand away. It wanted to feel her heart race, to receive its applause with a racing heart. Reaching her face, cradling it, she suddenly felt safe. Safety in such moments are crucial, it reinforces feelings so lapses in judgment can be forgiven. Past her face, it worked her hair. Strands fell back and forth like wavering reeds, magically cerise hands playing symphony to the captain's audience.

Suddenly, in the midst of the whimsical autopsy of the captain's exterior, the brilliant color faded and a figure came towards her. Slow deliberate breaths came from her as the color now evaporated. A face came before her. It was angelic. The kind of beauty painted so to last forever. It was the presence of a face so pure it must have taken bloodline centuries to perfect. Once again the captain stammered to ask a question riddled with shock. "My God, were you human at one time? It explains it. Tell me, I am wrong?"

"Captain, if tears could answer you they would. I show you my face now clean. God has nothing to do with this," the man before her said with geniality. "My name is Veles. Veles, in the 'Order of the Dragon.' I was taken from Earth in a time you would not even conceive to remember. I've seen 1492 as clearly as 2292. I watched from a very safe distance, waiting for that cursed star to burn out. It stood mocking me for too many nights. Eternity is not absentminded though. I wanted to return, reclaiming my land victorious. There is no choice for you, Captain. This is the evolution of mankind falling onto the periphery of extinction."

She sat knowing that this was not a king to greet his new queen. Veles seemed to scamper like a lizard around her as he asked a question. "Mrs. Harker, do you understand what lies ahead of you? A place where rats fester and bleakness is a ray of hope. I am sorry, I am taking you away from him forever. You are forsaken to a place where rank soil is sanctuary and disturbed earth holds you tightly. You will simply be alone. Beyond that are the things that rest on the outskirts of dread and consternation. This is not the ordeal of life and death you are accustomed to. There are no winners here. Fate plays a very cruel game."

She had no tears when he fell upon her, though peril had its place. Poetically it began. She became submerged in black as red faded from the room. Any whispered words mingled into unrecognizable phrases that can only be mustered at the crossroads of life like these.

Her ears were perched on the terrace of forever as she heard words hundreds of years dead, all chivalrous in manner and zealous in tone. The embrace charged the solar winds as they blew into obscurity, like a footnote in time being cataloged by things filling in the library of existence, resting on the borders of space, and floating in a place where the waters of a soul can only run black.

She began to stir a short time after. Realizing she was still sitting in the same cold steel chair from earlier, she saw a figure standing on the empty edge of the ship.

The sonic bliss had vanished, the silence bordering on insanity, languishing into the doldrums of dead air. She suddenly saw the kaleidoscope of Earth past Veles.

The planet's color seemed to be graying around the edges rapidly, like most elder statesmen, but some lush interior remained.

The sun no longer visible, a smaller star had taken its place, creating a reflection of the hull of the ship she was on. It showed a name, Donalbain.

She could see it lay on the deck below, meticulously placed for the quick retrieval and reinforcement of ego. She came to his side as he stood looking at Earth.

"You were right in your theory, Mrs. Harker. I was human at one time but for a very long time I have answered to other masters. They do not wish to present themselves in the light. Having waited for numerous galaxies to burn out, they claimed them one at a time. Black space is a welcoming audience for the first time performer."

She sat and listened to her master speak. Her amazement came that his pianist-like hands had an arachnid subtlety to them, as if each fingertip held venom.

He raised his right hand as he spoke. "This is not the return to my home I had longed for, you see. I am not so arrogant in death to think what lies before and beyond may not be what I remembered or even imagined. As I said, eternity is not absentminded."

"Veles, will you look past everything around you and return to your home? What if decay only extends its dead hand?" she asked.

"My dear, I have to. I only wish to perform one single task. What welcomes me beyond that I will accept."

"What is that?"

"The hills and the mountains of my home hold many endearing traits. Between them stands a road. I wish to walk it again as I did as a young boy towards my home."

"A road?" she asked.

"Yes, the Borgo Pass."

Triumphantly, it rang out through the hull. A long pause that followed seemed to search for nostalgia. Suddenly, he turned his back to Mrs. Harker and passed the sun, now performing its grand finale at the dusk of a play known as Earth.

Walking away, he spoke words that hung and echoed through the hull of the ship.

"Though I am no longer a boy, I will walk it as a monster."

THE DEAD LINE

KEVIN LEWIS

Carla Stratton had just entered her house when the phone rang. She was in no mood to answer it because she'd had the worst day imaginable—forgetting her umbrella and being drenched in heavy downpours notwithstanding. Being the owner of a real estate agency meant you're the boss. And in a tanked economy, that meant making tough decisions such as laying off employees—hard-working employees. Carla hated doing it but she was just thankful it had gone quickly and peacefully.

Still, it stung.

Setting her briefcase down on the round glass kitchen table, she grabbed the cordless phone and turned it on.

"Hello?" she said into the phone.

"He's coming for you," the voice whispered on the other end.

"Excuse me? Hello? Who is this?"

"My name is Amy Waters. It was too late for me. He was already in my house when I came home from work. He pinned me down and he…he came at me! When I woke up, I was standing over my own dead body. The man…the *monster* carried my body into his van. That was last week. But I've been trailing him. I saw him park a short ways down the road from your house. You have to get out of there!"

Carla wasn't going to take any more of this. "Listen, I don't know who you are, but I don't appreciate prank calls."

"This isn't a prank, if you will…"

Carla interrupted her. "If you call again, I'm calling the police!" She hung up.

Still rattled by the prank call, Carla basically skipped dinner—only having three glasses of red wine instead—and headed upstairs to catch up on some TV. She changed into her pajamas, which consisted of lightweight black jogging pants and a Red Sox T-Shirt. She then hopped into bed and rifled through her mail. Same old crap. Bills, bills, and more bills. One bill stood out, though. It was from her new and soon to be ex-plumber. Evan Bates was his name. He had come over a couple of weeks ago to fix her toilet.

Evan was a man one couldn't forget. He was odd from the start. Evan had entered her house wearing his plumber's uniform and a pair of sunglasses. He probably thought he looked cool in them because he never took the shades off. He was also a talker. He talked to Carla throughout his work time—how he was lonely because he had no family. Carla wasn't sure if he was trying to ask her out or not. Either way, she wasn't going to pay the bill because the toilet was still broken.

Asshole, she thought.

She placed the mail back on her bed side table, picked up the remote, and turned on the flat-screen television. She spent at least a half a minute flipping through the stations: sit-coms, adult-appropriate cartoons, and endless crime dramas that never held her interest, when she stumbled upon a breaking news story on a local station.

"This just in: police are investigating the mysterious disappearance of a Barnestable woman. Thirty-one year old Amy Waters was reported missing two days ago by her parents. Waters, an elementary school teacher, failed to report to work last week, and when her parents searched her house, they found their daughter's home broken into and ransacked."

Carla cupped her hand over her mouth. *What the hell?* As the reporter continued with the story, a picture of Amy Waters appeared on the screen. Carla thought Amy was very attractive. She had light brown hair, same as Carla, and wore short-rimmed eyeglasses.

"When police were called to the scene, they discovered blood on the floor and evidence of a struggle," the news reporter continued. "Police are calling this a kidnapping for now; although no ransom demands have been made at this time…"

She turned off the TV. She couldn't take any more of it. She got up from her bed and paced the room. *Who the hell was that on the phone? It couldn't have been Amy Waters. If it was, then it's definitely someone's morbid idea of a sick joke.*

It was silent in Carla's house for so long that when her phone rang again, Carla actually screamed. When she calmed down, she picked up the phone on the bed side table.

"Hello?" Carla nervously said.

"He's here!" the female voice softly said, still whispering in a panic tone.

"Look, I don't know why you're doing this to me, but this is harassment. I swear, you call me one more time, I'll…" Carla never finished her threat.

"Get out of the house!" the voice screamed.

The phone went dead.

"Hello? Hello?"

Carla dialed 9-1-1 but there was no dial tone. "Damn it!" she said. A loud bang sounded from within the house, startling her.

Carla gasped at the noise. The noise came again, and again, until she heard what sounded like something breaking through a hard surface. She slowly inched toward her bedroom door to listen more intently.

There was a clicking sound.

The front door! Someone was unlocking it.

She covered her mouth with her hand as she heard the door open and footsteps enter the house.

"Hello?" the intruder asked in a calm and patient voice. "Come out, come out, wherever you are!"

Carla didn't know why but the voice sounded oddly familiar. It was a man's voice, but that didn't narrow it down much. She knew she couldn't escape downstairs or by her bedroom window. The bedroom was so high up that if she jumped, she would either fall to her death or injure herself and be unable to flee her psychotic intruder.

She gently closed her bedroom door and studied her room for a possible weapon. No such luck. She then searched for her cell phone and realized it was recharging on the dining room table.

There were footsteps on the staircase. Her head spinning in a million directions, Carla quickly entered her walk-in closet and closed the sliding door just a crack so she could still see the bedroom. She closed her eyes and breathed heavily, waiting for what came next. It seemed as if it took her intruder forever to climb the stairs. The door to her bedroom opened slowly and the intruder stepped into the room. Carla couldn't get a clear look at him; he wore a black cloak with a hood over his head.

The cloaked man stopped in the middle of the room and turned around. Carla covered her mouth with her hand to stifle a scream, not only so she wouldn't be discovered, but because she recognized the intruder. It was her plumber. Evan Bates.

She couldn't believe it. He'd finally ditched the sunglasses, although she preferred the sunglasses to his current fashion statement. *What the hell's he in, a satanic cult?* she wondered.

"There's no point in hiding, Carla. We'll get you either way. We need you. I need you." He spoke with a calm voice, as if he was sure of the outcome.

Evan turned around and entered the bathroom.

Carla took a deep breath and made her move. She gently slid the closet door open and ran from the room. She had to try and escape.

Halfway down the stairs, she heard Evan yell, "I see you!"

Carla reached the foot of the staircase on the ground floor and entered the dining room through the living room. Her objective was to obtain her cell phone and call the police. But when she went to grab her cell phone, she discovered it was missing. Only the charger remained on the table.

What the hell? It was right here!

"You can't run from me," Evan taunted as he descended the stairs. She could tell he was taking his time, savoring the thrill of the chase. "None of them can."

Carla realized she could not escape via the front door, so she darted into the kitchen and exited through the kitchen door that led to the backyard. There was a chill in the night air. Of course, it was colder to her because she wasn't wearing a jacket. Or shoes. And the rain had also not let up.

Carla ventured into the woods bordering her property. She tried her best not to make a sound but the fallen leaves and branches crackled as she stepped on them.

"Carla," Evan Bates shouted into the rainy night. "I'm coming for you!"

She hid behind a tree. She was winded and needed a quick breather before she continued her escape. Carla breathed heavily, and the wind and heavy rain beat ferociously against her that she thought she was going to pass out. She stared at the direction she had just come. Evan was nowhere in sight.

Maybe he went around the front, thinking I would go for my car? she hoped.

She considered that option, as well, but she didn't think she would make it before he caught up with her. A friend of hers lived in a house on the other side of the woods, so Carla figured she'd try for her house and call the police from there.

Turning around to resume her escape, she was punched in the head so hard she lost consciousness. Just before she faded into oblivion, she realized the blow had come from yet another familiar face.

When Carla awoke, she saw Amy Waters standing in front of her. Carla immediately tried to stand up and run away from the woman who'd punched her in the head, but she couldn't. She was tied to a tree by thick rope, in a sitting position.

"What the hell's going on? Why are you doing this to me?"

"It wasn't me," Amy said.

There was something off about Amy. Her neck was bloody and her long-sleeved night shirt was stained. Still, Carla was too angry to care.

"It wasn't you? I saw you clear as day."

"Awake at last!" Evan's voice said.

Still wearing his black cloak, but with the hood down, he emerged from behind the tree. He was definitely built like a plumber. Medium height and athletically built. He had bleached blonde hair and his face was pale, which was new for Carla because it wasn't the last time she'd seen him.

Evan was also not alone this time. Another person dressed in a black cloak was with him, and when the two towered over Carla, the second person rolled down the hood.

Amy?

Carla was absolutely confused. It was Amy Waters from head to toe, although Amy #2 appeared horrible in a different way. Her hair, face, and hands were covered in mud, as if she'd fallen face-first into a pile of dirt. Carla was amazed the rain hadn't washed all of it away, unless she'd been shielded from the rain until recently.

"What the hell is this?" Carla asked the non-cloaked Amy.

"Who is she talking to?" the cloaked Amy asked Evan.

"I'm not sure."

"They can't see me, Carla," the non-cloaked Amy said. I'm dead. He killed me." Amy pointed her finger at Evan, whose eyes were transfixed on Carla.

"But there are two of you." Carla stared back and forth between the two Amy's.

"That's my body but it's not me. It's the monster he infected me with. I tried to warn you. I'm sorry. Maybe you'll succeed in warning the next victim."

Before Carla could ask more questions, Amy faded away, leaving Carla alone with her two attackers.

Evan nodded at Carla. "How's that toilet working out?"

Carla didn't answer his pathetic question. Instead she asked, "Where are your shades?"

"It's night time. I don't need them. Speaking of which, the night is almost over and we still need to feast. We're weak and oh so hungry. I want my family to be strong."

"Family?" Carla asked.

"Yes. That's why I need you. I lost mine so long ago, but that's all right. I'm making a new family now, and I want you to be a part of it. We'll have so much fun, Carla. You'll fit in just fine."

Evan stared at Amy Waters' body and Carla could now see the creature inhabiting it, as if it was superimposed over the young woman. "Shall we?" he asked his partner.

Amy looked down at Carla and grinned mischievously. Then the two crouched down and descended upon their meal, as Carla's screams filled the night.

WORLD ZOMBIE DAY

MARK M. JOHNSON

The mall was exceedingly busy for nine-thirty on a Sunday morning. However, this morning's crowd looked a bit more unusual than most days. Some were ordinary shoppers, often seen wandering the halls on any typical Sunday morning, but many others looked as if they might have risen from the autopsy table of the local morgue, or clawed their way free from their graves and staggered over to the mall for a little Sunday morning early Christmas shopping.

The many blood splattered and worm-ridden shoppers were on the move, heading deeper into the mall, while the ordinary folks just watched them pass with more than just a few incredulous stares.

The average-looking group consisted of mostly older men and women, and many snapped pictures and took video of the passing costumed dead. The bloodier group consisted of a very wide variety of ages. Young and old, and some entire families with grandparents in wheelchairs, shambled through the shopping mall like the risen dead on their way to a Sunday breakfast of living flesh. The news camera crew was also drawing quite a bit of attention from both groups as they moved through the miasma of pleasant aromas swirling in the air of the food court, on their way to the mall's center.

Occupying the reporter position of the crew, Dana McElroy led the group of three. She was cute, in a hometown girl sort of way, with her long light brown hair pulled back in a bouncing ponytail. Her twenty-four year old face looked fresh, makeup free as always, and her bright blue-green eyes sparkled with anticipation.

Dana's spunky, can do attitude and friendly personality had landed her this, her first job in journalism, her chosen field of study. Even though WBGN-TV Pittsburgh was a small network with only a limited news program, her boss had informed her that this interview might play nationally or at least on all the local stations, so she intended to do her very best.

Behind Dana, Pete Stavanger lugged the heavy camera equipment with his more than adequate arms. Pete's spiky blond hair, fierce expression and muscular build on a five foot six bulldog frame, usually gave people the wrong impression. He might look mean, but in reality, he was a cat-loving vegan currently harboring a severe crush on the girl leading him through the food court. Though he stood at least four inches shorter than Dana, he felt the two of them had hit it off as far as working together. They had shared some very good conversations in the past few weeks and he knew she was currently single. As they hustled through the mall, frantic thoughts of working up the courage to ask her out consumed his thoughts.

Bringing up the rear, a plump and balding man in his mid-forties huffed and puffed as he struggled to keep up with his crew. Dean Powlowski flipped through the pages of a black notebook he carried, until settling on the page with a printout of the Monroeville Mall's floor plan.

"Okay, guys," Dean called out. "It's just up ahead around the next corner."

"They're meeting us there, in front of JC Penny's, right?" Dana shouted back without turning.

"Yeah, the whole cast. All six of them in makeup and costumes," Dean answered as they passed around the corner and the center of the mall came into view. Aside from the few costumed stragglers still heading to the far side of the mall, where today's scheduled zombie walk would begin, the mall looked completely normal. The kiosk owners were setting up their stands and people moved in both directions, on their way to work at the many stores within the shopping Mecca. The mall buzzed with the low hum of early morning activity and conversation. Amidst all this, stood six people that immediately caught Dana's eye.

The six costumed characters stood in front of the glass security doors of the JC Penny's store. This particular location had historical significance in relation to the movie, *Dawn of The Dead*, which George Romero filmed in the mall many years before. Dana remembered this from her research concerning the event. She summarized as she approached the group, that this was probably why they had chosen this location for the interview.

Dana recognized them all from the hours of video she had watched of their late Saturday night TV program the 'It's Alive Show,' during her recent research in preparation for the interview. The show featured comedy skits by the cast, guest appearances by local Pittsburgh musical and performing acts, and they were the hosts for old horror movies showing on the stations. The host of the 'It's Alive Show,' self-proclaimed 'King of the Zombies' and this motley group's leader, Mark, AKA Professor Emcee Square, stood at the front of the group.

To his left stood Shannon—or Stiffy the Dead Clown—adorned in his clown makeup with a black clown nose, black Xs over his eyes, wearing a black leather jacket over a Death Mobile t-shirt and blue jeans.

Standing next to Stiffy, Eric—known on the show as Fritz III, the three-eyed hunchback—shuffled around in his ragged brown robe, looking just a little nervous, as if he were already in character while his two working eyes darted across the passing crowd.

Doug, also known as Pointy, the guitar-playing-opinionated-demon, stood at the professor's right, in his red polyester suit jacket and black bowler hat with two devils horns sticking out above the curled brim.

Peering out from behind Pointy lurked the creepy Nosferatu-like vampire called Helga Scheidenentzündung. Of all the characters of the show, Dana loved Helga the most. Playing Helga, Angela looked downright creepy with her long hooked nose, pointed ears and classic fanged buckteeth. Her silent darkly comic pantomiming never failed to bring Dana to laughing tears.

Bethany, who played Leah the Mummy girl on the show, stood off to Helga's right, just slightly away from the main group. Leah was fitting nicely into her role as the newest member of the cast. She looked quite fetching in her curve hugging mummy wrappings, with her long, beautiful dark hair cascading across her bare shoulders. Dana could see quite obviously why she was the favorite among the male fans of the show.

Prof. Emcee Square smiled and waved Dana and her crew over. He looked chillingly handsome in his trademark tuxedo and white-faced zombie makeup. Dana almost giggled like a little school girl at the spooky white contacts that covered his blue eyes. She suppressed the giggle with a welcoming smile as she held out her hand.

"Professor Emcee Square I presume?" she asked in her pleasantly professional voice. He took her hand in a firm comfortable grip and gave her a warm sincere smile that birthed butterflies in her stomach.

"Dana McElroy," he replied in a completely normal voice with a slight Pennsylvanian accent. It's very nice to finally meet you. I've enjoyed your reporting."

She was disappointed for a second when she did not hear the Transylvanian growl that she'd grown to love from watching the show. She quickly assumed that the accented growl was for the character only and she was hearing the man behind the makeup.

She found his true voice to her liking as well. She returned his warm smile. "Great to meet you, Prof," she giggled, using his stage name. "I love the show." She was worried to hear a nervous tremor in her voice as she felt something unspoken pass between them. She realized she was attracted to the crazy-looking man and let go of his hand reluctantly.

"Please, call me Mark," he said, holding her eyes for a few seconds. Mark turned and gestured to Pointy standing at his right. "Allow me to introduce my right-hand man and one of my oldest friends, Doug." Dana reached out to take Doug's offered hand, when a little girl in a black cloak stepped between them and stopped in front of Mark, interrupting the introduction.

"You have done well," the girl said in a child's voice stained with the inflection of someone far older. Reaching out, she took his right hand into hers. With her other tiny hand she threw back the hood of her cloak, revealing her long, almost white-blond hair, and the strange tattoos that covered her entire face, head, and every other visible part of her young skin all the way to her fingertips.

Mark smiled down at the little girl. "I'm sorry, sweetie, we're…" He stopped talking when his eyes met hers.

Everyone in the group immediately assumed that the unusual hieroglyphic-like tattoos were part of her costume, until they seemed to shift on her skin. The tattoos blurred, moved, then resolidified into new and equally bizarre shapes right before their eyes. Seeing this impossible transition made everyone who looked upon the girl swoon in a spell of momentary dizziness.

"Did you…" Doug started to ask as he reached out and touched Mark's shoulder for balance. Then Doug stopped talking as well when he saw the expression on his friend's face. Mark's mouth hung agape in mid-word, his face slack and lifeless, eyes distant and entranced.

When Mark gazed into the strange little tattooed girl's eyes, he saw his entire life play before his bewildered eyes. In an instant, he saw everything that he had experienced throughout his life, his triumphs, failures, regrets, the good times and the bad, the past, the present, and the future.

Within the deep wells of the little girl's ancient soul, he saw what was to come, for him, his friends, and humanity. The split-second vision drained him dry and left nothing but emptiness where his soul had been.

"Hey?" Shannon asked loudly, placing his hand lightly on Mark's shoulder as he cast a nervous, sideways glance at the girl holding Mark's hand, "Mark, you okay?"

"Aaahhhh," Mark droned out in a long, wheezing groan.

"Yes," the little girl whispered. "You see." She released her hold on Mark and turned, leaving him swaying as if he really were the zombie he had costumed himself to be.

"We had long planed to open the void and release them on your so-called, Eve of all Hallows," the little girl said as she stepped away from the small-confused group gathered around Mark. "But there are far too many innocents traipsing about on All Hallows Eve, and the Fallen have no power over them."

She turned around to face them again, holding out her arms and gesturing to the people all around them in the mall. "This festival though, your *World Zombie Day*, it suits the Order's purposes far better than they ever could have hoped to dream." As she looked up at the cast of the 'Its Alive Show,' they all saw the ancient emptiness of her deep dark eyes and fell back a step almost in unison. "They will make real your make believe, and then you and your costumed followers will join those who perish in sin, in service of the Fallen." She sighed wearily. "At long last, our waiting is over."

"Is this part of the Show?" Dean asked. "Because we're not even filming yet."

"No, man," Doug answered. "I've never seen this little chic before."

Hey, Pete," Dana called out. "I think maybe you should start…"

"Way ahead of you, Dana," Pete answered as he stepped up with his camera, already filming.

"Mark!" Shannon shouted, trying to rouse him from his daze. "Hey, wake up." Shannon shook him gently. Leah walked around the group and stopped in front of their entranced leader. She gently lifted Mark's drooping chin, closing his gaping mouth and lifting his eyes to hers. Mark's vacant eyes looked through her into infinity and Leah began to cry. Angela leaned out and glanced over at Mark with a confused look on her makeup-covered face, before returning her gaze to the little girl.

"Hey, what's wrong with him?" Leah tearfully asked her gathered friends. Their attention was solely focused on the little girl before them.

The little girl in question fell gracefully to one knee, and reaching out a hand, she spun in a slow circle, marking the floor with a stick of what looked like black grease paint but reeked of death. When she completed the circle on the floor, she remained inside of it, gently arranging herself to a sitting position. She took the black stick she'd used to draw, flipped it over, and planted it into the floor where it then stuck. Whispered words slipped through her lips as she passed a hand over the black candle made of human fat. A flame leapt up from its wick. An almost sad expression of reluctant resolve descended over her face.

"*Ego duco is orbis per scelestus cruor,*" she chanted while lifting a finger to her mouth. She bit down on it, savaging her own flesh and drawing blood. "*Ego liceor thee signum is orbis per insons inson-*

tis cruor." The tattooed girl touched her bleeding finger to the inside edge of her black circle as she finished her invocation chants.

The moment her bloody finger touched the black circle drawn on the mall floor, a brisk howling wind arose inside the corridors of the shopping center. The wind blew in from every direction, centering on the girl sitting within the circle, creating a whirling vortex around her.

Some people screamed, some stumbled and fell to their knees, as the torrent picked up and flung smaller objects through the air. Mark stood unmoving, as if nothing had changed. Leah clutched onto him and kept the wind from knocking them both over. Doug instinctively reached up to hold his hat on and turned in a circle, attempting to discern where the wind was coming from. Dana almost stumbled forward into the tempest churning around the circle on the floor, but Pete reached out a free hand to hold her back.

The driving wind tore at the little girl's black robe and she lifted her head, letting the wind blow her hair back as she closed her eyes and breathed deeply of the flowing air. With a loud whoosh, the maelstrom peaked, followed by an instantaneous silence, as a multicolored dome of shifting energy closed over her, sealing her within it.

The colorful shimmering dome resembled a giant soap bubble with hues of red, green, gold and black, all swirling across a surface that gave off a slight humming glow. The way the surface swirled gave the impression that the bubble was unbroken and continued on into the floor, making a complete sphere around the tattooed girl.

She was clearly visible through the translucent dome of swirling colors. She looked up and over her right shoulder, her dark eyes briefly scanning the gathering crowd around her. A shadow of uncertainty fell across her face, and then cleared, as her resolve seemed to reassert itself. She unceremoniously dropped the black robe from her shoulders, revealing her nakedness beneath it.

Everyone who gathered around the little girl inside the sphere had lived their lives believing that magic was all smoke and mirrors. Even though many of them attended church regularly, deep down in their secret heart of hearts, they did not really believe in the supernatural. Over the years, as human civilization grew in knowledge and sophistication, their minds had been bombarded with logic and science. Even most of those who openly claimed to believe in ghosts, spirits, the after life and even aliens, did not really believe…not really.

When their civilized minds beheld the little tattooed girl within her enchanted circle, the veil of disbelief that had covered their hearts for so long fell away. The walls of logic and scientific fact in which they all lived their safe little lives were shattered and destroyed by the sight. Deep down in the very cells of their bodies, in the supernatural genes that made up their souls, or in some dark forgotten corner of their minds, they knew real magic when they saw it.

They remembered.

A few cried out and fell to their knees in prayer, but most just stood frozen to the spot in exhilarated amazement, or complete terror. The little girl took no notice of them as she busied herself searching for something within the folds of her discarded cloak.

The black tattoos that covered the her body moved faster now, blurring, shifting and reforming every few seconds, as if trying to tell a long, complicated story in a limited amount of time.

Gazing at the unnaturally shifting tattoos for more than a few seconds induced dizziness and nausea in many of the gathered watchers, who turned and staggered away, spewing their breakfast onto the tile floor. However, the cast of the 'It's Alive Show' and all others who had come to the mall in costume now watched unaffected by the disorienting effects of the girl's strange tattoos.

"Hey!" Angela called out, breaking the stunned silence of the crowd. "She's got a knife!"

The little girl had indeed removed a wicked looking bladed dagger from the folds of her cloak. The blade looked ancient and razor sharp. Resembling a twisted black snake, it had glittering red jewels for eyes. The blade was the tail, and the hilt and handle formed the shape of the snake's curling body and head. The snake's mouth hung open with glittering white fangs poised to strike. The girl turned the knife towards her chest and held it high in front of her.

"Oh my God she's gonna…" Eric shouted in panic. Shannon broke through the bewildered paralysis that had held him and burst forward in an obvious attempt to prevent the girl from harming herself.

When Shannon tried to plunge his hands through the wall of the sphere, it was like grasping an electric fence. He gave out a short cry as a blinding bright light and explosion of electric-like energy flung him back and into the crowd. Then the little girl began to speak, her voice emerging from the sphere and amplified to the point of being deafening.

"*Of meus own mos!*" she cried out defiantly, her voice echoing through the mall. "*Testis pro Deus quod vir,*" she continued as many before her clutched their ears in pain. "*EGO Tribuo meus insons insontis vita.*" Her booming voice faltered slightly with thick emotion. "*Eximo Proeliators ex inritus,*" Her arms stiffened as she steeled her resolve. "*EGO solvo meus insons insontis cruor.*" As the last word left her lips, she drew the dagger forward with a swift, jerking motion. She screamed in pain as the knife pierced her chest and was buried to the hilt in her soft young flesh. Her body stiffened, shuddered, and then fell still. Everyone screamed with her and someone called out to God for help. The girl sat unmoving within the sphere, her head hanging lifeless. The shifting tattoos covering her body began to vanish, becoming fewer and lesser as they blurred and reformed. After a few seconds, the only marks that remained circled the dagger still clutched in her immobile hands. Then the knife began to move when her hands fell limply away from it.

Pete, finally overcome by the sense of foreboding that had been eating at him ever since he'd glimpsed the little girl, stepped away from his forgotten camera equipment and pushed past a few gawkers to reach Dana.

"Dana," Pete said in a hushed, hissing whisper. "I think we need to get the hell out of here."

Dana shrugged Pete's hand from her shoulder and stepped closer to the still glowing sphere. "It's moving," she said and pointed towards the dagger buried in the girl's chest. "Oh my God!" she shouted as her face twisted in horror. "It's alive!" The dagger moved. Twisting and slithering, it turned its bejeweled eyes upon the crowd and hissed. It undulated in the air for a few seconds and then withdrew into the girl's body, disappearing from view.

"Oh Jesus help us!" said an older women who had fallen to her knees to pray before the tattooed child. She made the sign of the cross in the air before her fearful eyes.

"I don't think Jesus has anything to do with this, lady," Doug said, sounding mechanically deadpan, like a recorded voice on the telephone.

The last of the markings around the knife wound vanished, leaving the girl's young pale flesh pure and unmarked, except for the unusually bloodless dark wound in the center of her chest. Then the wound began to blacken as if the flesh were decomposing at an unnatural rate. The blackness spread across her chest and in the air in front of her still body. Hundreds, thousands, millions, of tiny microscopic gnat-like black creatures crawled across her skin and floated in the air inside the sphere, only visible because of their vast numbers.

At first, the tiny black creatures only came from the wound in the dead girl's chest, and then they began to emerge from her nose, mouth and eyes. The girl's flesh seemed to darken from within then it fell away from her bones, melting away, becoming more of the small black creatures. The bones of the girl's body disintegrated as the creatures swarmed against the wall of the sphere and it began to expand under the pressure.

A few of the un-costumed people turned and ran from the expanding sphere, but most just stood transfixed. They may have wanted to run, their minds may have been screaming for them to flee, but they could not move as the now-blackened sphere expanded towards them. The sphere grew to twice its initial size, then three and four times, forcing the closer members of the crowd to back away lest it touch them. The sphere continued to expand until it seemed it would burst.

Then it did.

The sphere blew apart with a short burst of wind, like the last gasp of a dying man. The sound of rushing air caressed everyone's ears, and the distant echoing screams of the uncountable legion. The tiny black creatures exploded outward in every direction, filling the air and passing through flesh, concrete, glass, and steel like immaterial ghosts. The air inside the mall blackened for an instant, as if suddenly and without explanation everyone had gone blind. Then it was over: one second the air was full of black corruption, then it was clear as if nothing unusual had transpired. Nothing remained of the little girl but a circle of scorched tile on the floor.

"What the hell was that?" Dana said as she staggered back slightly dizzy. Her skin prickled and itched where the black things had passed through her. A cold white hand fell onto her right forearm and sank into her flesh, gripping painfully.

"Hey, that hurts," she said in protest and turned to look at the owner of the offending hand. Helga looked back at her with dark cold dead eyes. She hissed, showing her glistening razor sharp fangs.

Dana screamed.

"She thirsts," the professor said from beside Helga with an accented growl, his dead white eyes glittering with amusement.

"Hey get off her!" Pete shouted as he approached them aggressively. The professor reached out, caught Pete by the throat, and effortlessly stopped his advance by lifting him into the air.

Helga hissed again, and cowered away from the waxing morning light shining through the mall skylights. She dragged a screaming Dana closer to her and effortlessly tucked Dana under her arm like a side of beef. Their bodies blurred as Helga took flight, fleeing the burning light of day. A few yards away, the glass security doors at the entrance to JC Penny's were shattered as Helga and her first victim passed through them, a black blur of shadow. Helga disappeared into the store, seeking shelter from the purifying light of the sun. Dana's screams faded with her.

Pete struggled in the professor's grasp, his feet kicking in the air a foot above the floor. The professor grinned at him with rotting black teeth. "You live," he growled in his trademark Transylvanian growl. "I too need sustenance."

Pete's eyes bulged out from his head as his body withered in the professor's grasp. His tongue protruded as he gagged. Pete's hands raked at the professor's iron grip as his flesh wasted away in seconds until he was nothing more than an emaciated husk of dead skin and bones.

The professor sighed as he gently lowered Pete to the floor and released him. Pete wavered there for a moment, and then moaned and staggered away in search of the first taste of the living flesh his new hunger demanded.

Stiffy suddenly appeared next to the professor and slapped him on the back. "Oh boy," he said with amused fervor. "It's good to be back, *man*. I'm so hungry I could eat The Brady Bunch." Stiffy's black eyes glittered with twisted mirth as an oily-black serpent's tongue extended out past several rows of razor-sharp, shark-like teeth to lick his black lips. "But I'll settle for a family of four," he giggled manically as he pranced off into the mall.

Pointy gasped as his eyes shriveled in their sockets, leaving nothing but black emptiness, little wisps of black smoke curling away from them. Then flame began to rise inside his empty sockets as if his skull were nothing more than a hollow Jack-O-lantern sitting on his shoulders. The unholy inferno burst through the top of his head without burning his hat, his devils horns growing longer and twisting around the flame.

"You!" Pointy shouted. "You there!" He lifted his hand and pointed at a retreating Dean, who had dropped his notebook as he backed away. Pointy advanced on Dean, his new demon body blurring as he crossed the distance between them. Impossibly fast, he clamped his accusing hand over Dean's face. Dean struggled against Pointy's effortless hold on him, his screams muffled beneath Pointy's hand.

"Yes," Pointy hissed. "You have been a bad boy, Dean Patrick Powlowski, son of Michael. Your soul is forfeit."

Dean's struggles ceased as black smoke rose from beneath Pointy's hand. Pointy removed his hand and Dean stepped back. His eyes were gone, only empty sockets remaining, and he let out a groan of desperate longing as he staggered away.

A rasping groan drew the professor's attention away from Pointy and he turned to behold Leah, the Mummy girl. Her once voluptuously curvaceous body had withered away to nothing, her wrappings now hanging on bones barely held together by her dried, emaciated flesh.

"Ah, Leah my dear," the professor growled. "You'll be needing this." He reached up and caressed her wasted face. Entwining his hand in her long hair, he drew her to him and pressed his lips to hers. He breathed Pete's stolen life energy into her emaciated body. Her loosely-hanging wrappings swelled outward as her body filled them.

"Oh yes," she sighed contentedly, "That's so good." Her body stopped just short of her full form. "I need more," she whimpered in protest as she ran her hands over her almost restored curves.

"Of course you do, my dear," the professor growled as he gestured to the world around them. "There's plenty to go around." All around them, the screams, groaning, and cries of terror and pain were becoming louder with every passing second as the newly lifeless began to feed.

"Master!" Fritz cried with breathless urgency as he tugged on the professor's pant leg.

"Yes, what is it Fritz?" the professor asked in annoyance.

"We must flee."

"Flee, in our moment of triumph?" the professor said with a snort. "Whatever for?"

"The Adversary's forces, Master, they are aware of our escape. Even now they draw near and we do not yet possess enough souls to challenge them directly." Fritz began to lurch and jump from foot to foot nervously. "You are vulnerable, Master. We all are!"

The professor sighed in exasperation, "Yes. Of course, the Adversary." He turned slowly and surveyed the carnage taking place all around him with a pleased smile. "You are correct, Fritz, we must take our leave of this place."

Fritz bounced up and down in excited pleasure at having pleased his master.

The professor turned away from the madness and looked down at Fritz. "What of Helga?"

Fritz's third eye rolled in his head and his mouth fell open, drooling saliva onto the floor. The third eye focused on something distant and Fritz nodded. "She will rise with the falling curtain of night; they will not find her before." The eye peered harder, narrowing. "The reporter, Dana Bethany McElroy, she will thirst as Helga does." He smiled. "They will reunite with us under the new moon."

"Ah yes, very good, Fritz, well done." The professor patted Fritz on the head affectionately, then turned away and looked back into the crowd of living, dying, and already dead bodies swarming around them. "Stiffy!" he shouted into the chaos.

Stiffy looked back from where he was standing next to one of the mall's kiosk stands. "Yes, Professor," he whined sarcastically. He grinned savagely, showing his impossibly wide mouth full of bloody teeth. He held a screaming woman in his grasp and shook her to quiet her protests. "Pipe down, we're talking here."

"We have to leave, now stop playing with your food and come on!" the professor ordered.

"Aww," Stiffy moaned, his grin faltering. Then he smiled as he pulled open his bottomless pocket and stuffed the screaming woman into it. "Well, I'm saving her for later." He giggled as he tippy-toe pranced back over to join his comrades.

The Channel 11 news van raced through the intersection, turning onto Mall Road with tires screeching.

"My God, Joey, slow it down before you kill us!" Julie yelled in a worried, unsure tone. "I don't wanna be the news tonight!"

"We gotta get there, Julie. The riot's happening right now and we're the first ones on the scene!" Joey worked the steering wheel, swerving around a UPS truck. "This is gonna be big!"

"This isn't even my thing," Julie said, complaining as she caught sight of one of the many cars going the other way on Mall Road. A clown adorned in black and white makeup with Xs over his eyes was driving the car she noticed. She couldn't make out the passengers clearly but could have sworn she saw some kind of fire burning in the back seat. As the vehicles passed each other, the clown turned and looked her way. His eyes looked empty and he smiled at Julie with a mouth too wide and full of teeth to be real.

Julie shivered. "Their makeup gets better every year," she mumbled to herself.

"What?" Joey asked. He turned his eyes from the road for a second to look over at Julie.

"Look out!" Julie screamed back, pointing towards the front of the van. A police car had turned onto the wrong side of the road and was now barreling towards them. Joey screamed and spun the wheel, trying to avoid a collision, but it was already too late. The fleeing police car smashed into the passenger side of the van, sending it into oncoming traffic.

The impact threw Julie left and then right as the van rolled. Her head smacked into the door window, shattering it and nearly knocking her unconscious. The van came to a momentary rest on its roof seconds before another car crashed into it.

"Oh God," Julie cried as yet another car slammed into the already battered van and it tipped over onto the passenger side, bringing the ground up to meet her shattered window. She braced herself, squeezing her eyes closed in anticipation of the next impact, but it never came. She waited for what seemed like several minutes, but was only seconds, as she listened to other cars racing past the van.

Julie began to relax as the minutes passed and no other cars struck the overturned van. Breathing deep calming breaths, she took stock of her situation. The ground she could see under her was grass and dirt, so she figured the last impact had pushed the van onto the embankment alongside the road. She turned and looked up to her left and saw Joey hanging motionless from his seat belt.

"Oh God, Joey," she moaned. "Joey, can you hear me? Oh my God!" She began to sob as she struggled, then succeeded in releasing herself from her own seat beat.

She fell against the side of the van and then came up on her knees and reached up to Joey. His eyes opened and focused on her. He snarled and clawed at her arms, scratching them.

"Joey!" she shouted, pulling her arms back. "What the hell?"

Joey refused to reply. Instead, he began twisting and writhing as he tried in vain to free himself from his seat belt. Failing to gain freedom, he resumed reaching and growling at Julie, who crouched away from his grasping hands.

From outside someone began pounding on the van's front windshield. The rescuer got his hands into the edge of the window and pulled it away with a crackling of safety glass.

"Oh thank God!" Julie said, crying out as Joey managed to grab a few strands of her hair and rip them free. She reached out for help and the rescuer grasped her arm and pulled her violently from the van.

"Hey!" Julie shouted in surprised pain. "Take it easy! You almost pulled my arm off!" The rescuer continued to pull her up as she struggled to her feet in his grasp. She tried to get away as she gained her footing but her rescuer held tight, bringing her in closer.

"Hey let me go! I'm out already!" she yelled. Then she looked at her savior for the first time, and saw his eyes.

The slightly heavyset, balding man that she had taken for her rescuer gazed back at her with black empty pits where his eyes should have been.

Julie screamed. She pushed at his chest, trying to free herself from his grasp.

They struggled together in the dance of death on the side of the road as cars continued to pass by without stopping. He only held her tighter as she fought against him.

Pulling her deeper into his embrace, he blessed her lips with a kiss of gnashing teeth.

KILLING HEINRICH

SARAH E. GLENN

When Ilse de Milde woke up in the abandoned house, she pulled on her shoes. It was time to kill Heinrich. She needed to end things once and for all.

She'd tracked him from city to city in her quest. Finally, she'd gotten a lead from one of his women. Tears had slid down the girl's bruised face as she told Ilse about the cruelty of her lover. Heinrich's women always trusted Ilse, confided in her, when they saw the dark ring around Ilse's right eye, a permanent memento of Heinrich's loving touch. Providing a comforting shoulder was all she needed to do to learn where and when to find Heinrich.

This time, he had moved to a downtown apartment. The building had no guard or outside locks. Heinrich must have been feeling very confident. Ilse took the elevator to his floor, which was near the top of the structure. The height was perfect.

She walked by his door, placing its location within the overall scheme of the building. Afterward, she took the stairs to the top floor and jimmied the roof exit. The air was cooler, clearer on the roof. Rappelling down the side wall in the breeze was a pleasure. She sidled along the sills and ledges, checking for neighbors.

The apartment on the right of Heinrich's was empty, but showed signs of habitation. The entire wall it shared with Heinrich's apartment was hidden behind a massive stereo and television. She forced the window open and walked directly to the entertainment center.

So many buttons and digital displays! When she was alive, there were only two dials to a radio: one to find the music and the other to control the volume. She finally found the proper button.

One push, and pulsing music filled the room. *Wunderbar*. She turned the volume as high as it would go. Thumping came from the walls, both above and below, from irate neighbors. The most urgent pounding, though, came from the other side of Heinrich's wall.

Ilse unclasped her hair and spread it over her shoulders. She must make herself beautiful for Heinrich. He'd always loved her wavy tresses, either to caress in love or to jerk her to him during punishment. The carpet leading to Heinrich's apartment door was stained. How far he'd fallen. The play on words made her smile. She tapped hard on the faux wood, loud enough to be heard over the music.

Heinrich yanked his door open, a curse on his lips. He stopped short when he discovered the small blonde woman on his threshold.

"*Liebling!*" She gave him a brilliant smile and extended her arms. "It's me! Aren't you going to ask me in?"

Like an idiot, he did.

Her fist caught him below the breastbone, fast and sharp-knuckled. He fell to the floor, unable to speak or breathe. Ilse kicked the door closed and yanked him up by his shirt.

"Remember doing this, Heinrich?" She slapped his face hard enough to whip his head to the side. The imprint of her fingers was already forming on his cheek. Unlike her, however, he would not live to cover it up with makeup.

The man mouthed, "No," but the gasp was lost in the thump of the music coming from the next apartment.

He lied, of course. Heinrich lied a lot. He thought she didn't remember? He thought his other women didn't confide in her?

She would just have to teach him to be truthful again. Ilse thrashed him solidly with her fists and her feet. When he sank semi-conscious in her arms, she tipped his head back, exposing his throat to her fangs. His blood was sweet with pain.

From the hallway, she heard raised voices, keys sliding into the neighboring apartment's door. Time for this to end. She turned to the window overlooking the street. It reflected the lights of the living room.

She smiled.

When Ilse de Milde woke up in the crypt, she pulled on her shoes. It was time to kill Heinrich. She needed to end things once and for all. Before she left, she thanked the body for sharing its berth and replaced the lid on the sarcophagus. Her beds were becoming fewer and farther between.

The gates to the cemetery were closed for the evening, so she leapt to the top of the wall and vaulted over. She could have flown, but she preferred to spring, to stretch out, to swing up and over.

A short walk brought her to a road. Some cars hummed by, others rumbled and rattled as they passed, leaving acrid smoke in their wake. So many cars, so many more than when she began her hunt years ago. No one walked in the evening anymore; everyone drove, hidden in their ugly little cars. Ilse retreated to the shelter of the cemetery wall, where she let herself dissolve. The wind from the river lifted her tendrils of fog and carried her into the city. She floated, anonymous.

There was a time, though, when she spun bodily in the light, all eyes fixed on her bright costume. Cheers as she flipped through the air, the tug of the strong hands catching her. Heinrich's hands. They'd been brought over from Germany for their skills at *rhönrad-turnen*, but it was their work at the top of the tent, not its floor, that Ilse loved. She loved Heinrich, too, whose big hands caught her and saved her from the bare floor below. The audience paid to see the tricks, but also for the danger. Heinrich said that one day they would be headlining with their act, one day they would have their own circus. That day never came.

When she was close, Ilse began bringing her cloud-form together, becoming heavier. She descended, drawing closer to the rooftops below. Her feet solidified first, touching down, then the rest of her body. She squatted above the eaves of the house, gathering the shadows to her. She waited for Heinrich to come.

It might be tonight, it might be tomorrow night. This was the house where his women hid, fearful of his cruel hands. Heinrich had many women.

The night air was hot and humid. She had endured worse, though, with Heinrich on the platform near the roof of the Big Top. The heat of the day and the warmth of hundreds of human bodies collected up there, enough to choke you if the stench of sweat and animals didn't. Here, the smell of fried food and car exhaust permeated the neighborhood. She could also pick up the odor of a factory several blocks away.

She waited there, a beautiful gargoyle on the roof, for hours. Finally, Heinrich came. She knew who he was from the slam of the car door and the bitter scent of human breath mixed with hops. His heavy-footed shuffle slowed at the gate, then broke into a stumble at the stairs.

Ilse moved to the roof edge, peered at him upside-down.

Heinrich thumped the door once, twice. "Nicole!" he shouted. "Nicole, come out here!" He tested the handle; it wouldn't unlatch. His alternative was pounding the door anew.

He had disguised himself again, hoping to evade her detection. Now his hair was shaggy and unwashed, and he'd gained weight. The heat emanating from his form revealed a beefy frame and arms like sheep legs.

A light came on inside the house. Ilse hung lower, listening for the movements inside.

A woman's voice came through the door, muffled but loud enough to understand. "Go away. Leave, or we'll call the police."

Heinrich wouldn't stand for that, she knew. Her expectations were justified. "You got no business calling anyone! I just want to talk to my woman." He began smashing the door with hands and feet, breaking it apart.

His woman. One among many. But he only had one true wife. She hung from the eaves a moment longer, savoring his ignorance of her presence. Then she shifted one hand over the other, twisting her body as she dropped and swung forward, landing feet first on his kidneys.

Heinrich's face hit the door hard, leaving a bloody trail as he slid down. By the time he could raise his head, she was tucking an arm under him and grinning at his bloody nose. "*Guten abend,* Heinrich."

His weight pulled her to the left as she leapt for the roof again, but she compensated quickly. She carried him from rooftop to rooftop, border wall to ledge, fire escape ladder to penthouse skylights. Heinrich struck her legs and back. She ignored him. When he grabbed her leotard and it ripped, though, she boxed his ears. Professional-quality leotards, especially dark ones, were hard to come by. Perhaps it could be patched. The man continued to squirm, but he stopped as they began climbing higher and higher. Ilse took her time; she had all night.

Once, she had believed in him, trusted him, because she loved him. She loved him even when he began drinking after the shows, bitter over never getting 'discovered' by a major circus, frustrated at never making enough money to save, angry with the arthritis developing in his knees. She loved him even after he began sleeping with the women that followed him around at each stop, impressed with his muscles and prowess. She loved him even after he began taking his anger out on her, hitting her with those big hands, those strong hands that had always caught her.

Tonight, he would pay.

The breeze hit her full in the face when she pushed through the trees to the railroad tracks. Ahead was the old train bridge that spanned the river. In rail travel's heyday, it had been a busy junction. The sound of a whistle often interrupted a song by Merle Travis or Tex Williams on the radio. Now, it was long abandoned. Grass grew between the ties, and kudzu trailed over the struts and braces. The vines made for good handholds, though.

She dumped Heinrich on one of the girders. He clung to it and stared at her with eyes no longer dulled by alcohol and cruelty. "What do you want?"

"What I want, you cannot give back. But I can exact a price." His mouth opened as she did a double cartwheel along the narrow metal, graceful and carefree. She finished with a round-off and back-flip onto the next girder. "See, Heinrich? You left me for crippled, and put Maria in my place."

"I don't know what you mean. I'm not Heinrich."

"You always say that." Her laugh was almost childlike, belying the long sharp teeth. Then she was on him, lifting him bodily again. She hesitated at the edge of the bridge, then leapt, somersaulting over and over, speeding towards the lightless space below. At the last moment, she dissolved, leaving Heinrich to plummet through her mist into the harsh waters.

Ilse returned to the house. Lights burned inside, and had probably been on since the incident. She banged on it with the special knock. Ramona peeked through the eyehole before opening the door.

"Lise! Thank God it's you!" The heavyset woman pulled her inside and redid the lock on the door. "Nicole's ex came earlier."

Ilse nodded curtly and asked the appropriate questions: Did they call the authorities? Was anyone hurt?

"He left after we told him we were calling the police. He sounded like he was going to stay, but I guess he changed his mind."

Ilse nodded and sat next to Nicole. She put an arm around the girl, whose eyes were still red and swollen. "I think this will be his last visit to you, *liebchen*."

When Ilse de Milde woke up in the attic, she pulled on her shoes. It was time to kill Heinrich. She needed to end things once and for all.

She crept down to the occupied section of the house and looked for the women. She found them clustered together in the living room, talking in worried tones. They stopped as Ilse entered and regrouped to surround her.

Ramona pushed to the forefront. "We just got a call from Jessica." Jessica was one of Heinrich's women who had been brave enough to leave. "Her ex found her new house. He's driven by it the last couple of days, and now he's just parked out front, waiting. Her neighbor leaves for work soon, and she'll be isolated."

Ilse felt the old pain afresh. Heinrich had risen again. Surely as an angel had descended on her that night years ago, giving her broken body new strength and power, a devil must have done the same for him.

"Does she still have a restraining order?"

"Not anymore. It expired. What should we do?"

She gritted her teeth and headed for the door. "I'll handle it. I always do."

"There's something else you should know," Ramona said. "Jessica's pregnant. She thinks that's why he's out there."

Pregnant.

Ilse remembered being pregnant. When she learned she was expecting a child, hope had blossomed anew in her heart. She thought Heinrich would be pleased. He would see the future reborn. He would stay home at night.

Instead, he was furious. How could she have allowed this to happen? Didn't she realize she would be unable to perform during the summer, their busiest time?

"You plot against me, jealous woman. You want revenge, so you plan to ruin me!"

The next day, he brought one of the Italian girls to rehearse with them. "We must train someone to replace you, since you have been so foolish."

Her name was Maria—were they all named Maria?—and her eyes followed Heinrich's every move. He insisted on teaching the girl personally, despite Ilse's offer to show her their routines.

She fought the nausea and the heat for weeks as the circus crossed Oklahoma, then rolled into Texas. Maria subbed for her on slow nights.

No time for leisurely floating. She shifted to bat form, which she despised. The twilight vision, the squeaking for direction, the flapping wings weren't like flying at all. Tonight, though, it was necessary. Her wings beat the air, forcing her up through the hot heavy air. Much like that last night in Texas, when Heinrich insisted she perform. It was a big night for the circus and the tent was packed. They were paying to see The Flying De Mildes, not some no-name girl.

Below her, Ilse's weak eyes spied whirling lights; a great spinning wheel. A circus? But no, it was merely a carnival. The state fair perhaps? Was it that time again? The Furies were teasing Ilse with her dream, or perhaps merely reminding her of that final night of flying.

The moves were harder, the tucks and rolls less neat, but the crowd clapped and Heinrich urged her to do more daring stunts. She began the long swing for a double flip, let go of the trapeze, and hurtled through the air. She straightened out her torso, reached out her arms...and no hands met hers.

Ilse desperately cried for Heinrich, who was holding his hands just out of reach. Grinning.

The bat lacked the omniscience of the mist, but it wasn't hard for her to identify which house below was Jessica's. It was surrounded by flashing lights. She folded her wings and dove, almost as fast as her heart was sinking.

Men were wheeling a body out of the house, the face covered. Police were searching the small yard around the home. Another officer was talking to a woman with a microphone. Jessica hadn't been in the neighborhood long. Yes, Jessica had moved to escape her ex-husband. Yes, her ex-husband had been seen in the vicinity. No, it was too soon to draw conclusions.

Many voices, many scents. Ilse perched on a gutter and began sniffing. There were many scents here, but only one was unaccounted for. A human scent intertwined with smoke, sulfurous smoke. Heinrich's.

The scent tracked back to a cooling spot by the curb and spots of oil on the street. Here, the human smell blended with exhaust fumes, burning oil, and lemon car freshener.

Ilse listened to the different voices, following the conversations with her acute hearing. Where was Heinrich now?

"I'm going to go have a word with Mr. Bradley while the Sarge finishes up with the TV lady. We'll be lucky if the paper hasn't beaten us there."

Ilse leapt from her spot in a flurry of fuzzy wings and arced above the officer, who was headed towards one of the cars with flashing blue and white lights. When he selected one, she landed on the lightbar and burrowed underneath, clinging to the metal with her claws. The engine started and they lurched away from the house. The lights turned off and air whistled over her, instantly cooling her small form.

Their arrival at Heinrich's could have taken minutes or hours; her sense of time came from scenes, the sliver of nights between slumber. Below her, through the roof that separated them, she heard the officer call for backup. Bradley might be dangerous.

The car came to a halt in a suburban neighborhood. The officer checked on the expected arrival time of the other policemen. Ilse detached from the lightbar and flew around the houses, landing on each sill to catch the scents.

Here, there was the car with the oil and the lemon freshener, and the stench of Heinrich. She circled the house, screeching with frustration at each closed window. The back door opened quietly then, and Heinrich slipped outside. He ran across the lawn and over the fence of a neighbor's home. He was disguised as a *schwarzer*, a black man. Perhaps he believed it would help him elude the authorities...but never her. She would always know him.

He twisted and turned through the driveways of the subdivision, with her flapping behind him. Was he so intent on escape that he couldn't hear her beating wings, her cries of fury? Heinrich's stride finally slowed. He stopped and reached in his pocket for one of the tiny phones everyone but Ilse carried these days. She heard the small beeps of his call, then a woman's voice.

"I need a ride," he said between gasps for air. "I'll meet you at the grocery store on Sixth. My car broke down, doll."

The bastard. He had killed one woman tonight, and was asking another for assistance? Time to strike. She landed behind him, took human form again. When he snapped closed the cell phone and turned, she was there.

Her claws raked across his chest, knocking him back and down. The phone went skittering across the pavement. Ilse pounced on it and ground it under her heel. Heinrich scrambled to his feet.

"Hey, lady, what's your problem?" he shouted.

She grinned at him and swung her claws again. He grabbed her arm and pulled, sending her into a neighbor's chain-link fence. He followed up with a punch to her stomach.

Unfortunately for him, Ilse had stopped feeling pain years ago. At least physical pain. She leapt, wrapping both arms and legs around him, and squeezed. He seized her hair and yanked, but it didn't stop her teeth from going into his neck. She endured his scratches and blows until he slumped against her.

The fall permanently damaged her back. She would never fly again. The fall had caused a miscarriage. She would never bear children again. Heinrich never came to the hospital, nor did anyone else. The circus moved on, leaving her behind. Alone.

Ilse straddled the bench, watching as he stirred and began to move. He rubbed his chest, then lifted his head to check out the dried blood on his fingers. The seat rocked.

"*Liebling,* you might want to think before you move next time," she said.

Heinrich ignored her, straightening, and the seat rocked again. He stared up at her, then over the edge of the safety bar. Below him were trailers and kiddy rides, all dark and silent.

They were in the top seat of the Ferris wheel.

"You're crazy, woman! What do you want?"

"To play a game," she said, standing. She braced one foot on the bar and one on the back of the gondola. Gently, she wiggled it.

"Stop that!" He slapped at one of her legs.

"Why don't you join me? It would be like the game the lumberjacks play with the log in the water, where they spin it and try to throw the other one off."

"You trying to get us killed?"

Ilse couldn't help but laugh. "You never stay dead, Heinrich. Get up, play."

"My name isn't Heinrich."

"You always say that, too." She shoved one foot hard, and the bench rolled ninety degrees. He grabbed for the bar, yelping like a dog.

She rocked the other way, and only his lurch to the seat kept the gondola from flipping over entirely.

"That's the spirit!" Ilse shifted back and forth, singing a song she remembered from her childhood. A song she would never sing to her own child. She grabbed the seat and bar with her hands and began spinning in earnest. Round and round, sky over packed dirt. Heinrich flew shrieking into the air, kicking all the way down. It reminded her of the first time she'd killed him, in Dallas. He'd kicked the same way after she'd flung him off the trapeze. He never insisted on 'no nets' again.

When Ilse de Milde woke up in the abandoned building, she pulled on her shoes. It was time to kill Heinrich. She needed to end things once and for all. If only he would stay dead...

THE MEEK SHALL INHERIT THE EARTH

SAMUEL J. GUSS

Letter to the Editor
New York Times
June 25, 2017

In the end it wasn't supernatural or divine intervention that is wiping us out with the undead. Nor is it exactly due to natural disease and viral infections, though we did play a part in that of course. It was the ants. The Brazilian Carpenter ants discovered at the beginning of the century.

Those of us old enough and nerdy enough to remember reading academic science journals in college, can recall with clarity the time we read about the remarkable discovery that two breeds of Carpenter ants in the Brazilian rain forest had mutated alongside a fungus to form zombiefied ants.

The find was an amazing find and excited us entomologists beyond measure. A moving, living organism that was dead, controlled by chemical processes of its decaying bodily structures and microbes found in certain types of fungus.

It was something out of a horror story.

No one saw it coming and what was at first laughed at as 'science fiction meets urban fantasy horror' became a mass hysteria that would shake humankind to the core.

See, while the ants brought us here to the verge of extinction, it was us, the scientist that had to go probing around with it and our governments to go weaponizing it.

On my desk, in a reinforced planetarium is a small mound of these creatures. Stumbling around, bumping into leaves, tiny sticks and peat moss until a live ant comes too close. A chill races up the spine to see how the zombie ants detect it through pheromones, and lunges towards it as one, sinking their mandibles into the neck of the unsuspecting ant.

It's over in no time and in a few minutes; a new zombie ant climbs unsteadily to its little legs, partially eaten, guts hanging out as tuffs of meat, turning mossy.

The U.S. Government still denies this claim, but I was there. I was recruited. Fresh out of my Master's degree at Harvard in Entomology—the study of insects—a black van pulled up at graduation and a man in a suit inside asked me my name and upon receiving it, invited me for a ride.

It was surreal, like a dime-store detective novel as the offer was made. It wasn't the money, though at the time I was hard-pressed financially, and trying to figure out how to pay the huge college debt I'd collected over my eight years, along with keeping the electricity on in my studio apartment.

It was the opportunity to play god with denizens small as my thumbnail and bring about a naturalistic way of controlling the enemies of our nation. It worked, too.

The thing about messing with life though, isn't the successes we have had in our history. The eradication of polio, bubonic fever and other common viruses in our history are testament to these successes. Before the outbreak, we were on the verge of wiping out cancer, AIDS and even the common cold.

Truth be known, we even had the ability to inoculate ourselves from this most viscous of diseases, but it works to well as population control and as a 'means to an end' to keep those in power on their thrones.

They are inoculated of course. Even I and other fellow scientist are as well. I don't have to worry about ever becoming a zombie, though I find it hard to sleep at night, realizing that I'm among the privileged few who can say that.

With an estimated ten to the seventeenth ants in the world (that's a one followed by seventeen zero's) and at this time about thirty percent are zombiefied, there is no place safe in the world, except Antarctica and in specially constructed bio-centers such as the one I work in.

No one is safe. All it takes is one person to be bit by one of these little buggers and within hours that person is out there infecting others.

We've seen and controlled other species from getting infected, and more or less it's not even the ants anymore, but flies, fleas, rats, spiders, mosquitoes and a ton of other insects of global and regional varieties. Yet, we do nothing other than send out the flamethrower technicians to burn away nests, swarms and tides of these insects, while sniper teams take out the humanoid infections.

The thing is, there is a cure. We're just not making it public and we need to use it now or lose it.

Just like any virus or bacteria, this zombie chemical process mutates, and within a few generations it will have moved past our efforts to kill it like we are now, and a new cycle will have to be explored and studied and eventually—hopefully—used.

They won't go public with it, as it's too efficient in controlling the population. The Red states are gone forever and while politically we may not miss them, millions of people died in a reported uncontrolled infection of the South East.

Uncontrolled? Hardly. If it was uncontrollable, then the entirety of the continental United States would be infected.

So, why am I writing all of this? In the hopes that someone will read it, believe it, and distribute this information. The average person only knows that zombies exist because of failed scientific experimentation.

The truth is: it is controlled. It actually came from nature and was perfected by, and used by, us.

The cure is known and used but needs to be made publicly available and distributed amongst the masses of our little six-legged friends, otherwise all will be lost. In the meantime, don't let the bed bugs bite.

Editor's note:

The esteemed Dr. Redstone wrote this shortly before his suicide. His press secretary stated that Dr. Redstone had become paranoid in his final days of trying to work out a cure for the contagion we have unfortunately come to live with. It is presented here as an example how the disease can eat its way into the normal, rational thought processes of a rational human being.

THE CATALOGUED ROOMS OF QUINCY MANOR

NICKOLAS COOK

(Taken from the unfinished notes for a manuscript written by Professor Pravari Kayshun, Feb. 2045)

An introduction.

Since the Second War of Northern Aggression, many rumors—most unsubstantiated, except by the gullible and the unscientific—have surrounded Quincy Manor.

If one were to put any faith in them, the stories range from the fantastically absurd, to the cosmically terrifying. Because of the current diametrically opposed political climate, and because there have been several technological disadvantages since the Downfall Year of 2026, it's believed by many of my learned colleagues that no one person, or group, has been able to gain entrance to the decrepit domicile. Subsequently, the multitude of rumors has been left to seed and blossom in the festering ignorance of a lost age of man.

As my readers may already be aware, Quincy Manor has become somewhat of a Holy Grail for us in the business of 'Room Cataloguing.' It's rumored that the great abode housed over one hundred separate rooms, each with its own individual character and furnishings.

Some ancient volumes that survived the Great Burning Times, between the years 2028 and 2031, have come to surface among us like half-rotted fish floating up from the Stygian depths of time. But these manuals give only meager hints at best of the manor's contents. They have been deemed mostly faked, or too unreliable to be taken seriously, except by the novice cataloguer.

I write this introduction as prelude to revelation.

For evidence of the singular commonplace truth of Quincy Manor has been placed in this author's competent hands. The fire seared manuscript, like many a forgotten artifact from that before time, has undoubtedly seen its share of trial and tribulation, and may have escaped confiscation or destruction simply because of its mundane appearance. However, this author regrets to inform that the much-lauded—and to my regret, highly publicized—photos that came into my possession with the manuscript have been lost, purposely misplaced, or indeed, outright stolen by unknown authorities. Although they may yet turn up in the black market for some future thief of a collector to paw through at his avaricious leisure, for now—for us—we have a partial documented history of the home, and this detailed description of the rooms.

But before we move forward to the beginning of this long awaited tome, I must beg the reader's forgiveness as I set the stage for its presentation. Think of this, if you have become impatient, as a curtain about to be raised. And now a man, neatly combed and dressed in a black suit and tie, has entered stage right. He stands before you, his pale hands clasped before him. He smiles down benevolently at the eager and responsive faces of his audience-to-be. This smiling and genial man is myself, dear reader. My prelude concerns how this extraordinary manuscript came to me.

How the Manuscript Came to Me.

University Soledad sits upon the ancient hilltops of my ancestors. Nestled within the dusty ruins of Atlanta, it's where I teach and study the craft of 'Room Cataloguing.'

Two years ago, a somewhat dirty-looking individual approached me as I was walking between classes to get some fresh air. A man, who we shall call Thomas A, had hired this beggar to deliver a message to me. I'm not sure if I ever knew Thomas A's real name, for he was a man given to subterfuge and deceit, and trusted no one.

But the beggar was easy enough to surmise. If I had to place his age, given his physical appearance, which was cloaked in dirt and neglect, I would guess he was somewhere between forty and fifty years of age. He carried about him the tell tale signs of radioactive poisoning: missing teeth, the gray-toned bald patches on his head, and a violent case of the ague that ran rampant through his body.

His filth-encrusted, spider-like hands thrust a crumpled piece of paper at me.

The fact that this man had honest-to-God paper was astounding enough, but his unkempt state lent the moment a sense of unreality that can hardly be digested by anyone except the scant handful of the population that can remember paper.

I must admit that I stood in a state of shock for some few moments, until the vile creature murmured something unintelligible and pressed the wad of forgotten luxury into my open palm. I took it, still unable to articulate my surprise. My fingers seemed to work by themselves to unravel the stained and crushed paper.

This is what I read:

"The Room Of Ancillary Dreams juts forth from the inner sanctum of the..."

From there a dark stain so discolored the page that I could make out no other words in the first line. Scanning the rest of the page, I read a disjointed description of one of Quincy Manor's many fabled rooms. Handwritten, in a neat, thin style, it seemed perhaps more feminine in character than male. Although the sex of the author may be debated for many years to come, we'll never know for sure.

Needless to say, I was shocked to hold something of such profound magnitude. I can say with professional humility that my hands shook, as if the beggar had passed his affliction across to me with his prize. I asked where he had come by it. He shook his head and pointed at his throat. At first I didn't understand, but he kept tapping his throat and shaking his head, until I finally gathered he was mute—perhaps another byproduct of his time spent in the Burning Lands beyond. Once more, I repeated my need to know how he had come about the paper. For an answer, he rummaged through his tattered clothing for a moment, and with a stench that wafted to my sensitive nose, he handed me a scratched and much-used vidbox.

He held out his crooked, shaking hand for money, and in my haste, I tossed him half a week's pay without care. The beggar gave a shrill hiss of delight and bounded away in a shambling run.

I looked at the vidbox, my breath trembling, my heart thumping with excitement. I prompted it to play and a rather unclear vid began to unravel. There was no picture, static fizzed and popped on the screen. There was only a man's voice, altered by a purposeful distortion to mask his identity. In a high warble, he gave me instructions.

I won't bore the reader with the convoluted directives, and the outrageous price suggested by Thomas A., but I will only say that, in the end, I became the owner of a tome of knowledge so groundbreaking for my field that I can still scarce believe it. Even now, as I sit to write about what I've discovered in the last two years of my researches and laborious translations, my mind sometimes stumble over its revelations. I have to remind myself that this is not some fantasy created for the simpleminded. This is true enlightenment, cosmic and holy, all encompassing. For if these rooms may exist in our staid universe of ruthlessly straight geometry, then what else may exist beyond our irksome view of that universe? Indeed, may we any longer call this a *universe*? Why not *bi*verse or even *quad*verse? Perhaps we should even consider recognizing this as an *etern*iverse.

Forgive my heady words, but these revelations caused me to forget myself. And now, dear reader, I share them with you.

The Rooms of Quincy Manor
Catalogued by Prof. Pravari Kayshun
(Note: Make sure Quincy's dialogue is translated for vid dissemination processing, as per University Dean's request)

What do we know about Quincy Manor?

Among the many insubstantial legends of its other worldly nature, we do know for a fact that in 1856, Colonel Theolonius Quincy set about its ten year long construction—and this we know because pre-Second War of Northern Aggression documents verify it—with the help of one hundred slaves and a two hundred strong company of hired men. This was pre-First War of Northern Aggression—otherwise known by the misnomer: The Civil War— so materials were plenteous and to be had for little money. Labor was just as profuse, for many Southern males were without work due to the Southern decrease in the import/export ratio between the two politico-economic cabals. One of the many reasons for the First War of Northern Aggression.

As many a collector knows, surviving County records have it that the first post of Quincy Manor was set in the early morning hours of October 31, 1856. This strangely chosen time for the beginning of construction has only added fuel to the fire of its legend.

Why would Col. Quincy choose the witching hour to begin his new home?

The absurd myth, which still enjoys much belief among cataloguing circles, has it that early in life Quincy made a bargain with the Devil, and that for the attainment of wealth, military fame, and a good, healthy wife who would bear him many children, he sold his immortal soul.

And in some respects, it would seem his life followed this beguiled course. By age thirteen Quincy's father died and left the family fortune in his ready hands. Age sixteen, he enlisted in West Point Military Academy and quickly rose through its ranks. It seemed as if Quincy's life was indeed being guided by, if not some demonic entity, than at the very least a celestial star. By age nineteen, he had wealth and was beginning to gain some measure of military fame. The only component missing was the wife.

Quincy's journals tell his logic at this point. His home was deep in the swampy forest of Florida, so he worried that it would take something more extraordinary than marital companionship and riches to lure a wife into its antediluvian humidity. "What woman's childlike heart can resist a dwelling where dream and reality, nay logic and magic, become one..." (Taken from the 4th edition of Luban and Grunden's publication of 'The Quincy Journals').

Where did he get the plans for such a domicile? What earthly imagination could have conceived of such an otherworldly construction?

If possible, this is even more shrouded in legend and myth than Quincy's life after the home was completed, for it's here that his journals cease any discussion of the house, or even what took place after the last nail was hammered in to the last board.

If the folklore is to be believed, the Devil offered something extra—for a further price.

But we're not here to speak of superstitious suppositions, so I won't speculate upon such silly mythology. I will, as far as I'm able, stick to documented fact.

We do know from the famous Dr. Franklin Davis (see appendix) that Quincy had visitors during, and after, the construction of Quincy Manor. The prolific Dr. Davis was impressed enough to make several entries in his copious and markedly well-preserved journals of the wonders that he witnessed within the walls of the colonel's abode. Most of these entries we can give little credence, for their nature is well beyond belief. As the good doctor was well known to be an addict of his own medicines, we must take the most incredible of his entries with a grain of salt, and think upon them only as subconscious metaphor. To do otherwise would be ludicrously unscientific, and would dilute the fantastical elements of the house itself.

This entry, for example, can hardly be considered whole truth:

Today, Quincy brought me to the Room of Corners! I have never seen, nor heard, anything so incredible in my life. I should have known by my host's forced geniality that something more than what science could explain lay behind the simple white door. My mind still reels at the sights and sounds of what lay beyond the threshold. God! How can it be? It cannot. But it was there.

The room seemed perfectly normal when we first entered. I remember Quincy grasping my hand tightly in his own. He warned me, "Do not look behind the corners." I did not understand what he meant, for the room was a simplistic square shape; no corners other than those that made up the shape. Not even a hidden shadow, because the sunlight was bright beyond the white-curtained windows.

And then the corners moved!

As incredible as that sounds, this rooted and solid room began to alter its shape. No longer were there four corners. They began to multiply.

First there were eight of them, then sixteen, and then more than I could keep track of. The room surrounded us. The door to escape was swallowed by these impossible new angles. I was lost among them. All I could feel was Quincy's warm fingers wrapped tightly around my hand.

Each corner seemed to swim forward for inspection, and then just as suddenly, to warp and become more corners. My mind reeled. But the worst horror was yet to come. Quincy told me not to look behind the corners. I should have listened to him. I heard something sigh from beyond one of the blossoming bends of wood and plaster and paint. I couldn't help myself. Dear God! I could not stop my eyes from focusing on the originator of this almost luxurious sigh of contentment. I wanted to know this contentment for my own. It bubbled up from the deepest part of me that I had to know this sensation, that if I could only see around this bend, then I too, could experience it.

I will never forget those bright and knowing eyes staring back at me. It felt as if their preternatural light was stabbing through me, through every fiber of my being, dissecting me as I have many a specimen in my laboratory. I felt more naked and alone than I have ever felt in my life, as if the cosmos beyond was one large hungry entity, intent upon supping on my writhing and useless soul.

I must sleep now, if I can. I must find some logical explanation for this phenomenon. Lack of sleep. Bad food. Overwork. Any of these, and all of them, could explain my experience.

As one may see from the entry, Dr. Davis's mind could barely grasp the incredible geometry of the Room of Corners and it must have spun off into a strange fantasy. This, with the professed lack of sleep and overwork—and an unspoken admission, but historically proven, enhancement of self-administered hallucinatory drugs—must be the cause for his impossible vision. No sane mind could credit such a sight as truth. One can make an argument for the incredible geometry. After all, the universe is comprised of such angles and formulas. But we must seek logic in his experience. Science does not validate the existences of such things as this sighing creature beyond the corners.

There is no God. There is no Devil.

As many know, there are purported to be something between one hundred and one hundred and ten rooms in Quincy Manor. No one knows for sure the exact number. The architects and the builders worked on separate parts of the vast mansion, so they could never come to a true number between them. As stated before, the colonel didn't allow records for public viewing to give us the exact number. It's believed that no one ever saw all of the rooms—perhaps not even the bride for whom Quincy created the mysterious domicile. She died during a breeched childbirth, leaving the old man without wife or child.

Over the decades, fellow practitioners of room cataloguing have devised a list of major and minor rooms, based on folklore and what little true documented evidence we possessed up to this point. The uncounted number not withstanding, the Quincy Manor Manuscript—as it's now known in 'Room Cataloguing' circles— gives us detailed description of twelve of the major rooms, their colors, layouts, shapes, furniture, and even sometimes, the design and fabric of the wallpaper and curtains.

The major rooms the manuscript illumines for us are: The Room of Ancillary Dreams, The Room of Oracles, The Room of Stairs, The Room of Corners, The Room Alight, The Candied Room, The Room of Mirrors, The Room Obscured, The Room of Forgotten Children, The Room of Accidental Geometry, The Room of Secondary Light and The Flowered Room. All of which had various numbers of offshoot minor rooms that tunneled, cocooned, or in some cases, purportedly lay in the same space at a different angle unseen from one side but easily viewed from another.

Since the late Dr. Davis has already given us a taste of his perception of what lay within The Room of Corners, we'll move onward to The Room Obscured, and speak of what the manuscript details.

Its description is vague, but enough is given that I believe we can excise the pertinent details from the extraneous fantasy.

The tome delivers this passage to the curious. (Excerpt 'The Quincy Manor Manuscript' page 234):

Beneath The Room of Stairs, lies The Room Obscured, so named because few know of its existence. Those who knew are no longer able to speak of it. The room is locked at all times, hidden from prying eyes by several right angle cuts along the walls to keep it from the casual observer. Within the room, its solitary denizen lies in wait for those foolish enough to seek ingress—or egress—without the proper protection. The red door bears no symbol for those with earthly sight. But for those with eyes that may see beyond there is much. Beyond the red door, the room appears to stretch upwards twenty yards and outwards at least as far. The walls are of black painted oak, cut at the height of the full moon, and blessed by He Who Walks the Knife of Night. Each plank lies close to the next, so that no light or air may enter or escape. I allowed no windows, for fear of the full moon causing more harm than good, so there is only the light that the curious visitor might carry with him.

However, I do not advise light. I have tested the room myself, sleeping on the cold, hard floor in anticipation of that which makes itself known. It doesn't want light. It detests it. In fact, it requires deepest darkness to exist in this world. I have spoken in a fashion with the room's only true occupant. It has shown me marvels beyond...

The rest of the description continues in much the same manner, always speaking of the mysterious occupant as if he isn't human, giving us tantalizing structural details along the way. For a Room Cataloguer, the meat of the description is found between the lines of such insane ramblings. We have a large open room, black oak walls, no windows, and seemingly no furniture; surely one of Quincy Manor's more austere rooms. The details of the right angles to hide the room are all the more fascinating when one considers that the room is situated under the stairwell. After researching the entire manuscript, I find that The Room of Stairs above stretched down at thirty-five degree angles. This leaves a space that could hardly have allowed for a room the size described hidden beneath it. Using every mathematical resource available, I am still unable to make the angles work. If only the accompanying photos were available, the reader could see for himself, indeed, one room did sit upon the other.

But we will come back to this impossibility later.

Next we move to The Room of Forgotten Children.

There is a folktale about this particular room that has been passed down among generations of Room Cataloguers. It begins after Col. Quincy's wife and stillborn child died, leaving him alone and emotionally bereft at his sudden loss. The legend says he decided to people his house again, to install the youthful laughter he could never enjoy from his own child. Weeks passed, and strange lights and sounds began to emanate from the house. Worried locals reported odd visitors at all hours of the night to the mansion. Blood-curdling screams were heard coming from the dark woods surrounding the Quincy land. Then several local slave children were reported missing. Their bodies were never found. The townspeople pointed the finger of blame at Quincy Manor, but the well-paid local authorities protected the old man against the impropriety of an official investigation. There was no proof Col. Quincy had anything to do with the disappearances, only supposition and hearsay from superstitious locals.

The manuscript doesn't deal with any of this history, and we have no proof that any of it is more than a fantastic fable.

What 'The Quincy Manor Manuscript' does tell us is that the room is twenty-seven by twenty-seven by twenty seven, width and height. If one is to take the number twenty-seven and divide it by three, we come up with three times three times three. Some ancient religious texts tell us that the number three multiplied by itself twice gives us the perfect anti-trinity. Another jumble of numbers will give us the number 666. The folktale states that nine children were reported as missing in a twenty-seven day period of that year. Is this all simply a mathematical coincidence?

Another excerpt ('The Quincy Manor Manuscript' page 27)

The Room of Forgotten Children now resounds with that lost laughter. I have become a father of sorts. They will need to feed soon.

This is the only entry in reference to the room. Mysterious, full of awful portent, but certainly no proof exists that it's anything more than a reactionary gibe at the charges leveled against him. And it's there that we leave this mystery. Whatever Col. Quincy left within The Room of Forgotten Children, we will never know. There are no remaining definitive histories of the era. Much of what is detailed here is nothing more than information gleaned from superstitious folklore passed from one generation to another, later recorded by internationally famous folklore professor, Dr. John Miller, during his 2015 expeditions into the Blasted Zones.

It's in The Room of Secondary Light we see the unknown architect's ingenious use of glass and wood; and yet another impossible challenge is posed to the solidity of Euclidian math.

(Excerpt from 'The Quincy Manor Manuscript' page 589)

As per the instructions of 'He Who Walks the Knife of Night,' I have made the proper signs and created a doorway to a world of secondary light. The doors, both physical and ethereal, remain locked to all but myself. If one moves too close to the outside walls, a faint pulse can be felt emanating from within. To see what the secondary light reveals would drive any other man to the brink of madness. I alone may stand within the radiance of the tainted, sickly green light that throbs with something like life. Something beyond it does know sentience, if not a recognizable life force. And it's aware of my inspection. It watches me from beyond. I keep the stone altar installed near the open portal, in the hopes that the force beyond the nauseating green light will make known its desires. The altar was chiseled out of a massive riverbed stone from an antediluvian time when great beasts walked the earth. The signs and sigils span its mass, interwoven into patterns that no mortal man may look upon without fear of insanity. I dare say, even I, its creator can hardly stare upon the thing without the sense that I am falling into a bottomless well of darkness and meaninglessness. It's the ultimate instrument of angst and hopelessness. How may one live knowing that such things exist? One can only wonder at the intellect that must lie beyond us that may create such things.

And then as a direct contradiction to this most obvious malevolence:

('The Quincy Manor Manuscript page 411)

The Room Alight bears the number of power. Seven windows look into the East; seven to the West. The curved glass is designed to capture the warm morning sunlight. They store the stolen light into a set of specially constructed 'perpetual' mirror angles, so that the light is made to bounce between the glass units. By night, the moonlight meanders past the stained glass windows, and is also captured in the mirrors. Sometimes, in the wee hours of the morning, I can hear the lights dancing with one another in an oscillating frequency, one that exists almost beyond mine ears ability to hear.

Once again, we see mathematics play a role in Quincy's notes. In fact, this morbid obsession with math and measurement seems to dovetail with his vision of the mansion as a place of power.

It would appear to the cautious researcher that Quincy's unhealthy fixation with the domicile overrides his reason, and begins to meander into madness.

But this is a shared madness— at least for your author. My own obsession has prompted a query to the government to allow for an excavation of the land upon which the Quincy Manor once stood.

Months from now, we may know for sure the extent of his madness; we may plumb the rotted vegetation and recover a blurred picture of the lost framework, the squares and angles, of the lost Quincy Manor.

(Addendum to Prof. Pravari Kayshun's final paper on The Quincy Manor)

It's said that madness is like an infection, and for Prof. Kayshun, Colonel Quincy's madness did, indeed, become his own. After waiting for eight months for the 'proper papers' to come through at the university, Kayshun was denied transport outside the city and denied funds to continue his quest for answers about

Quincy Manor. We can only assume that his frustration drove him to become an outlaw.

As reported in every major news vid for the weeks following his abandonment of good reason and morale behavior, we know he stole transport—along with a handful of graduate students and interns working under him at the university—and left for the outlands, in search of the last great mystery of our age.

From the vids sent back along nefarious routes to his colleagues and friends, we also know that he claims to have been successful in locating the manor's ruins. But whether we may trust the dim close-ups, the wobbly shots of a bleak and overgrown wetland jungle, and the sudden departure from sanity that these vids show, who knows?

It's interesting to note that one shot—one that has appeared time and time again on news vids in subsequent years—does allow a 1.4 second glance at something no biologist, anatomist, nor physicist has been able to explain. It's the impossible shape of something bulbous and cratered rising from a pool of pulsing green light. There is no sound, but the jostling of the vid would indicate there was a great disturbance caused by this unknown shape.

This was the last vid his friends and colleagues ever received from him. A search party was dispatched later that week, but to no avail. Shock troops from the Northerner Aggressors drove them away before a proper search might be made.

Many believe that this spilt second shape is only a trick of light and angle—a modern-day sleight of hand for the gullible—sent back along by the good professor to tantalize his expectant audience.

It's said that, in his obsession with finding his Holy Grail, Prof. Kayshun would not accept the reality that anything beyond our mundane world ever existed within the walls of the ruined manor, and that he had created this self-styled illusion to keep himself enthralled with the mystery, a mystery that was undoubtedly sinking into a dank morass of the swamp of humidity, mosquitoes and wasted time.

Was this shape real?

Did Prof. Kayshun finally find his answers?

What lurks within those swampy depths of the ruins of Quincy Manor?

Prof. E. Vocashun

THE UNWELCOMED

DAVID BERNSTEIN

Jared sat on his windowsill looking up into the clear night sky. He wondered how far space went and if someone else—maybe a boy like him on another world—was doing the same thing. A bright explosion lit up the sky, followed by bursts of what appeared to be lightning. Streaks of flame fell to the Earth, one landing not far off in the woods behind his house.

He ran downstairs and told his parents what he saw. His father went outside with him and together they stared at the heavens. There were no more explosions or bursts of lightning, only the twinkle of countless, far-away suns.

The next day Jared went hiking in the woods toward the direction he thought the flaming thing had landed, taking his dog Jeff, a Jack Russell Terrier, with him. Together they scoured the region and came upon a clearing in the woods. The locale was singed; the trees all vaporized into charred sawdust. In the center of the area lay a silver sphere about the size of a bowling ball. He approached the object. Jeff began barking, staying back and outside of the burnt area.

"Come on boy," Jared said, but the dog was slowly backing away.

Jared saw his reflection in the metallic sphere, making him appear elongated. The thing was unblemished, as if newly made. He placed a finger on it. The surface was icy-smooth to the touch. Jeff continued barking. Jared, using both hands, thinking the sphere heavy, and lifted it off the ground. Surprised, the object had the weight of a soccer ball, but felt solid like a ball-bearing. He turned around to show Jeff it was all right, but was met with a low, menacing growl. "What's the matter, Jeff?" He began walking toward the dog, bringing the sphere close to its face when Jeff yelped, turned, and ran toward home. "Crazy dog," he laughed.

He smiled, elated with his find. It had to be from the explosion he'd seen in the sky last night. Maybe it was a piece from a secret government satellite or better yet, from an alien spacecraft!

He walked back home, making sure his parents didn't see him with his new prize. A note was left on the kitchen table telling him they had gone out for the afternoon and would be back in a few hours. He was glad to see Jeff sleeping under the table.

Jared went upstairs to his bedroom. He probably wouldn't have shown the sphere to them anyway, not wanting to take the chance they would make him give it to the authorities. He at least wanted a chance to show it to his best friend, Brett, before he had to offer it up.

"Brett," Jared said into the phone, his voice urgent. "Get over here now. I've got something cool to show you."

Twenty minutes later, his best friend was at the front door, pounding away to be let in. Jared opened the door and led Brett up to his bedroom. He'd kept the sphere in his closet and now took it out for Brett to see. It felt heavier than when he'd first found it.

"Where'd you find this thing?" Brett asked, sliding his fingers along the surface.

"In the woods behind my house." Jared told him about the explosion and the shooting flames and finding the area charred, completely void of life, with the sphere in the middle. "Jeff won't go near it."

Brett tossed the sphere onto Jared's bed and wiped his hands on his shirt. "Dude, dogs are good at sensing things. What if that ball is letting off dangerous radiation or something? We could be dying already."

Jared hadn't thought about the possible dangers. "Nah, it's fine."

"Put it away. If I see you're fine in a few days I'll feel better about it," Brett said.

"Thanks a lot," Jared shoved his friend playfully, then placed the sphere back into his closet and covered it with a blanket. "You want to eat over?"

"Sure."

Later that night, after his parents came home, Jared's mother cooked dinner. Jared and Brett remained silent about the sphere while they ate. During dinner, Jared asked if Brett could sleep over. "As long as it's all right with his parents," his mother said. Brett called and received permission.

Later that night, while Brett was in the bathroom getting ready for bed, Jared went to his closet, uncovered the sphere, and gazed at it. He wondered where it came from and picked it up as if studying it would help render an answer. The object was definitely heavier than before when he'd showed it to Brett. A horrifying thought occurred to him. What if the sphere was sapping his strength? Maybe it didn't weigh any more than it originally did. Perhaps he had simply grown weaker. He put the sphere back, covered it with the blanket, closed the closet door, and ran across his room to the pair of fifteen pound dumbbells he kept under his desk. He lifted one with ease. A sigh of relief escaped his mouth. Brett and his radiation nonsense had scared Jared into believing the sphere was dangerous. He laughed, putting the weight back.

For the next couple of hours the boys played video games, working hard at conquering levels. After completing the game, they watched television, flipping through the channels when a news broadcast caught Jared's eye.

"News, really?" Brett asked, confused.

Jared shushed his friend, intently listening to the broadcast. The anchorwoman was talking about an explosion in the sky the other night. The scene cut to a field-anchor speaking to a man wearing a blue jacket with the word NASA on it.

"One of our satellites fell out of orbit last night. It broke apart during its descent, the pieces scattering about the region, but a few objects fell out of the projected area. If any pieces are found by individuals, they should not go near them as they might be radioactive, and immediately call the authorities."

Jared turned off the volume as the broadcast cut to an accident on the Thruway.

"You see," Brett said, turning toward Jared. "That thing in your closet might be dangerous."

Jared rolled his eyes. "No way. They're just saying that so they can get their expensive equipment back. Besides, you saw the thing, it's just a metal ball-bearing, nothing mechanical or complicated.

"What're you going to do with it?"

"Don't know," Jared shrugged. "Maybe sell it on Ebay."

Brett shook his head. "Well, keep it away from me."

The boys continued flipping through the channels until finding a cheesy action movie. After the movie ended, they went to sleep, Jared in his bed, Brett on the floor in a sleeping bag.

As the boy's slept, in the closet, the sphere began vibrating, six small holes appearing on its surface. One-inch long centipede-like creatures crawled from the holes, ten in total. They slithered their way under the gap of the closet door and along the floor, their tiny legs scurrying quickly in a continuous blur, then separated into two groups of five. One headed toward the bed, while the other group went to the sleeping bag with Brett sleeping soundly.

They climbed up the blankets draped off Jared's bed then up his pillow, stopping at his ear. The lead creature squirted a numbing agent from a hole on its head before it and its brethren entered Jared's ear canal.

Once deep inside, past the drum, they linked together, end to end, becoming one, and burrowed into an artery and released a plethora of eggs. While this was happening inside Jared, Brett was also being infiltrated in the same manner. Once the organisms were emptied of their eggs, they dissolved into a liquid-goo that would be absorbed by Jared's body.

The following morning, the boys were starving as if they hadn't eaten for days. Jared's mother served pancakes, eggs, toast, cereal, sausages, bagels, and three glasses of orange juice each before Brett returned home. Jared left the table, his stomach ready to burst, and went to the living room to watch television. Shortly after the large meal, he began feeling ill. His face was flush and his forehead felt warm.

"You better go lay down, sweetie," his mother said.

Two hours later, Jared was lying in sweat-soaked bed sheets. His skin felt as if it was on fire. He writhed in agony as his stomach churned nauseously. When his mother came in to check on him, she gasped at the sight of her son. She grabbed an old glass thermometer she'd had for years and placed it in Jared's mouth, but he bit down, shattering the thin glass.

"Spit it out!" his mother cried. "Don't swallow the mercury, Jared!" She slapped his cheeks, trying to get him alert. He was hardly able to hear, let alone comprehend her words. He chewed the bits of glass, grinding them into smaller pieces, the liquid mercury sliding down his throat.

Jared's mother sat him up, bent him over, and began thumping his back with her fist. "Spit it out!" she kept shouting, not knowing he'd already ingested it. Jared's father entered the room.

"What the hell's going on in here?" he asked.

She ran through Jared's symptoms and how he'd chewed the thermometer.

"I'm calling an ambulance," Dad said and left the room.

Jared began screaming in agony, reaching out blindly into the air, but as suddenly as his screams began, they stopped. Small bumps, the size of golf balls began appearing across his skin.

His mother screamed. "Forget the ambulance! We need to take him now."

Jared's skin began rippling, the lumps undulating before they began bursting open. Yellow pus, mixed with fleshy chunks of gore, exploded from each one, releasing the newborn centipede-like creatures. A group landed on Jared's mother. She cried out and jumped backward, brushing the creatures off her.

Jared sat up as his father entered the room. He looked upon his son with horror, Dad's face scrunched up as if ready to sneeze. Jared let out a screech before his skin split open along his arms, revealing shiny onyx insect appendages. His fingers became tentacles, each one a foot long.

Jared tore the skin from his face along with his scalp as if they were latex, revealing an insect-like head. It had bulbous eyes like green marbles and fierce looking mandibles that opened sideways, showing multiple sets of sharp teeth.

He screeched again as hundreds of the offspring scurried along the floor, trying to climb up his mother's legs. She began stomping them, leaving green and yellow gobs of goop and crushed insect parts. The monster that had once been Jared screeched again before jumping off the bed and springing to its feet. His socks were shredded cotton, the insect-thing's three pronged talons having torn through. Large spikes, resembling curved daggers, protruded from the back of its legs.

The creature launched itself at Jared's mother, knocking her down, pinning her. It sank its tentacle fingers into her face, the squiggly appendages revealing themselves as they spread across her skull. It pulled its arm up, tearing the woman's face off, leaving exposed bone and muscle. She lay screaming as Jared's father grabbed his son's baseball bat and cracked the creature across the back of the head, breaking off an antenna-type protuberance. The creature squealed, turning around. A third arm, with a scythe-like end, sliced Jared's father from groin to head. The man's body split in two, revealing heart, lungs, intestines and gallons of blood.

Jared's mother still lay on the floor, crying out in pain, her fingers caressing her skinless face. The creature lowered its face to hers and from its mouth released a dark liquid. Within seconds she fell motionless, but still lived. The centipede babies crawled onto her, entering any open orifices they found, some making their own. The creature that was once Jared turned and ran out of the room and down the stairs. It heard noises from outside—more hosts were approaching. It burst outside ready to attack, but was met with a hail of bullets. M-16's and M-60's tore through its carapace. Green slime exploded from each hole a bullet made. The creature writhed on the ground, squealing like a pig being slaughtered before succumbing to death.

"Check it out, Captain," a man said.

"Yes, sir." The captain, along with a few additional personnel, approached the fallen alien. "It's dead, sir, like the others."

After checking the house for more aliens, the military men left the bodies they'd found inside and set it ablaze before confiscating the sphere. The alien's carcass was carted off in a secure bio-bag, headed for a lab in D.C.

"Sir," the captain said to his commanding officer. "We have another report of a sick boy. Just down the road."

"All right men. Let's move out. We've got an invasion to stop. Let's show these things they're not welcome on our planet."

SHADOWS

ELISE HATTERSLEY

What wakes me up is the sensation of someone sitting down next to me on my bed. *Mum?* I think incoherently, but my mum doesn't live here; I'm an adult now, and people don't sit on the side of my bed. Silence follows, and I give it up as the final shred of a dream. Drowsiness begins to take over my body again, and the comfort of my familiar bed helps to soothe me back down into sleep. I know this house inside and out and its familiar creaks and soughs are like a quiet lullaby.

The soft tread of careful footsteps on the carpet brings me back, and I open my eyes. Staring into the shadows of my bedroom, I try to breathe slowly, imitating sleep. Is there someone in my room? Will they kill me if they realize I'm awake? Is it a burglar?

The silence spins out again, and I begin to relax, ascribing the sound to the neighbor's noisy son and the distorting effect of near-sleep. The tightness of fear starts to let go of my throat.

Adrenaline bleeding away, I feel exhausted again, and my eyes begin to close when I see a shadow move. A shadow that, I suddenly understand, shouldn't be there at all.

My body bypasses my brain and I sit up, my mouth open in an aggressive yelp, my hands coming up to protect my chest.

They are everywhere…and more are coming.

Hanging from the walls, the ceiling, cluttering up the corners. Some crouch on my chest of drawers or lurk, cat-like, atop my wardrobe. The ones perching on my footboard and headboard remind me of vultures, but the suspicion of a humanoid body is common among all of them. Their shadowy shoulders just reach the top of the mattress, and they crawl and lurch along the floor, the walls, the furniture. Their hands are long, I see, with thin, tapering fingers. From the mirror on the wardrobe door, more are stepping into the room. Most are silent, but occasionally I hear the soft sound of a foot touching down on my side.

The mirror itself doesn't shatter or ripple—as if there was no glass, and the room's reflection is actually another, backwards room cleverly concealed by the wardrobe's doors —a bitter Narnia.

A movement catches my eye and I look beside me where one sits obscenely close to me on the bed, its face within a hair's breadth of mine. Seemingly made of shadow, it looks like swirling smoke. Eyeless, mouthless, noseless, it should be bereft of expression, but I sense a malevolent smirk curling the corners of an inexistent mouth.

It takes me by the arms and puts me back down on the bed so effortlessly that I might as well not struggle. I try, and my muscles scream with the strain, but my arms don't move at all and the long, cold fingers dig into my flesh.

They swarm, and their flocking blots out the world. I try to scream, but one crawls head-first into my mouth and forces its way down my throat.

Tears spring into my eyes, and I feel a smoky, ethereal tongue lick its way up the track on the left side of my face before those tapered fingers slip into my eyelids and pull them up, and the owner of the tongue finds its way into my skull, scraping its insubstantial body past my eyeball and pushing out further tears.

As they descend upon me, sliding themselves up my nose, into my ears, into any and every available orifice, I see memory after memory play itself out.

A man murders his wife for over-cooking his food; his children watch as he hangs himself from the oak tree that still grows in my back garden. A woman dies alone and her cats attempt to eat her, and while she lies rotting in the kitchen, her husband fucks his mistress in his office before returning home and ignoring the corpse. Children hide under the floorboards and wait for their stepfather to sober up and put the gun away, not sobbing quietly enough to keep from being found.

I am them, they are me, and I feel their fear, their despair, their rage, and their darkest urges. Memory after memory finds its way into my brain, and my weeping, silent though it is, shakes the bed and rattles the headboard against the wall.

The flow of creatures tapers off after what seems like an eternity. I feel my chest heave, feel my skin stick out at odd angles where an elbow or a knee pokes at it from inside before melting away and weaving itself into my flesh. I have been soiled, impregnated with the horror of these memories.

The hands that have held me to the bed all this time let go. I look at him—I think it's a him—and he looks at me. The dampness of sweat and urine makes the sheets cling to me, and again I sense a grin on the face he doesn't have. Then he raises his hand—I flinch—and tips an imaginary hat at me before slowly, deliberately, inescapably forcing himself into me.

I see my bedroom, the long-ago wallpaper bearing *My Little Ponies*, and the little girl they drove mad. The way she slowly lost all hope of escaping them and ended up in a state of permanent catatonia. I feel her pain as she withdrew, never to return, so deeply into her own mind that they can no longer touch her, dirty her with the filth they are made of.

I remember a little boy, before her, and another little boy before him; a succession of children stretching back for decades, with the occasional adult-sized gap when someone ignored the convenience of the larger bedroom for this one's coziness, like I did. And then it comes rushing back to me, and I remember every single night this has happened before, every time I've come to this point and known that the only way to live with this, without risking another child's mind and soul, is to forget.

I lie in my bed for what seems like hours, as a slow-motion dawn starts painting the curtain's pattern on the ceiling, and I consider my options carefully, as I now know I've considered them time and time again, night after night after night, since I moved in three years ago.

I make the same decision. I remember too well the way those kids felt, how futile their children's defenses were against the memories forced into them each night.

I fall asleep and find a blissful oblivion, again.

The morning is just like all others. My sheets are crinkled and smell suspect, so I strip the bed and throw them into the wash, thinking vaguely about how much I sweat in my sleep.

For a moment, a whiff of ammonia comes to me and I almost remember…something. Then instinct kicks in and I shove it aside, roughly, not wanting to know what lurks in the depths of my mind.

I get on with my day, relishing the bright sunshine as it pools on the floor near the windows. The house is comfortable around me, familiar. There's nothing like knowing exactly where you belong.

There's no place like home.

SINS OF THE FATHER

NICKOLAS COOK

Danny leaned into the cold steel bars, his face pushed carelessly between two of the time-worn bars that made up the cell door, and kept the world locked away from him. If he moved an inch either side, his sensitive nose could pick up the scents of men decades before him, their smells, their despairs, their acceptance of the inevitable days and nights in prison.

Danny sometimes liked to play a game of trying to figure out who had his cell before him.

Well, 'liked' was probably the wrong way to describe what he did to occupy his stretches of time between the structured blocks of time sanctioned by the powers-that-be, the nameless, faceless assholes who now controlled every second of his existence.

Yes, the word 'like' was pretty much an anomaly in a place like this. You did the things you had to do to survive. One rarely liked to do them.

Love for anything or anyone was an even thinner reality behind tons of concrete and steel that had been his home for the last three years, and unless some miracle occurred, it would be for another ten years, at least.

He used to think about those numbers a lot—how many days he'd done, how many more he still had to do to satisfy the bastards who'd put him here—but now it just left him numb and confused. He'd been here for a time; he was here now; and he was going to be here some more. Days and nights that were not his own and days and nights he'd never get back.

Eat up, boy. He could hear that voice in his gut tell him whenever he got the urge to feel sorry for his plight, his father's voice.

You done fucked up, son. You gots to take your just desserts like a man. Sometimes it's sweet as apple pie. Most times it's shit on a stick. But you make your own desserts, boy, and ain't nobody can help you eat it up.

Danny would've liked to punch the old man in his face whenever he found himself being lectured by that familiar rasping inner voice. But how could you punch a dead man?

Besides, there was always a little part of him that knew the voice was at least partly right.

He'd been the one who carried the gun; he'd been the *Billy-badass* who pulled it during an argument with his ex; and he was the one who threatened the stupid bitch with it when she'd gotten on his last frazzled nerve. The fact that the loudmouth bitch had been in the right only compounded his self-loathing about the matter. But she'd sassed him in front of his friends. She'd just about cut his balls off for all his boys to see with her big fat mouth, cutting him with her mocking words, laughing in his face when he warned her—warned her!—fair and square to shut the hell up.

Danny realized he'd fallen into the familiar moment of his past that continued to harass him when he was dumb enough to let it catch him unawares. He loosened his white-knuckled grip on the cold bars and stepped away, angry at himself for allowing memory to come swimming out of the deep green sea of his soul and give him a nasty nibble.

He had his back to the bars when another familiar voice broke through the tumultuous silence.

"Hey, there, boy," the man said. "You got some mail here." Before Danny could turn all the way round to face the smirking guard, a small white-stained envelope came sailing inside. Like all mail that came into the prison, it had been opened and perused by the guards, to ascertain that it contained nothing illegal, no coded escape plans, no devices for making bombs or anything that would allow a prisoner to escape his cell.

Sometimes the letters or postcards were even censored by one of the prison staff, if they read something they thought might be considered code. Even love letters got the black marker treatment sometimes. Especially if the jerk reading the letter was a miserable son-of-a-bitch who thought it good chuckles to delete some steamy passage, some far away sexual hope, from a lover or wife on the outside.

It gave some of those bastards a real thrill to steal even that tiny pleasure from their charges. After all, they were all guilty of something, so why shouldn't they be punished in any small way possible, whenever possible?

Some of the guards, assholes like Yancy, who'd thrown the letter at him through the bars of the cell door, lived for those little moments where he could stick it to the inmates in ways no judge or jury would ever have thought of, small ways of killing the soul.

Yancy tapped the bars with his nightstick, sending a sharp echo through the small cell. He gave Danny a smile that made his heart hurt and his skin crawl. "Hey, fuckhead, my condolences." Then he laughed and walked away, leaving behind the stench of his cheap aftershave and garlic breath. Danny felt a doom-ridden chill creep up his back as he bent over to retrieve the abused parcel. His hands shook as he turned it over to see it was from his mother.

A quick, unbidden flash of memory struck at him from that green depth where he tried to drown all his past, the time before his life had become steel bars and tirelessly precise work, sleep, shit, and eat schedules. It was one of the many times when the old man had been at him and his mother with his fists and his rage. With unwanted memory came the remembered terror and uncertainty. Time didn't dull those moments in the least. Such emotions always remained razor sharp as a vicious backstroke from a cold knife. They always left him a little breathless with their insistent violence, juggernauts that refused denial.

The crumpled envelope lay in his hand like a ruined bird, fragile and tattered.

Danny slowly pulled open the ragged slit, and as if in a dream, slipped the sloppily folded letter from its ruptured belly. The paper came apart easily because someone before him had already read it, stolen this private moment from him like they'd stolen everything else from him since the second he'd been forced inside. That was probably the thing he resented the most, that thievery of his most intimate moments, his pain and anguish, his joys and loves. None of them were his alone anymore.

Spying eyes watched his every movement, every day and night. If he took a shit, a piss, if he dared to even capture a stolen moment of masturbatory pleasure for himself in this hellish place, they knew it. They told him what to eat, what to drink, what to watch on television, how much he could watch on that television, what music he was allowed to listen to, who he could talk to, when he could talk to them, what he could say to them.

For a second, Danny felt all that boiling up inside of him like rotting vomit; it threatened to overflow, spew forth in some burning response to his situation.

The letter still lay in his hands, waiting to tell him something he didn't want to know, perhaps something he couldn't handle.

Danny forced his numb hands to finally hold the opened letter before his eyes and he read it yet again.

Dear son,

I got to tell you something and don't know how do it. So I suppose the best thing to do is just do it. Son, I'm sorry to tell you that your daddy's dead.

They tell me he was workin' in Georgia somewhere and he got hit by a tree that came down the wrong way. I know you loved him and he loved you, so I know this isn't easy to here.

I hope to see you soon.

Mom

Danny read the letter several more times, feeling a slow combination of emotions roll over him like venomous waves. Tears sat in his eyes, shimmering but not falling. The cell seemed to constrict around him for a moment, like a throat working to swallow him for good.

The letter fell from his hands, and hit the dirty concrete floor with a quiet feather-like rustle. His hands came together in an unconscious prayer; his body shook as the emotions ran through him. Shadows rose up from the corners of the cell.

Danny fell to his knees and began to laugh.

Loved him? Loved that fucking bastard?

As usual, his mother had no concept of how he really felt about anything. She wanted to believe that all was well, that they had been, and were still, the All American family.

Here he was in prison for damn near killing his ex-girlfriend; his father and mother utterly estranged for nearly a decade, and she still believed there was nothing wrong.

All is well. Nothing wrong, here. Don't look too close. Or pick at the scabs. Don't peek behind the curtains.

A series of memories killed his laughter, turning his ironic reaction to bitter venom at the back of his throat.

His father making him hold down the chicken while he chopped off its head. The warm stinking blood exploding from the dead animal's neck, showering the small frightened boy, in his eyes, lips, in his hair.

His father laughing at his horror at the headless dancing body, the crazy flapping wings, the head, its eyes opening and closing, black eyes looking at Danny as the head died.

His father slapping his mother, calling her names he didn't understand, ripping at her t-shirt until it fell to pieces around her shoulders, exposing her naked, blood-stained breasts; Danny turning away in dismay and terror, hearing the screams as he continued to beat her until she couldn't stand up anymore.

The shotgun was held against his chest; his father was drunk, could hardly stand up, wavering on his feet, the weapon, cold and hard against his quivering flesh, as the old man smiled at him, his eyes barely able to focus on his son. "Think you smarter than me, do you? Show you…by God…show you…you little bastard…"

The old man looking at him from the truck cab. Warm summer rain splashing against the windshield. The Greyhound bus waited in the terminal; slow people were boarding it, heads down.

Danny watched them, wondering if any of them were feeling the mixture of fear and excitement he was feeling. "You leave now, you don't come back. You hear me, boy?"

Danny turned his attention to his father's grizzled, Whiskey-sodden features, eyes bleary and yellowed. All he felt was for the man who sat next to him was cold distance. No hate, no rage. Just nothing.

"I won't ever see you again," he said.

"No…no, you won't."

Danny found the letter next to his leg, and slowly picked it up.

A sound of shuffling feet drew his tear-heavy eyes into the corridor. Through their shimmer, he could see Yancy. The tubby guard was watching him again, smiling down at Danny as he kneeled on the stinking cold concrete floor of his cell.

Yancy's voice was mockery and hatred rolled together. "Oh, did the tough little boy get some bad news?"

Danny stared at the guard through the bars. The sparse cell light gave the man stripes of dark and light—a painted vulture.

Danny crumpled the letter in one fist and threw it at Yancy with such sudden violence that the man actually flinched and tried to duck away.

The paper of course only bounced off the steel bars and fell back into the cell, but Danny still felt a small triumph.

"Go fuck yourself, Yancy."

LEAVE FULFILLED

CHRISTOPHER NADEAU

A Tale of Promised Enlightenment Told in Three Parts

1

The first thing I notice about him is that his face is missing. His voice is the same and it looks like he's wearing his favorite red shirt, but there's no face, meaning no mouth and no eyes. I don't understand how he's talking to me but that's the least of my troubles. He says he's come here to lead me out of bondage.

I tell him I'm not in bondage. I'm free. He laughs. It's an odd occurrence coming from a blank white slate. He tells me that's part of my problem. He extends a hand and insists I allow him to show me something important. Against my better judgment, I accept and everything vanishes.

2

The place he brings me to is not a place but a realm filled with bizarre imagery and a seemingly endless expanse of open land. There is no sound here except my breathing and my faceless companion's gentle footfalls. I walk behind him because I'm afraid of where I'll wind up if I don't.

As we walk, I want to leap forward and bash his skull in with my fists clenched together into a single weapon. Where does this smug son-of-a-bitch get off telling me I'm in bondage? What is he in? What makes him so goddamn superior?

He turns and faces me and my resolve crumbles.

"We have arrived," he says.

I laugh, I think. The place where he stopped walking is no different from the rest of this no-place shithole. My faceless friend merely stands in place, as if expecting me to say something or make a move. All I can think to do is stand there and stare back.

3

I don't mean to kill him. I don't. It just happens.

Something about him just standing there, faceless, like a detached torturer performing an experiment. It drives me over the edge.

I don't know how to get back

Now I'm stuck in this place that isn't a place, this realm my idiot friend thought held all the answers. This is not enlightenment. This is not freedom from bondage. This is nothingness, emptiness, solitary seclusion!

I step over his unmoving body, prepared to trek out into the endless expanse, only to find myself in a familiar room. An old friend jumps up from his kitchen table and emits a high-pitched yelp.

"My God, is that you?" he says.

I cock my head to the side and ask him what he saw. He says one moment he was alone, the next he wasn't.

He frowns. "What happened to your face?"

I smile but he can't see it. Offering no explanation, I extend my hand and tell him I can free him from bondage.

"You just need to come with me."

ONCE MIGHTY

CHRISTOPHER NADEAU

We were the Scourge of the Open Seas, the greatest threat to any sailing man who crossed our path. We laid waste to vessels three times our size and rarely lost a man doing it. Everyone feared us, aye, and it was earned.

Not anymore. Not since we sailed into the Hole.

It wasn't planned. We knew nothing of it when we set sail for the Western lands and ran across a British naval vessel heading in the opposite direction. My first mate took one look at the ship and said, "Not that one, Cap'n."

I looked at him as if he'd gone mad. We'd been sailing for weeks with neither land nor other ships appearing to break the monotony. The men were starving and surly; there was talk of revolt.

With one final glance at my first mate, I announced to the crew that fortune had smiled upon us this day. The resulting cheer convinced me I'd made the right choice. I should have listened to my first mate; his instincts were never wrong.

For upon that vessel resided a pervasive emptiness and things born in the dark.

We felt it as soon as we crossed the plank and set foot on her hull. We'd thought the crew was hiding below decks but we soon realized the ship was unmanned. Though it was not without its occupants.

My first mate looked at me and gritted his teeth. "Orders, Cap'n?"

I shrugged. This empty place bears no landmarks, nothing to distinguish supposedly different sections of the great black sea upon which we sail. Which way is North or any other direction and why should it matter? It seems as if all directions are the same here, none of them leading to salvation.

Even this man of the sea longs for the sweet sensation of unmoving surfaces beneath his feet.

I chuckled and patted my first mate on the shoulder. "Onward! Till there be daylight."

The first of my men started screaming at such a high-pitch he was heard from the gallows. By then, most of the boarding crew was on the other vessel.

The screaming crewman couldn't be understood but we all felt his dread. It rippled through the air and through us like the coldest sea breeze.

When we found him, there was nothing but a punctured, fleshy balloon in a pool of drained fluids.

All of the crew came aboard to bear witness, leaving behind only those screaming from the galleys for release. It was as if they sensed they would soon be abandoned.

"Do ye think we be dead, Cap'n?" asked my navigator.
"Perhaps," I said.
His eyes narrowed. "I'm not yet ready for that."
I smiled. "Nor I, lad."

What emerged from the bowels of that ship was a silent war of dread, things born of the dark in an uneasy alliance with a hungry abyss. Their soundless assault ripped into many of us, turning once vibrant, strong men into quivering, oozing mockeries.

I must admit to cowering in a corner, my sword held limp at my side. This was no British crew defending its vessel; it was the abyss crawling out to feed on the damned.

My brave, battle-hardened crew withered before its onslaught.

Some of us were spared.

"Do ye see that?" cried the navigator. " 'Tis some sort of convergence!"

I squint in the direction he's pointing and can swear I see it, too.

Up ahead, the black waters merge into a single point, as if we've reached the end of our journey. What if there's nothing beyond it?

It swallowed us. It reached out and filled us with cold and despair. Our bodies were no longer our own, our minds mere blank slates to be controlled. We understood at once its unquenchable hunger, its need to envelop and merge with us.

We became its sustenance in a different way than the others. It sent us into the dark places to keep it company and we did what we always did. We sailed the sea in search of…something.

"My God, Cap'n!" my first mate said. "We're comin' to the end of this!"

"Aye." I leaned forward and lowered my voice. "But what next?"

"It matters not. So long as this nightmare ends!"

He's right. Moments later, we reach the point of convergence and pass through into the next great mystery.

The hunger travels with us.

THE BACK ROADS

P. DAVID PUFFINBURGER

"We'll be there tomorrow," Brent said.

"We had better be, my ass is tired of sitting," Paige said.

"Oh no, we can't have that pretty little ass hurting," he joked as he put his arms around her and rubbed her butt, making her purr.

When they opened the motel room door, allowing light to spill inside, they saw cockroaches scatter in all directions.

"Hey, I'm not sleeping here!" she said, disgusted.

"Yeah we're getting our money back. This place is gross."

Brent went to the office and banged on the bell over and over until the manager came out from a back room.

"Hey, man, our room has roaches in it. I want my money back," Brent demanded.

"Well, that's too bad, 'cause you ain't gettin' it back," the manager snapped. He was an old fat redneck wearing a wife beater shirt and a pair of sweat pants that were too small for him.

Brent reached across the counter and grabbed him by his shirt, chest hairs, and skin. "Look, asshole, you're gonna give me my money back or I'll beat the shit out of you!"

"Okay, okay, calm down. You made your point. You can have it back," he said with his hands in the air.

After Brent got his money back, he went to the room to see if Paige was ready to leave. She met him at the door, ready to go. "Let's get out of here before we get cooties," she said.

He took the bags and went to the car. He popped the trunk on his 2003 Camaro, and threw them in. A pickup truck full of rednecks drove up, stopped under a streetlight, and stared at Paige for a few minutes while Brent was packing everything up. When they didn't drive away, Brent became angry and yelled at them, but they just laughed and then finally drove off. Brent finished loading the car and they left the motel. He turned down a road he thought went to the highway, only someone had moved the sign so it pointed the wrong way.

He drove for a few miles until spotting a sign: **Craton 8 Miles**.

"Craton. I've never seen any signs for that town before," Brent said.

"How often do you come this way?"

"Once, but I never stop when I'm by myself, I drive all night," he said.

"Well good, maybe they have a decent hotel to stay in."

Headlights came up behind the car, the driver using his high beams. They were so bright that Brent had to look away from his mirrors. Then four more lights came on and the brightness of them made both Brent and Paige shield their eyes.

"I think it's those redneck assholes we saw earlier," Paige said as she turned around and peered through the lights.

"I'll pull over and let them go by."

Brent pulled over onto the shoulder of the road, but when he slowed down, the vehicle behind him stopped as well. Then another pickup swung around and blocked him in. He was trapped! Brent looked at Paige and their hearts started to pound in their chests. The seconds felt like hours and they both held their breath. Sweat formed on Brent's forehead as he waited for what might come next. Paige bit her lip, her hands clenched tight. The vehicles just sat there.

There was muted laughter and then the trucks drove off. When they did, Paige saw the one parked behind them had been the same pickup truck from the motel.

They sat there for another five minutes, both of them letting out a sigh of relief, then Brent started to pull out. As soon as he did, headlights came on and a horn blew. Another pickup had been there with its lights off, waiting for them. Brent and Paige both screamed, thinking for sure the vehicle was going to hit them.

Brent's drove back onto the shoulder, and the headlights from the other vehicle lit up the road and the inside of his car. Brent stomped on the gas pedal and the Camaro spun its tires but couldn't get traction. When it finally did, it took off with the other vehicle right behind it. Both vehicles sped down the road at high speed. Brent spotted a sign: **Simpville best barbeque in West Virginia.** Brent turned down the road of the sign and drove even faster.

"Brent, slow down!" Paige screamed

"I can't! Those assholes are right behind us!"

The truck behind them started to slam into the back of their car. Paige began crying and screaming. "Make them stop, make them stop!" she shrieked. Her face was soaked with tears, and snot bubbled out of her nose; her high-pitched screams in his ear didn't help the situation.

Someone had removed the guard rails that protected cars from going over a high drop-off, and they'd removed the 'sharp turn' sign, so Brent didn't know the turn was there.

The aging muscle car went flying through the air. When it came down, it landed in a thirty foot drop-off, a hollow that had been cleared of trees. The car flipped over and over again, finally coming to rest upside down almost at the treeline.

Minutes later, Paige crawled out with minor cuts and bruises all over her body. She stumbled around to the driver's side to get Brent, but he'd been knocked unconscious. He was still breathing, so she knew he was still alive.

Headlights appeared at the top of the ridge and she began to panic. She didn't know what to do. She didn't want to leave Brent, but she knew what would probably happen if she stayed.

The men in the truck were running down the hill towards her, and she could see them by their pickup truck's headlights, their flashlights bobbing up and down. She pulled on Brent and tried to wake him up but he wouldn't move.

"Brent, wake up! Please wake up! They're coming!" she cried as she watched the rednecks close the distance between them. She shook him harder, trying to wake him, until the rednecks were less than twenty feet from her.

Knowing if she stayed she'd be caught, she had no choice but to run, so she dashed into the woods and hid behind a fallen tree.

"Hey, city boy, I see you wrecked that pretty little car of yours," a fat guy said to Brent.

They forced open the car door and dragged Brent out. Paige watched from her hiding place and held her breath.

"Ha, looks like you're in deep shit now, boy," the leader said as he poured beer on Brent's face to wake him.

"Paige…Paige, where are you?" Brent mumbled, out of it but still calling for his girlfriend.

"Paige is the bitch's name, huh? Well, we ain't seen her so she must've got thrown from the car," he said. "You boys look around for that sweet piece of ass we saw at the motel," he told the others.

Four of the five rednecks walked away to do as they were told.

"Now, boy, where's your wallet? And anything else you got that might be worth somethin'?"

The man that stayed with the leader started to search the Camaro and took anything of value. The leader searched Brent's pockets and took his wallet, and counted his cash. They took his cell phone, IPod, watch, and his GPS.

"Well now, city boy, you have two hundred bucks on you, that ain't bad. Most of you dumbasses have no cash nowadays. They all use their debit cards and credit cards. That don't help us none. You see, we take from people like you so we can support our families. Ain't got no jobs around here. This shit ain't personal, boy, even when we kill you, it's just business." The leader started laughing.

Up on the road, an old Cadillac pulled up and stopped. The driver got out and ran down the hill and into the treeless hollow. It was the manager from the motel.

The leader wasn't happy to see him. "What are you doin' here, you dumb shit? Why ain't you at the motel? What if some more people come by?" the leader asked the motel owner.

"That asshole grabbed my chest hair and pulled out half of them, now I want to be the one that kills him."

"You can kill him if you want."

The motel owner pulled out a revolver and with a wide smile, pointed it at Brent's head and pulled the trigger. Blood, skull fragments, and brain matter splashed all over the car, splattering the paint.

The motel owner and the redneck leader laughed as Brent's blood spurted out of the mortal head wound, his arms flopping over on the ground for a few seconds as nerve endings shut down.

From her hiding spot in the woods, Paige held her mouth closed with her hand and cried for Brent. He was her first boyfriend, and had taken her virginity, and now he was dead. She slumped behind the tree and held herself, wanting to scream. She couldn't stop crying. She wanted to run but knew that if she did, they would find and kill her, too.

The four rednecks returned after searching the area for her.

"She wasn't thrown out of the car. She must have got out and now she's hidin' in the woods," said a large man nicknamed Mudd.

"Good. Now we have something to hunt," the leader said, rubbing his chin.

They all got very excited at the thought of hunting her down. First they would rape Paige, then kill her when they were finished with her. She heard their plan and took off running into the woods. As she ran, saplings cut her legs and branches slapped her face. Her heart pumped hard and fast, and in her mind she mourned for Brent.

"Paige….Paige!" they yelled as they searched the woods for her.

She could hear them behind her and she kept going. She'd fallen in the mud and splashed through a stream. She was covered with mosquito bites. She'd fallen down more times then she could remember. She never stopped to feel sorry for herself, knowing she had to escape. She needed to get help. The rednecks would pay for what they did to Brent.

As she ran, thoughts about what they would do to her if she was caught spurred her onwards.

Then, up ahead she spotted a light through the trees and though exhausted, ran faster, her destination the flickering light. Maybe it was a farmhouse or a ranger station, anything where she could find help.

"Paige, where are you honey? We ain't gonna hurt you, sweetheart, so come on out!" the leader yelled.

They were getting closer to her and Paige let out a little squeal of fear. She was terrified, and charging through the woods at night didn't help either.

The light was getting closer. She ran full speed to it, tripping over debris on the forest floor. Picking herself up each time, she stumbled forward, her arms before her so she wouldn't crash straight into a tree and knock herself out. When she finally reached the light, she saw it was the porch light on a small house. She jumped over the railing lining the home's property and started beating on the front door.

"Hello, hello can you help me?" she called out.

She beat on it over and over, until finally someone opened it.

"Good Lord, girl, you're gonna beat my door down!" said an old man around seventy. His clothes were filthy and he only had a few teeth left. His hair was greasy and he had a nose so large it had to be a result of heavy drinking. He smelled terrible but to Paige he was the most beautiful person she'd ever seen, for he could help her.

"I…I…need your help… I need the police!" Paige cried.

"What's the matter, girl?" he asked.

"People are chasing me. They ran us off the road then killed my boyfriend!"

"Oh my Lord," the old man said. "I'd better call the police then."

He went into the house and picked up an old style, rotary telephone, then dialed 9-1-1 and waited for the police to answer. After a full minute, Paige looked at the phone, her eyes following the cord, until she saw that the phone wasn't plugged in. The end of the cord was lying on the floor.

"You lying bastard, you're not calling the police!" she screamed.

"No, I'm not, I'm stalling for Teddy and the boys to get here. He's my grandson, you really think I give a shit about a whore like you? Ya see, I'm in cahoots with him and you're as good as dead. Well, he'll probably fuck ya first." The old man began to laugh. He dropped the phone, staring at her with lust, then went to grab her breasts. She kicked him in the groin.

"Ooomph, you fuckin bitch!" he hissed, falling over.

She turned to leave the house when the front door was kicked open. Teddy was standing there with two of his goons behind him. Paige turned to run but he grabbed her hair and threw her to the floor. She hit the floor hard but used the force to keep moving. She crawled a few feet and then ran to the back of the house. She opened the back door and jumped off the small landing. She could hear Teddy yelling commands to his two men to get her, but she was too fast and was on her way around the house and down the driveway before they reached the back door.

She thought she would follow the dirt road but decided to stay in the woods so they wouldn't see her. She did keep the road in sight, however, as she stumbled through the brush and dry leaves lining the road. Headlights appeared behind her and she knew it was the rest of Teddy's men returning from the crash site. She ducked down as they pulled into the driveway, and watched Teddy and his men get in the pickup truck and take off. They drove right by her hiding place; it was the first good luck she'd had all night.

She walked in the woods by the road for more than an hour. Her legs and feet hurt from walking, her skin hurt from being scratched up, and the memory of Brent getting killed weighed heavy on her mind. She cried until her eyes hurt.

With the sun beginning to rise, Paige came upon a small town, though the name 'town' would have been pushing it. The place was more like a community. There was a grocery store that doubled as the post office, a two-story restaurant with a hotel that boasted the best barbeque ever, and a police station. That was what she was looking for. She ran to the police station. Pushing through the wooden front door, she ran inside and stopped short in terror. Teddy was sitting there with the sheriff of the town.

"There she is, we knew you'd come here, they always do." Teddy said, both men laughing.

"Get her out of here before anyone sees her," the sheriff said to his deputy as another man moved up behind Paige.

The last thing she saw was a fist coming at her face, then everything went black.

She woke up tied to a wall.

"I see you're finally awake, sweetheart," Teddy said with an evil grin.

The room was almost pitch black, only a lantern in the corner pushing back the darkness. It was a basement or somewhere else underground. The smell of mold and rotten potatoes was strong. It was almost enough to make her pass out. She looked around and the only thing she saw was Teddy. He was standing in front of her with a knife in his hand. He tried to kiss her but she turned her face away. She could smell beer, stale cigarettes, and body odor wafting off him. She was half dazed and couldn't think straight. When he tried to kiss her again, his lips met hers and he stuck his tongue in her mouth. She snapped fully awake and gagged when he tried to suck on her tongue.

"Did you like that, baby?" he asked. There's more where that came from."

"Let me go!" she screamed and spit in his face.

"I'm gonna play with you a little, and there ain't shit you can do about it. I suggest you treat me with some respect or else." He punched her in the stomach to make his point. She gagged and sucked in air that wouldn't come, bile dripping from the corner of her mouth from the blow. It hurt to breathe now and she wondered if he'd cracked a rib.

"I'm gonna start with him first," he said then walked over to Brent's body. The corpse was lying on a wooden table, naked. Brent's eyes were open, the dim light reflected in the dead orbs.

Teddy took a knife and stuck it in the corpse's chest and began to gut it.

"Leave him alone you bastard!" Paige screamed.

Teddy looked at her and smiled.

"Don't worry, honey, you're next," he said.

He went back to cutting Brent, the knife going deep into his chest. She continued to scream and call for help, so he stopped working, walked over to her, and slapped her across the face. Then he returned to the body and resumed his task.

The next cut he made was in the stomach. He cut deeply and then began pulling out Brent's intestines, tossing them into a bucket on the floor. Teddy pulled them out one at a time, laughing and playing with Brent's guts as Paige cried and pleaded for him to stop.

Paige closed her eyes. She couldn't believe this was happening. She was terrified that she was going to die in this dismal basement. She started to go into shock, as

Teddy continued to cut up the body like it was a deer or a pig. When he was finished with Brent, he came for her next. He laughed and sliced the knife across her pretty face; she screamed in pain.

"You two will be served up at the restaurant as steak. More city people passing through town will eat ya until there's no evidence left."

When Brent was cut up in sections, Teddy wrapped up the meat and prepared to take it to the restaurant.

"I'm takin' lover boy to get eaten, and when I get back I'm gonna fuck you raw, then cut you up while you're still alive."

He walked up the wooden stairs on the far side of the room, and a second later, heard a door slam closed and a deadbolt being thrown.

She pulled on her bonds as hard as she could. Blood rolled down her arms but she didn't care. She had to escape. When her blood had soaked the ropes, they became slippery, and she was able to pull her left hand out, though she left a layer of skin behind. She untied the rope on her other hand, and by the time she was finished, ten minutes had passed.

"Where you goin, bitch?" Teddy said from the stairs.

"Leave me alone!"

"Leave you alone? I can't do that. We've got people to feed. You're gonna be turned into barbeque; we're runnin' low," he said. Before she could move he was down the stairs and across the room. He punched her in the throat and everything went black again.

When she came to this time she was naked and felt a horrible pain in her crotch as Teddy fucked her. She tried to scream but her throat hurt from where he'd punched her. Then Teddy made a face and groaned, and she felt him ejaculate inside her. She was tied to the wooden table, her back sticky with what she knew was Brent's blood. When Teddy was finished, he reached over her head and picked up a large, razor sharp knife. He didn't hesitate as he placed the blade to her throat and slid it across her jugular in a smooth even swipe that showed how skilled the man was at killing. Paige felt the knife slide across her neck and cut deep, then felt her hot blood bathe her shoulders and chest. It warmed her up and she smelled a copper aroma that overpowered the odor of mold. Then she grew cold.

The last thing she saw before succumbing to death, was Teddy staring down at her with a smile on his face.

THE VAMPIRE HUNTERS' CLUB

MARK RIVETT

Dr. Tanya Zirkel stood at the head of her dinner table, surveying her Carnegie Mellon University colleagues. With a neutral smile, she spoke over the din of academic discussion that rolled through the teachers and administrators gathered at the table for food and wine. "My friends I sincerely apologize, but we must cut this fantastic evening short."

Dr. Cloverson glanced up from his chair at his beautiful host in her elegant black dress. "But Tanya…" The expression on his face was one of true disappointment as the ninety-year-old man attributed the monthly gatherings for keeping his mind sharp where his frail body had long ago become bound to a wheelchair. "It is scarcely past one in the morning. Is everything okay?"

The discussion slowed but failed to stop at Tanya's announcement. It could take upwards of twenty minutes to pull the intellectuals and scholars away from their alcohol-fueled banter, and—as urgent as the situation was—Tanya didn't want to risk those keen inquisitive minds latching on to some detail or some barely-noticeable body language. It was one thing to assume the lives of her colleagues weren't at risk, it was another thing to know with certainty…and Tanya did not. Her heart thundered in her chest, and every cell in her body wanted to scream, "Get the fuck out!"

Instead she smiled back at Dr. Cloverson with her crystal blue eyes and maintained her cool steely demeanor. "My sister took my brother-in-law to the hospital with chest pains. He seems all right, but I have to pick up my mother and meet them there." The lie was well crafted, straddling the line between emergency and nagging importance; exactly where it needed to be in order to express the urgency of the situation, but not enough that anyone would bother to actually follow up.

The guests began to quiet their conversation, drain their wine glasses in long deep draughts, and stand to leave.

"Oh my! Your sister is young like you. How old is her husband?" Dr. Parjat asked with genuine concern, as she laid a hand on Tanya's ivory arm. "I could make some calls…"

"Oh thank you, Bairavi. I'm sure everything's fine. My sister has a tendency to exaggerate the seriousness of health-related issues…but better safe than sorry." Sitting at a dinner table with more than one medical doctor world-renowned in their specialty usually had more advantages than disadvantages. It was unlikely that any would actually pry too far into Tanya's personal life, but it was still a calculated risk.

Ten minutes passed in what seemed like an hour. One by one each guest stood, offered their hope that her brother-in-law would be fine, and took their leave.

Two Philosophy instructors helped Dr. Cloverson's wheelchair down the ornate stone steps to the street-lit sidewalk below, all the while debating the finer points of Socrates and Aristotle. Tanya stood in the doorway, watching her guests each make it safely to their car while casting quick, subtle glances up and down her street.

Soon, either a dark blue Corvette or a collection of police cars would be pulling into view and there were innumerable reasons why her dinner guests needed to be gone when that happened. It was unlikely that Dr. Troy Burgeon was the type of monster to involve the police, but the details of what had transpired at his place weren't entirely clear. Again, it was a calculated risk that the three missing female Women's Studies students were already dead or monsters themselves, and the very last thing Dr. Burgeon wanted was police involvement. That cold hard fact meant the situation was more dangerous—not less.

One Hour Earlier

"Be quiet, Nathan," Cheryl hissed through whispered breath as Nathan struggled to squeeze his girth through the open window.

"You should have left me outside to keep watch," Nathan sighed back. He was not an athlete in his most physically fit days and three years of studying medicine at CMU hadn't helped that fact. "We shouldn't be doing this anyway. You guys are nuts!"

"Tanya said we needed to keep an eye on Dr. Burgeon, and that's what we're doing." Morice, by contrast, could easily be mistaken for a college football or basketball player despite the fact that he had spent the whole of his CMU education buried in Sociology books. "How long do you think before someone else disappears?"

"Goddamn it, be fucking quiet," Cheryl hissed again. Her short multi-colored hair and tattooed sleeves lent her a no-nonsense demeanor that cast her already no-nonsense attitude as the de-facto leader of the group. "Do you understand what kind of shit we can get in?"

Nathan pulled himself through the window and on to his feet. "You mean sneaking into what we think *might* be a vampire's mansion to spy and look for three missing CMU students? What other kind of trouble could we get in? This isn't *exactly* like every vampire-story- gone-wrong-that's-ever-been-written or anything." Nathan was scared, and when he was scared, his default setting became sarcastically sensible.

"Try breaking and entering as well as burglary, asshole," Cheryl whispered. "Now don't say another word unless Dr. Burgeon is fang-fucking you in the ass!"

Morice was ignoring the exchange. He moved silently around the dark hallway with an ability that suggested this was not the first time he'd done this. With gentle steps, he moved from one concealed area to the next, paused, peered through an adjacent doorway, and advanced down the hallway toward a dull orange-lit room.

Nathan got the hint from Cheryl and attempted to mimic Morice's movements down the hall. His heavier frame and lack of athleticism made his advance almost clumsily comical, if not for the fact that a blood-sucking monster of the night could jump out and kill him at any moment.

With a sigh, Cheryl followed suit, her miniature frame easily finding shadows, cubbies, and alcoves to conceal her progress.

Long moments passed before Morice made it to the end of the hallway and silently glanced around the corner into a fire-lit room. His shoulders tensed as he moved but relaxed when confronted by the vacant study. He had half-imagined Dr. Burgeon to be expecting them, waiting casually in a chair to deliver some patronizing comment before pouncing.

Nathan caught up to Morice and followed his glance as he walked casually—and recklessly—into the room. He made his way past an antique love seat positioned in front of the fire place, then glanced down at a coffee table and cocked his head inquisitively.

Cheryl appeared from behind Morice and locked her eyes on Nathan with a questioning gaze. She was about to chastise him for his lack of caution when he reached down and picked something up from the coffee table. With a furrowed brow, Nathan held a half-full wine glass up in the firelight, the unmistakable imprint of a woman's lipstick on the brim.

Instantly all three minds connected on what the lipstick meant. Their heads turned and their eyes focused on a large, dark staircase that led to the second level.

"What do we do?" Nathan whispered as he set the wine glass down with a quivering hand.

"Shit!" Cheryl rubbed her brow. Her conviction smashed headlong into mortal terror as to what waited up those stairs. Someone, a woman and probably a fellow CMU student was up there with a killer, but for all her bravado and school-kid daring, she hadn't truly prepared herself mentally for a face-to-face confrontation with a vampire…none of them had.

Morice thought for a moment as he unconsciously rubbed his lower back. "We gotta see what's up," he whispered in response.

"Guys! What if we're wrong? What if Dr. Burgeon is with his girlfriend? What if he recognizes us from campus! We could be expelled!" Nathan pleaded in hushed tones.

"And what if we're right? If that was your sister up there, what would you want us to do right now?" Cheryl asked.

With great care, Morice took one silent step after another up the staircase as he peered up into the darkness of the second floor. If Dr. Burgeon was a vampire, it was extremely unlikely that he hadn't already heard them. Yet, if they still had the advantage of surprise, Morice intended to preserve it.

For the first time, Nathan noticed the odd bulge in Morice's rear waist band, and he nearly fainted. He glared intensely at Cheryl and motioned with his eyes at the unmistakable outline of a pistol hidden beneath Morice's shirt. The reality of what was actually occurring began to press in on him, and on some level, Nathan started to feel disconnected from his body. He was no longer a sarcastic care-free college kid. In this moment, he was a burglar with an armed accomplice.

Cheryl shrugged with her eyes back at Nathan and began to silently follow Morice up the stairs. Nathan followed.

One by one they made their way to the second level where a single long sliver of light cast through a cracked door to barely illuminate the hallway. The mansion was eerily silent, and the trio gathered in the hall to calculate their next move.

Committed to her cause, Cheryl took the first step into the pitch black corridor. Her heart felt like a jack hammer and every moment was a prayer she wouldn't step on a creaky floorboard or brush up against something that would give her away as it tumbled to the ground. Morice and Nathan followed warily.

An eternity passed before Cheryl made it to the partially open door, no more than an inch. She strained to peer inside as Morice and Nathan flanked her. The narrow slit revealed almost nothing of the room's interior.

"Guys…" Nathan whispered, hoping for one last opportunity to convince his compatriots to retreat.

Cheryl answered by reaching out and gently pushing the door open to reveal more of the room. The groan of the hinges on the door may as well have been a baby crying in a silent theater, but as it opened, a horrifying sight revealed itself.

A single antique lamp cast gentle yellow light through the room. A young woman lay nude on a king-sized bed, her arms and legs restrained by ropes tied to the head and baseboard. Her eyes were closed and she appeared to be sleeping if not for the huge blood-red stain that spread outward from the cream-colored sheets beneath her body.

Nathan, Cheryl, and Morice stood stunned as they took in the scene. None knew what to do. At best, they were dealing with a psychopathic CMU teacher who victimized his students. At worst, the possibility they had all known, but had yet to truly embrace, was reality; a vampire was using his faculty position to prey on vulnerable women.

And then her naked chest rose in one labored breath.

"She's alive!" Cheryl gasped.

With complete disregard for caution, Morice gripped Nathan's wrist and burst into the room. "Help her!" he growled through clenched teeth.

Nathan staggered into the room. "What?"

"Help her! You're Pre-Med!" Cheryl followed them into the room and began looking around for nothing in particular. All at once she felt a bizarre mix of rage and helplessness as she stormed about, unsure of where to direct her emotion.

Morice's eyes darted around, looking for signs of Dr. Burgeon. "Where is…"

Before Morice could finish his thought, a closet door exploded into shrapnel of wood and a pale naked form tackled Cheryl to the floor.

"Untie her!" Morice shouted to Nathan as he pulled his pistol from his waist band.

Immediately Nathan began to struggle with the knots that bound the half-dead girl to the bed. His actions were driven less by a sense of duty and more by a complete shut-down of mental faculties. Morice's order was the only thought that ran through his terrified mind and he simply lacked the capacity to act outside the only tether holding him to reality.

Cheryl's scream echoed through the mansion and Morice trained his aim on the figure that rose from the floor holding the miniature form of his friend. Dr. Burgeon stood in the middle of the room, pinning Cheryl in a bear hug from behind. He looked with sinister eyes at Morice as a toothy smile washed over his face. Unnaturally long canines hovered precariously over Cheryl's bare shoulder as the monster stared down the barrel of a gun.

"I know you," Dr. Burgeon said slyly. "You're one of Dr. Zirkel's minions, aren't you?"

Morice looked down the sight of his pistol and directly into the sinister eyes of Dr. Burgeon, the doctor's gaze staring unflinchingly back at him. The body of Cheryl hung between them in a death grip. "Let her go."

Nathan had untied one wrist of the helpless girl and began working on the other. His uncanny ability to block any distractions out and focus utterly on what he was doing served him well. Still, the knots were tight and it took meticulous effort to untie them.

"Put the pistol down, kid." Dr. Burgeon responded with a fanged grin. "You don't want to do this."

Cheryl struggled in vain against the strength of the vampire who held her.

Morice's mind raced. If he put his weapon down, Dr. Burgeon would kill them all, but if he fired, there was no way he wouldn't hit Cheryl.

"Come on kid, put the pistol down." Dr. Burgeon took a step toward Morice with his human shield. "You're what, second year, third year CMU? You have a great future ahead of you. You don't want to do this. It's no big deal. We can just forget about everything."

Nathan finished with the girl's wrists and began to work on the knots around her ankles.

Morice took a step back as Dr. Burgeon approached. He glanced from the fanged monster to Cheryl and back again. "What do I do?" Morice asked no one in particular, the gravity of his impossible situation paralyzing him.

"Put the gun down and you and your friends can go. I promise. We can forget about all of this. I'm just a teacher, you're just students. No one has to know about any of this." Dr. Burgeon's fangs withdrew and he looked less like the monster he was and more like the trustworthy teacher he had been in the CMU classroom.

"I got it," Nathan stammered as he untied the last knot.

Cheryl closed her eyes tightly and screamed, "Shoot him!" She knew if Morice followed her command she was dead. "Shoot!"

Four gunshots thundered in the room. The first caught Cheryl in the shoulder, passed through her body, and lodged in Dr. Burgeon's chest. The second shot slammed into her chest and a red pool expanded through her shirt. Realizing that Morice had elected to trade Cheryl's life for the remaining three, Dr. Burgeon discarded his human shield and dove for Morice. The third shot pierced Dr. Burgeon square in the chest, knocking him back. The fourth passed through his right eye socket and left a gaping hole that erupted blood and fluids. He dropped to the floor.

Nathan hoisted the young naked girl over his shoulder with an exasperated huff. He wanted nothing more than to run, but a flicker of compassion forbade him from abandoning the scene, and for the moment, held his terror at bay. Without a word, he made for the hallway.

Morice lunged to grip Cheryl in one arm as she fell, blood pouring from her gunshot wounds.

Dr. Burgeon growled as he regained his footing. The wounds he'd received were far less dire to his vampiric constitution and he glared with one blood-red eye at the man who had taken the other. "You're going to regret that, kid!"

Morice answered by firing three more shots into Dr. Burgeon's chest. The vampire staggered from the force of the wounds but continued to glare at Morice.

"I know you," Dr. Burgeon gasped. "Vampire Hunters Club... Tanya..."

Morice hoisted Cheryl over one shoulder and followed Nathan into the hall and down the stairs. All the while he watched behind him for the monster that would undoubtedly pursue him into the night.

Nathan had left the front door open, and Morice could see his heavy-set frame waddling toward the car they had parked across the street. As quickly as he could, he ran down the front steps and watched as Nathan opened the car door and dumped the naked woman into the back seat.

Lights from neighboring houses were turning on, no doubt in response to the gunshots that had just destroyed the quiet suburban night. Morice spun around and around as he made his way toward the car, training his gun on any sign of Dr. Burgeon, before dumping Cheryl in the back seat next to the other woman and diving into the passenger seat.

"We have to get to a hospital!" Nathan shouted as he fumbled for the car keys. "Holy shit! We have to get to a hospital!"

Morice kept his eyes behind him as the shadowy form of Dr. Burgeon slipped into view, framed in the yellow interior light of the mansion. "We can't go to a hospital! We can't! Dr. Burgeon will find us. He has to. I shot Cheryl. We're so fucked!" Morice's thoughts moved faster than his mouth. The best they could hope for was not to get pulled over on the way to the hospital. Even if they dropped the two women off anonymously, there would still be surveillance cameras that would easily identify the vehicle, and its occupants, Morice and Nathan. If Cheryl ended up in an emergency room there would be a ballistics trace. The other woman was most likely the victim of Rohypnol and already looked like a classic rape victim well on her way to a rape-murder victim. All those things spelled doom for Nathan and Morice, even excluding the fact that there was a highly intelligent and well connected vampire who wouldn't take too kindly to being shot in the face and having three, possibly four, CMU students roaming around with the ability to identify him. Excluding the myriad of mundane reasons they couldn't go, there were plenty of supernatural ones.

Nathan started the car and peeled away. "Well what the fuck, man! They're dying!"

Morice thumbed his pistol for a moment as he looked back at Dr. Burgeon, who no doubt would be following them shortly. "Dr. Zirkel! She'll know what to do."

Nathan fumbled in his pocket with one hand and retrieved his cell phone, his other hand on the steering wheel while speeding through the Pittsburgh suburb. He flipped open the phone and thumbed the buttons. "She's going to be pissed…"

"Just get us there, man. And slow down. We don't want any attention," Morice said. There was no alternative. Dr. Zirkel had been running the Vampire Hunters Club for years. She would know what to do. She had to.

"Lay her on the couch!" Morice ordered with a growl.

Nathan huffed as he carefully and quietly pushed his way through the back door into the basement study. With a groan, he dumped Cheryl's limp body on the couch and watched as her blood oozed down the fine upholstery onto the expensive tile floor. He couldn't even recall his phone call, warning Dr. Zirkel of their arrival or the drive here, so when he looked down at his blood-covered clothes, his eyes went wide with panic. "What the hell!"

Morice, also drenched in Cheryl's blood, grabbed a thin blanket and covered the naked body of the other nearly dead girl laying on the love seat across from Cheryl. Her breathing was so shallow that Morice didn't know if she was still alive. "Quiet!" he hissed.

The study door flew open and Dr. Zirkel, clad in her black evening gown, paused for a second, and surveyed the scene. Her insightful blue eyes, framed by her long dark hair, darted about the room, calculating the best course of action.

"Did he see you?" she asked as she closed the door behind her, and marched into the room. She felt for a pulse on the girl lying on the love seat.

Nathan stood dumbfounded and continued to stare blankly at the gore that painted him red. "Dr. Zirkel, I'm sorry, but do you have a shower I can use?"

"Yeah, he saw us. I'm pretty sure he knows about the club now. I mean, *really* knows." Morice mumbled with a mixture of fear and exhaustion. His adrenaline had worn off during the car ride over and he was left with a sickening, almost drunk feeling as he pondered the gravity of their situation. "Is he coming for us?"

"Nathan honey, there's a laundry room down the hall you can scrub up in but you can't use the bathroom upstairs yet. I have to get rid of some guests first." Dr. Zirkel crouched next to Cheryl and felt for a pulse on her also. She bit her bottom lip as she stood and glanced back and forth between the two girls. "He's not going to be able to sit on the fact that there are people—students—out there who know the truth about him. You can't go home tonight." She paused for a few seconds as she thought, then said, "I have to get back to my guests. There's some rope in the tool shed in the back yard. Tie the hands and feet of these two and I'll be back shortly."

Nathan seemed to move unconsciously as he disappeared down the connecting hall.

"Cheryl isn't bit," Morice said. "I shot her."

Dr. Zirkel sighed. "So the police may be coming as well… what happened? and be quick."

As fast as he could, Morice related the events of the previous hour: their fateful decision to break into Dr. Burgeon's home, the attack, and their escape. The strong athletic boy who had likely taken and received his share of beatings in the bad neighborhoods of Pittsburgh—but rose above it through pure strength—choked with tears as he spoke to his teacher. All the while his eyes were locked on Cheryl…slowly bleeding to death on the couch.

Dr. Zirkel sighed again. Her Vampire Hunters Club had done the right thing by coming to her, but that didn't make things any easier. "Tie her up first." She motioned to the girl that had been bitten by Dr. Burgeon. "Then try and put pressure on Cheryl's wounds to stop the bleeding." She looked at the pale body of the young student lying on her couch. "And try and get Nathan back to his senses. We're going to need him. I'll be back in a few minutes…and stay quiet."

Tanya breathed a heavy sigh of relief as the last of her dinner guests took their leave and she finally closed her front door. No police cars had come barreling down her street, and Troy Burgeon hadn't shown up in his blue Corvette. She had time to think.

She'd suspected Dr. Burgeon of being a vampire ever since he joined the faculty at CMU but hadn't anticipated how cunning a killer he was. He preyed on mostly foreign students that had a plausible excuse to fly home unexpectedly back to some obscure African or Asian country so no one ever suspected a thing when they vanished. Or he chose students into the Pittsburgh night life. Only when the last three Women's Studies students disappeared did she take the initiative to set her Vampire Hunters Club after him. Those students were also her Sociology students, and while most CMU administrators and the police might have dismissed the disappearance of two strippers and a single mother on welfare as not entirely uncommon, she knew better. These young women had made it into CMU, and that alone should have been enough to ring alarm bells within the Pittsburgh Police department, but it hadn't.

Tanya closed her eyes and took a deep breath. She needed to focus, put herself in Dr. Burgeon's shoes for a moment, and think.

With a nod to herself, she marched away from the door, through her dining room, and into her fire-lit foyer. The dull orange light danced over the two antique chairs and single end table that decorated the room. She ran her hand over one of the four ornate glass pillars located in each corner of the room and thought for a moment about how much she was risking. Her faculty position…her success…her students lives…her own life.

Wouldn't it be easier to turn a blind eye to the existence of vampire predators and simply enjoy everything she had accomplished?

"No," she whispered. She marched into the kitchen, fumbled through the tool drawer, retrieved a few select items, and returned to the basement to tend to the gruesome and desperate scene.

"I…I can't!" Nathan protested as he squirmed in his skin.

"What? You're Pre-Med! What the hell did you think you'd be doing?" Tanya glared at her student as she clutched a pair of needle-nosed pliers in her outstretched hand.

"In a hospital, yes, but not in a goddamn study in some basement!" Nathan glanced around the room helplessly as he came to the realization of what he would be required to do. His eyes rested on Cheryl. "Why can't you do it?"

Tanya was losing patience. Morice had bound Dr. Burgeon's young female victim, and she would need tending to shortly. Either she would recover or she would rise as one of the undead and Tanya hadn't quite decided exactly what to do in the event of the latter.

"Goddamn it, Nathan! We can't take Cheryl to a hospital," she said. "Someone has to pull the bullet out, and that someone has to be you! Unless you grow a pair right now, she's going to die!"

Morice had wrapped Cheryl's wounds with some towels he'd found in the dining room. The gunshot in her shoulder had stopped bleeding, but the wound in her chest hadn't. Blood continued to pool on the floor, and periodically she would wake up, beg feebly to be taken to a hospital, then pass out again.

Nathan had never been the target of Tanya's rage before, and he quickly withered in front of her. "Okay, okay," he said. With a shaking hand, he reached out and took the pliers from his teacher. "Uh…" he paused for a second. "Help me take her shirt off."

Tanya reached down, dug her hands into the collar of Cheryl's shirt, and tore it open, exposing her naked blood-soaked chest. The bullet hole directly beneath her right breast hemorrhaged blood in perfect rhythm to the beat of her dangerously weak heart.

"Damn it, Nathan! Do it!" she ordered.

"What do we do about her?" Morice looked down somberly at the restrained girl who lay unconscious on the love seat. The girl had grown paler and paler with each passing second.

Tanya considered the girl for a moment. Her face was lost among the hundreds of anonymous students who Tanya had encountered day-to-day, but felt she looked familiar. Abruptly, she reached down and lifted the student's lip to expose her ivory teeth and pink gums. The elongated canines were unmistakable—she'd died and now would rise as a blood-thirsty vampire.

Morice sighed. "Do you have anything I can make into a stake?"

"There's a hatchet and some firewood outside." Tanya motioned to the back door of her study. "Be quick."

"Dr. Zirkel?" Nathan's voice trembled. He held a malformed bullet in the gore-stained pliers. The easy part was done. Now stopping the bleeding would be the next challenge. "She's going to die, Dr. Zirkel. We have to get her to a hospital," Nathan whined.

Morice and Tanya exchanged glances as they considered the situation. Now that the bullet had been removed, the police wouldn't be able to trace the shooting back to Morice or connect Cheryl's wounds to any bullets that would undoubtedly turn up at Dr. Burgeon's home. The doctor might be able to use his University status to investigate any gunshot victims that had been admitted to local hospitals, but that was a risk they would have to take.

At that moment, the doorbell rang and Tanya's heart jumped into her throat. Nathan and Morice stared wide-eyed at her. Their minds blanked in terror, and their only hope was that Tanya could provide instruction. Each second passed like an hour as they came to the realization that the situation had just become very dangerous.

"Nathan, get Cheryl to St. Clair. Tell them you found her lying in the street in Dormont and you don't know her," Tanya said in frantic whispers. "If it's the police, I'll keep them occupied long enough for you to sneak out the way you came."

"What if it's..." Morice began.

"Get this other one staked." Sheer force of will propelled Tanya out of the study and up the stairs to the front door. "If you hear me scream...run." She caught one glimpse of Morice's concerned and questioning face. She let it go unanswered.

Was it the police? Was it Dr. Burgeon? Tanya wondered. Her black high heels seemed to thunder in the silence as she made her way up the stairs and across the hardwood floor. She had always been good in pressure situations involving only herself, but there were so many other people who were involved now and that fact multiplied the things that could go wrong exponentially. What if Cheryl died before she reached the hospital? What if Nathan couldn't deliver a convincing story, cracked under pressure, or got arrested? What if the other girl rose as a vampire before Morice could kill her and broke free?

Without contemplating her arrival, she soon found her hand on the lock to the front door. The glow of the dull yellow streetlights gently penetrated the translucent stain-glassed entry designs. A million terrible scenarios played though her mind as she turned the doorknob, unsure of what or who to expect.

"Hello, Tanya." Dr. Troy Burgeon stood on the porch, leaning casually on the door frame. His body and face bore not the slightest evidence that he'd been shot multiple times a mere hour ago, and his lips curled into the familiar smug grin of superiority Tanya had learned to loathe. "Do you have a moment?"

She considered for a second the legends concerning a vampire's ability to enter a home without invitation. "Hello, Troy, it's awfully late. What can I help you with?" She knew any protest to his arrival would go nowhere. She was still dressed in her evening gown and every light in the house was still on.

With a lop-sided grin, the doctor smoothly slid past Tanya into her home, deliberately making a point to enter her personal space. His female students might have swooned at the calculated move in normal circumstances, but Tanya was not one of his female students.

"I was hoping you might have a moment to talk about your Vampire Hunters Club, Tanya. I have some concerns," he said.

"Concerns that can't wait until tomorrow? I'm just about to call it a night, Troy. I have a noon class on Saturday…if you want to swing by around 2:00 that would be fine." She smiled internally, knowing the impossibility of him visiting her during the day.

He ignored the implication that he should be on his way and sauntered into the dining room to survey the evidence of the evening's gathering. He ran his finger over a half-empty wine glass sitting on the table among a dozen of others. "How come you never invite me to your dinner parties, Tanya? I'm hurt."

"My CMU friends don't like you, Troy." She disguised the truth as a joke, knowing his ego would forbid him from recognizing reality. "You wanted to talk about my Vampire Hunters Club?" She closed the front door and followed her CMU colleague into the dining room.

"Do you really think it's a good idea to have a Vampire Hunters Club on campus? Students running around with wooden stakes, looking for vampires...don't you think it's only a matter of time before someone gets hurt?" He made eye contact with her and flashed his usual flirtatious smile.

Tanya glanced back with a grin and moved to keep the dinner table between herself and the vampire as she made her way to the foyer. Undoubtedly, he would read her smirk as an invitation to follow.

"We can't all teach Women's Studies and Sexuality, Troy," she said. "It takes effort to capture the attention of our students for the rest of us. Besides, no one's running around with stakes, crosses, or garlic. The club is merely an exercise in theory...a creative way to grab the imagination of young people and get them to think outside their comfort zone."

Dr. Burgeon laughed as he matched pace with Tanya on her way to the foyer. "Theory? Think outside their comfort zone?" he said. "Come on. You don't have even one student who might take things a bit too far? You've seen these kids—Goths, Emos, whatever the hell the current black-clad fad is these days. Your kids are weird."

Tanya ignored the insult. "My kids have all been accepted to CMU and that's quite an accomplishment. Think about it. History students can imagine history from the perspective of a creature that lives through the ages as an immortal. Sociology students can think about how a predator might prey on society's lower class. Criminology and psychology students might get some insight into the mind of a true killer. Hell, engineering students might even ponder what it would take to create a Vampire death-trap." She waltzed into her foyer and took a seat in one of the two chairs. "It's all merely a way to teach without the students even realizing they're learning. I have very strict rules about stakes and crosses and whatnot. Would you care for some wine?"

His eyes lingered on Tanya's legs for a moment before he reached over and grabbed a half empty wine bottle from the dinner table. "Why thank you, Tanya. I'd love some." He drank deeply, smiled as he offered the bottle to Tanya, and followed her into the foyer. He shifted his eyes from her legs to a glass column that seemed somewhat out of place in the room and may as well have been a portal to the 19th century.

Tanya smiled as she waved the wine away. "No thank you, I've had quite enough already." She grinned at the implication that she was alcoholically disadvantaged to the predator standing before her. "So you've driven to my house in the middle of the night to talk about my Vampire Hunters Club? Come on, Troy, what's going on? Why are you really here?"

He took a seat in the chair opposite Tanya, his brow furrowed as he considered the other glass columns placed in each corner of the room. "I had some kids break into my home tonight, Tanya. I recognized them. They were your Vampire Hunters Club kids."

"Oh?" Tanya feigned surprise. "What happened? Did you call the police?"

"No," he answered immediately. "My neighbors did that. But I thought I'd swing by your place and get a little insight from you. If there's a group of students on campus that actually believe in vampires then that's a problem. I'd like to know their names so I can talk to them."

The firelight cast long shadows through the foyer, and Tanya's heart thundered so loudly she had little doubt that he could hear it. Here she sat in her home, with a vampire mere inches away from her. Her only defense; the hope that she'd chosen her protégé's wisely. If she had, she would live. If she hadn't…

"Their names? The records at CMU would have their addresses…their parents' addresses…are you worried?" she asked as she stared with a smirk into the firelight, her index finger on a small switch imbedded in the side of her chair.

Dr. Burgeon laughed angrily. The question was innocent enough but he read its meaning. "Well, Tanya, let me explain to you what's happening at this exact moment so you can wrap your mind around how truly screwed you and your Vampire Hunters Club are…" He stood up in front of the fireplace and glared down at her. "I was shot multiple times…which was shitty enough in and of itself, but you see…the sound of a gunshot going off in my neighborhood tends to attract the police. When those police use the sounds of gunshots as an excuse to invade my home without a warrant, that's a problem. It takes time to dispose of a body, you see, of which I happen to have more than one either marinating in a drain-cleaner bath or stuffed in a freezer." His eyes bore furiously into Tanya in an attempt to drive home his point as he revealed to her his true nature, a merciless and cunning killer; a nature he had not yet realized Tanya was already well aware of.

She continued to run her finger over the switch in her chair. She maintained her neutral academic tone despite his attempt to intimidate her. "So, now that the police have found your victims, it seems to me that you're the one who's pretty much screwed," she said. Her thoughts drifted to Nathan speeding through the streets of Pittsburgh with Cheryl. He and Cheryl would be safe. At least for the moment as Dr. Burgeon would certainly not be exercising his University privilege at any hospitals any time soon.

"I really liked it here," he said. "I taught nothing but night classes. The sluts in my courses may as well have been lambs to the slaughter. Seriously, Tanya? A Vampire Hunters Club?" He'd gradually raised his agitated voice to shouting and Tanya hoped her neighbors wouldn't hear.

Tanya looked up at the vampire before her. His hair had become frazzled and his fangs reflected the firelight. He looked more animal than human and she knew he would pounce on her at any moment. "Oh, Troy, you're so, so stupid."

He hadn't expected that reaction from her. In all his existence, he'd been the one in power. No one dared insinuate that he was stupid, let alone tell him directly to his face. "You're fucking dead, bitch."

Tanya flipped the switch on her chair and bright light washed over the room. The four glass pillars projected intense ultraviolet light in all directions. Instantly, Dr. Burgeon shrieked in agony as his flesh burst into flames. He looked frantically around the room for refuge.

His desperation was answered by three thunderous clangs as every exit to the foyer was sealed off with hidden steel doors. Even Tanya's eyes struggled to adjust to the sudden wash of brightness and relief washed over her that her Engineering students had taken her assignment seriously enough to build a reliable death-trap. Shielding her eyes, she stood from her chair and backed away from the writhing inferno of flesh before her. The trap had worked, but the vampire might still have a sliver of fight left in him.

Dr. Burgeon was paralyzed. His screams echoed through the room and he fumbled toward Tanya helplessly as his body disintegrated. Within moments his screams devolved into gurgles, then mumbles, and finally silence. The odor of burnt flesh permeated the air as Tanya looked down on all that remained of her former colleague—a smoking pile of ash.

Without a word, Tanya made her way over to the fireplace mantle and felt for a second hidden switch. With a flip of her finger, the lighting returned to normal and the steel doors withdrew. The only evidence of what had just transpired was the nauseating stench in the air and the black remains of Dr. Burgeon.

She grew calmer with each passing second. There were still loose ends, to be sure, but there would be no forensic investigators combing through a pile of ash on the floor looking for evidence of foul play. Vampire mythology was a double-edged sword. On one hand, modern vampires made vampire hunting difficult by blending into society, using the police, and otherwise acting human in nearly every respect. On the other hand, once you actually killed a vampire, there was very little precedent for murder by sunlight, or much difficulty in disposing of what amounted to a burnt-out campfire.

Tanya made her way to the pantry to retrieve a dustpan, broom, and air freshener. As she did, she passed the entry that led to the basement stairs. "Morice?" she called. "Are you still down there?" The thought that the vampire girl might have gotten the better of him still lurked in her mind.

A second passed. "Yeah, Dr. Zirkel. Is everything okay?" Morice's voice echoed up from the basement study. He had certainly heard the commotion and was awaiting confirmation that his mentor had come out alive.

"I need some ideas on what to do about a blue Corvette parked in the front of my house registered to a now permanently missing murderer." She made her way back to the foyer and began sweeping the remains of Dr. Troy Burgeon off the floor. "Any suggestions?"

THE GHOST IN ROOM 315

KEVIN LEWIS

"I didn't think it would be this big," Beth Cooper said as she gazed at the massive structure that was Mandrake Castle.

"What did you expect?" her husband John, said as he found a spot in the parking lot. "A Bed & Breakfast?"

Beth did not answer. She was enthralled at the hotel. Although not as big as most famous castles, Mandrake Castle was fairly large. It was a gray, stone Victorian with a turret in the front corner. The castle and spacious grounds were surrounded by Douglas fir trees.

"Isn't it beautiful?" John asked.

Once again, Beth didn't answer. She was gazing at the room below the turret. She didn't know why but the room seemed to beckon her.

"Earth to Beth? Hello?"

Beth came to and stared at her accountant husband of ten years. Although both in their mid-thirties, Beth was always amazed at how youthful John looked. At thirty five he still looked like he was in his mid-twenties with perfect skin tone and his thick head of black hair didn't appear be falling out anytime soon. Beth was the same age but she felt as if she were fifty. She was tired constantly and, after the horrible diagnosis, wasn't taking proper care of herself. In high school Beth was very popular and beautiful but, as of late, she didn't feel beautiful. She was downright depressed. "I'm sorry," Beth answered her husband.

"Are you okay?"

"I'm fine."

"All right. Let's check in."

Once they unpacked their luggage, which only consisted of three suitcases, one for John, and two for Beth, they walked around to the front door. It was night when they arrived at the castle so the front lawn was lit with outside floodlights. Beth remarked to herself that the grounds appeared to be well kept. The grass was green; of course one could also thank good old mother Washington nature for her constant assistance in that matter.

When they reached the front door, John walked ahead and opened the door for his wife. "Thank you," Beth said.

The front lobby was decorated with an array of Halloween decorations to accommodate the October holiday. Cobwebs were draped along the archway that led into the side living room. Artificial pumpkins and corn husks were displayed on table tops and the window sill that overlooked the front lawn of Mandrake Castle.

John and Beth walked up to the front reception desk that was manned by a young woman who appeared to be cramming for a college exam. The young woman didn't seem to realize that anyone was at the desk so John rang the skeleton head bell. *These people are really celebrating Halloween*, Beth thought. At the sound of the bell, the young woman gazed up at the couple, closed her book, and sat up from her chair behind the desk.

"Welcome to Mandrake Castle," the young woman said in an obviously rehearsed welcome greeting. "My name is Kristy. How may I help you?"

"Hello there. We're the Cooper's. We have a reservation."

"Can I see your reservation?" Kristy asked.

John dug in his pant pocket and handed Kristy the piece of paper. Kristy typed some information into the computer and, after a brief moment, extracted two keys on the board behind her.

"Here you go," Kristy said as she handed the two keys to John. "You're in room 305."

"Is that the room below the turret?" Beth asked. She had no idea why she asked the question. All she knew was there was something fascinating about the room.

"No, that's room 315," Kristy answered.

"Oh, can we switch?"

"I'm afraid you can't. It's…occupied."

Beth found Kristy's answer curious. It was as if she hesitated before finishing her answer. Beth was going to inquire more about Kristy's hesitation when John asked, "Sweetheart, why are you so interested in that room?"

Beth just shook her head irritably. "I don't know. What's with all the questions?" Beth didn't wait for John to answer. She picked up her luggage and headed for the staircase, leaving a speechless John behind.

John met up with Beth in the third floor hallway. She stood in front of their room, her luggage placed on the maroon rug, her hands folded across her chest. John set his luggage down as well and hugged his beloved wife.

"Beth, sweetheart, I'm sorry. Don't be upset. This trip is supposed to be a break for us."

"I'm not upset. It's just…I don't know. It's everything."

Beth couldn't say what she wanted to say. That she was still emotionally distraught over the doctor's diagnosis after her last miscarriage—that she would never be able to bear children. Hell, Beth knew John was still distraught as well. This trip was to give them a fresh start. Beth was starting to wonder if they had set themselves up for failure.

John placed the key into the lock and opened the door to room 305. John entered first, followed by Beth. Beth glanced around the room. No great shakes; the wall was a typical cream color and the wood furniture needed drastic upkeep. The small room was definitely not as impressive as the hotels she was accustomed to in New York when she would visit her younger sister, Jenny, who was happily married, with three adorable children. But Beth was happy too, right? She sometimes wondered about that as well.

"Come on, honey." John placed his hand on her shoulder, reeling her back to reality. "It's late. Let's go to bed."

Sleep never came for Beth Cooper during their first night at Mandrake Castle. Beth kept tossing and turning in their double bed. The bed was far from comfortable. The mattress was as hard as a rock and the pillows were too light and fluffy. It was as if she was resting her head on the mattress and not on a pillow. John, on the other hand, was asleep the moment his head hit the pillow. Throughout their ten years of marriage, Beth realized that nothing could stir her husband from sleep. Ambulance sirens could be blaring outside, and he would sleep right through it.

Beth decided enough was enough. She needed something to knock her out. Beth hopped out of bed and entered the bathroom. Slowly opening the medicine cabinet so as not to wake John, not that it would, Beth took out a bottle of night time sleeping pills, and closed the medicine cabinet. She stared at herself in the mirror and shook her head in frustration. *Maybe this was a mistake coming here. Maybe there's just no hope for us.* Beth didn't want this to be true. She loved her husband dearly but they were both struggling to make their marriage work because they couldn't have children. She often suggested therapy but John wouldn't have it.

Beth popped two pills in her mouth. As she downed them with a glass of water, she heard sounds emanating from outside the bathroom. They were soft, playful sounds…laughter.

"John?"

No answer. Not that she was expecting one.

Beth entered the bedroom and found John still sound asleep in bed. The laughter continued. This time Beth deduced that the laughter was coming from the hallway. Beth slowly opened the door and stepped out into the cold and dark hallway.

"Hello?" Beth asked the empty hallway. "Is anyone out here?"

Once again she received no answer. Beth folded her arms across her chest for the cold was getting to her. She closed the door and returned to the comfort and security of her husband in bed.

Still, sleep never came.

"You heard voices and saw no one?" John asked Beth during breakfast the next morning. John and Beth had decided to forgo eating at a breakfast restaurant and instead tried Mandrake Castle's continental breakfast. They sat down at a round table for two in the downstairs dining room and drank weak coffee and munched on a muffin and a bagel.

"It was laughter. The more I think about it, it sounded like a teenage girl's laughter."

John frowned at the mention of "girl". Beth mentally shook her head. *He still thinks I'm fragile over the ordeal*, she thought.

"Don't look at me like that," Beth finally protested. "I know what I heard."

"Come on, Beth. What parent allows their teenage daughter to go romping about in a hotel at night of all times?"

"Who's to say the child's parent is still alive?" a voice remarked from beside them.

Beth and John turned and discovered an elderly woman listening intently to their entire conversation. She appeared to be a frail woman with white hair and wrinkles covering her face and hands. Beth figured she was the kind of woman who had no family around and very few friends so she'd talk to anyone who showed the slightest interest.

"I'm sorry. I don't think we've met. My name is Beth Cooper and this is my husband, John."

Beth and John stuck out their hands to shake the old woman's hand. The old woman weakly extended her hand and Beth could clearly see the woman's veins.

"My name is Veronica Bardwell. I used to work here back in the sixties but, as you can see, very much retired. Anyway, when I was working here, I used to hear sounds, especially if it was dead quiet. It was laughter, just like you heard last night, dearie. A teenage girl's laughter."

"That's exactly what I heard!" an excited Beth said. She looked to John who just rolled his eyes in annoyance. "But who could it be?"

"Well," the old woman began. "Are you familiar with the castle's history?"

"To be honest? No."

"The castle was built by former Port Carlington mayor, Robert Mandrake, as a retirement home for him and his wife, Lucy. Robert only lasted a year in the castle, suffering a massive heart attack. When Lucy died of cancer three years later in 1895, Mandrake Castle was converted into a hotel. Well, what the previous owner explained to me when I worked here was that, back in the early 1900s, a young woman tragically died here. Mary Billings was her name. She was only thirteen, but her mother, Roberta, had her working odd jobs at Mandrake Castle. Roberta was a tyrant. She ran a tight ship and had Mary working at all hours of the day *and* night—cleaning the floors, dusting the furniture. Mary never had a normal childhood.

"One day, Mary was cleaning room 315 when, somehow, she fell out of an open window. Poor Roberta was so distraught over Mary's tragic death that she left the hotel. But people say Mary's spirit still lingers here in Mandrake Castle. She wants to be a normal teenage girl and have fun. Oh, my! Look at me. Here you two are trying to have a vacation and I'm scaring you with a ghost story. I'll be on my way. It was lovely meeting you."

"Yes, thank you. It was lovely meeting you too" Beth said as Veronica Bardwell slowly sat up from her table and sauntered away.

When the old woman was out of earshot, John whispered into Beth's ear, "That woman is bat-shit crazy."

"Stop it, John. What if she's right?"

"Are you kidding me? It's just a ghost story to scare the tourists. You don't seriously believe that crap?"

"What if it is true? That poor girl."

The second night at Mandrake Castle was no better for Beth. She tossed and turned and still couldn't fall asleep. John, as usual, slept like a baby. Two hours and no sleep later, Beth once again heard the laughter in the hallway. This time, she decided to investigate further. She stood up from bed and entered the dark hallway. With no flashlight to guide her, Beth carefully walked down the hallway, following the direction of the laughter.

"Hello? Who's there?" Beth asked the darkness. Once again, the darkness did not answer her.

Beth rounded a corner and suddenly came face to face with room 315. She stopped dead in her tracks. Taking a deep breath, Beth grabbed the doorknob and opened it. To her surprise, it opened with no fuss. She figured the door would be locked. Beth slowly entered the room, flipped on the light switch on the wall beside her, and eyed her surroundings. It appeared as if the room had not been touched in years. The furniture, which consisted of a king-size bed with two night stands on both sides, and two bureaus, were all covered in dust. There was no television set—only an old radio that appeared to be from the early 1900s.

"Are you looking for someone?" a voice asked from behind Beth.

Beth spun around and came face to face with a teenage girl. She had light brown hair and wore a faded white blouse over a black skirt. The white blouse appeared not to have been laundered in ages. Something, however, was bizarre about the girl. Her face was pale white, as if she were sick.

"Are you lost?" Beth asked the girl.

The teenager shook her head. "No I most certainly am not," the girl said in a very proper and old style language. "I live here in this room. At least I have for a very long time."

"My name is Beth Cooper. What's your name?"

"Mary Billings."

Beth was stunned at the answer. "This is a joke. Mary Billings is dead."

"I know I am dead, silly."

"Stop it! You're playing a cruel prank on me. This is someone's idea of a sick joke."

The young girl suddenly ran through Beth so quickly, Beth had no time to react. Beth stood in place, shocked and amazed at the same time at what had transpired. There was no pain for Beth felt nothing except for a brief moment of absolute coldness, which subsided once Mary appeared outside of Beth's body. Mary's body clearly was not solid at all. It was…Beth couldn't put her finger on it. Nothing. It was as if Mary was a hologram in a science fiction story. Only this was real life. Beth turned around and faced Mary. Mary just giggled.

"How could this be?" Beth asked.

"I don't know. It just is. One minute I'm cleaning the window to this room and the next I see my dead body lying on the ground below. All I can hear are people screaming at the sight of my body. My mother was one of them. She was so horrified at what happened, she quit her job the next day and took my body back to Seattle where she was born and raised. Only I never really left this place. My spirit, that is."

"Oh, my God." Beth couldn't think of anything else to say. *This is why hotel management won't check the room out to guests. They know it's haunted, or have received too many complaints regarding the haunting.*

"At first, the hotel tried renting this room out, but I put a stop to that. I died because of this room so why should anyone else find joy in it. Through time, staff pretty much realized I was haunting their hotel, particularly this room, and wasn't going to leave. So they decorated this room all for me. They never threw my belongings away after my mother fled, so they transported everything I owned to this room. A few times, they tried contacting my mother. They told her they believed her daughter's spirit was still residing in the hotel and that she might want to try and communicate with me through a medium. To try and make me leave. My mother would have no part in that. She refused to come and see me."

Beth shook her head. *How could a mother abandon her daughter like that? Even her daughter's spirit?*

Then Mary's face became rigid. "I didn't want to see my mother anyway. She was a horrible person."

All of a sudden, the lamp flickered on and off. Beth turned from side to side to see what was causing it. She then figured it was Mary's rage that was causing the electrical chaos.

Mary continued. Her fists were clenched in utter anger. "All life was to my mother was work, work, and work. I had no childhood, no friends. All I did was work at this dreadful place. I hate this place. *I hate her*!"

Beth heard a loud crack and then the lights suddenly stopped flickering. She turned to her right and, standing on a round table by a couch, was a cracked photo frame. Beth walked over and picked up the photo. It was of Mary and, who Beth deduced, was her mother."

She thought about offering to have the frame replaced for Mary, but thought better of it.

"Then why don't you leave?" Beth asked. "Move on?"

"It's not so dreadful anymore. There are all kinds of people here: adults, children, and teenagers. But it does become lonely. They don't hear or see me. There's no one here to love me."

"You poor girl." Beth felt horrible for her. This ghost girl had no friends and no mother to love her. *It must be unbearable*. "But, if no one else can see you, then, why can I?"

"Maybe you *want* to see me?" was Mary's only answer.

Beth paced the stuffy room, her hands folded across her chest from the cold air. "I can't believe this is happening. I mean, my husband thinks I'm insane."

"You're husband doesn't appreciate you," Mary replied, her tone much more stern and intense. "I heard him speak to you this morning at breakfast. "He does not understand the unexplained. And he does not understand you and what you're going through."

Beth nodded her head in agreement. "It's been a difficult year. Ten years to be perfectly honest. We had been trying so hard to get pregnant. A couple of times we succeeded, but I ended up miscarrying both times. Then, last year, my doctor told us we'd never be able to conceive. That nearly killed us. We both wanted a child so badly. I suggested we adopt but John would not consider it. 'The baby would never be truly ours!' he'd say. So, it'll just be the two of us."

Beth began to cry. She cupped her hand over her face. Mary stepped over to Beth and offered her a comforting hand. Beth took it, although never made contact.

"It's all right," the ghost girl said. "I'm here to listen. I care."

Beth nodded her head. "Thank you."

Realizing the time, Beth bid Mary good night and exited the room. Upon departing, Beth shut off the light and closed the door, leaving Mary in total darkness. Beth returned to her room and discovered John still asleep. She crawled into bed and, thinking of her ghostly encounter with Mary, actually fell asleep.

Breakfast the next morning was tense at best. Beth and John talked nonstop of Beth's conversation. At one point, Beth was on the verge of tears. "She's real! You have to believe me!"

"Beth, you're talking nonsense," John whispered. Beth could tell he was embarrassed at their topic of conversation. "Ghosts aren't real."

"Yes they are real. Mary Billings' ghost still resides in this hotel. Her mother was so horrible to her when she was alive. Even in death Mary is still lonely."

John shook his head in irritation. He sipped his cup of coffee and stared Beth straight in her eyes. "Listen. I'll hear no more of this ghost talk. If you're that obsessed about it, we'll leave and stay at another hotel."

Just like Mary said. He doesn't care about my feelings.

"No we can't. Look, I'm sorry. I don't mean to act this way."

"I know you're upset about the diagnosis."

I'm the only one upset about the diagnosis, you bastard?

"We both are. Listen, let's get away from the hotel and take a scenic drive for the day? What do you say? We'll do some shopping, see the sites?"

They drove into the main section of Port Carlington. As they drove through the main street, Beth thought about how much Port Carlington, as well as most of Washington, resembled Maine. The countryside with its spacious fields and mountains reminded Beth of her childhood in northern Maine. The center of town was like any Maine town, north or south. Small, family owned cafes, antique and used book stores lined the main street. It was just like growing up with her mother. Beth's mother was a kind and loving woman, unlike Mary's mother. That thought brought a frown to Beth's face and John noticed it when they pulled into the public parking lot.

"Come on, honey. No frowns. We're supposed to have fun."

But there was no fun to be had for both of them. All Beth could think about was leaving Mary alone in Mandrake Castle with no one to socialize. The thought pained her so much she thought she was going to vomit. When they entered a quaint clothing store, Beth appeared to be on another planet. John picked out a beautiful scarf to show Beth. She wasn't interested.

She couldn't stop thinking about poor Mary Billings.

After a silent and awkward dinner at a local restaurant, Beth all but forgot the name, they returned to Mandrake Castle where they immediately went to bed. At least John went to bed. Beth, on the other hand, waited for her husband to fall asleep, tip-toed out of the room, and ventured down the dark hallway to room 315.

"Mary," Beth said as she entered the room.

Mary was waiting for her. "I missed you," the ghost girl said.

"Me too," Beth said, and then dropped her head, as if in shame.

"What is the matter?" asked Mary.

"It's my husband. He thinks I'm crazy for believing in you."

"You're not crazy. He's crazy for not believing in *you*. You believe in me, don't you?"

Beth was actually pondering the thought when she heard a familiar voice behind her. "Beth, what are you doing?"

Beth abruptly turned around and stared face to face with John. "John, what are you doing out of bed?"

"I'd like to ask you the same thing?"

"I wanted to talk to Mary?"

"Jesus Christ, Beth. Do you hear yourself? There are no such things as ghosts!"

"No, you're wrong!" Beth shouted at her husband. "Can't you see that Mary is real? She is here in Mandrake Castle. Her spirit never left. Mary is so lonely. All she wants is a mother to love her. I can give her that. Finally, I can be a mother to someone!"

Beth could tell her husband thought she was insane. John shook his head in disappointment and frustration. "You're delusional, honey. Can't you see that?" John offered his hand to his wife. "Let's go, sweetheart. Let's get away from this place. This isn't healthy for you."

Then the lights began to flicker on and off again.

Mary.

"Do you see what I mean?" Mary said. Both John and Beth stood silent. Beth could tell John heard Mary's voice.

"What was that?" John sternly asked the old room. "Who's there?"

"Behind you!" Mary eerily whispered in answer.

John turned around and faced Mary. Her pale and dead face stared right back at him.

"Oh, now do you believe?" she sarcastically asked him.

John began to back away from the ghost. Mary followed his every move. Beth stared at her husband. His face was sweating from fear and his hands were shaking.

"Can't you see what he is doing to you, Beth? He's deluding your mind into thinking this place is bad for you. That *I'm* bad for you.

A lamp on a nearby table shattered, untouched by human hands, enveloping the room in darkness.

"He doesn't want you to be happy," Mary said. "He just wants to bring you down. Rule your life until you are weak."

The cracked photo of Mary and her mother began to shake on the table, as if it was preparing to take flight.

John inched toward the window. He held his hands out in front of him in a defensive maneuver, although Beth wondered how that tactic would stand up to a ghost. "Stay back. I'm warning you."

Mary giggled at the frightened man. Then her giggle turned into a grimace and John's face fell flat with horror. *"YOU'RE JUST LIKE MY MOTHER!"* Mary screamed and the intensity of her scream thrust forward not only the cracked photo but John as well with such force and speed that he smashed through the window. John screamed all the way until he crashed on the ground below.

Beth ran to the broken window, her hand cupped to her mouth in horror. John lay on the ground in a pool of his own blood. His dead and terror-stricken face seemed to be locked on his wife. Beth also noticed the cracked photo by his side.

"All of the bad energy is gone from this room," Beth heard Mary say behind her. Mary meant not only John, but her mother as well.

When sleepy guests began to congregate, Beth stepped away from the window, turned around, and discovered she was alone in the old room.

"So, have you seen anything strange in this place?" the husband asked the hotel clerk upon checking in.

The young couple had wanted to stay at Mandrake Castle the moment they researched its bizarre history on a haunted hotel web site. They were interested in the paranormal and all things that went bump in the night.

"I haven't seen anything personally," the hotel clerk said. "But, I've heard from other employees and guests of strange occurrences."

"What about the psycho wife who pushed her husband out the window?" the wife asked.

"Well, that was never ruled a murder. There was never any evidence."

The young couple both looked at each other and sighed. Disappointed, they picked up their luggage, and walked up the staircase to their room.

The elderly woman heard everything as she sat on a club chair in the reception area, sipping her tea. Being a lifelong guest, she was accustomed to the constant thrill seekers and ghost adventurers that plagued the hotel after the tragic death of the man nearly forty years ago.

It didn't bother her. Life went on.

The old woman set her tea cup down and climbed the stairs to the third floor. She rounded the corner and walked until she arrived at room 315. She extracted her room key, opened the door, and entered the room she had lived in for the past forty years.

She stared around the room, gazing at the photos on the wall.

They were all of her. She felt a chill in the air, and when she turned around, Mary was before her; still young and happy as ever.

"Mary," Beth Cooper said in a hoarse voice that came with her age.

Mary smiled. *"Hello, Mother."*

AN AUTOGRAPHED POSTER OF CLAIRE DANES

AARON GUDMUNSON

The tag on the velvet Elvis painting read $45. It was one of the ugliest things Rick Enders had ever rolled his eyes across, but the need to possess it was sharp and immediate. The king stood twelve inches, his jumpsuit sparkling with miniature rhinestones, feet poised in that patented pose that made girls swoon those decades past—and a few still today.

Elvis's signature sneer was brushed on ever so delicately, and the blocky sunglasses seemed reflective. Yes, Rick needed this painting. He already envisioned a place for it in the Rock n' Roll Room on the third floor of his house.

"Take your order?" barked a voice at his side. He looked up at the face of what surely must have been Broom-Hilda's older sister. His appetite for grilled tuna slipped away, but his appetite for bargaining had just yawned awake.

"Yes, you can." He checked her name tag. "Meryl." Her face pinched at the sound of her name, as if hearing it from this man was profanity. "I'll take tuna salad on rye, no tomato, home fries and a Diet Coke."

"Anything else?"

"Yes, actually," Rick said, his smile widening. "This painting."

"That?" Meryl said, jabbing at it with the stub of her pencil. "Ain't for sale, mister."

Rick's smile vanished. "But there's a price tag on it."

Meryl grunted, peeled the sticker off the frame, gave it a once over through her bifocals, then stuck it to the back of her order pad.

"Meryl, may I speak to your manager?" Rick asked in a tight voice. He hated being refused a sale. Being refused anything, for that matter.

Meryl stabbed the pencil at the window and the ancient sign by the highway that read **Meryl's Place** in blue neon. "I am the manager." She waddled off, bumping through the kitchen doors, buttocks hunching against one another like the shoulder blades of some horrific beast.

Turning, she gasped to see Rick Enders still standing there, looming, smiling distastefully around capped teeth. "I'm not leaving without that painting."

"I told you," she said, regaining composure. "It ain't for god-damn sale. You can check out a place up the road called Tuck's Treasures. He's probably got a dozen of them things."

Rick stepped closer. He looked prepared to kiss his hostess, or perhaps bite her. "I don't want to go to Tuck's up the road. I'm asking you, madam."

"Ask all you want," Meryl said. "That painting ain't leavin' my restaurant."

"And I ain't leaving without that painting."

"I'm calling the police."

Rick snatched the phone from the wall and yanked out the cord, wrapping its coils around his fist. "Hear me out, Meryl. It's in your best interest."

"Why the hell do you want that old painting for?" she rasped.

"Why the hell don't you want to sell it to me?" he asked, pulling his wallet from the inside of his jacket. Meryl didn't reply in words; the lines of her face trembled and dewdrops sparkled on her eyelids. Rick removed a hundred dollar bill and held it out.

She snuffled and scrubbed a gnarled hand across her nose. "Ain't got change for that."

"None expected," he replied. "Do we have a sale?"

She nodded once, sharp. She snatched the money and stumbled back, putting the grill between them. "Take it and get out, and if I ever see you in here again, I'm callin' the cops."

"Pleasure doing business with you," Rick said and returned to the dining room to collect his purchase.

Perhaps it was his background in sales that made him such an astute bargainer. Maybe it was his assholism. No doubt about that—he *was* an asshole. Not that he faulted himself for it; that particular quality served him well. Perhaps it was why, after eight years with the company, he'd been promoted to vice president of marketing and was able to rehab a four-story Victorian outside Galena, dedicating each of its nineteen rooms to something he loved. He'd been a champion salesman since earliest memory, beginning with a Tom Watt kit as a Cub Scout. He'd sold more than enough useless trinkets to finance his trip to the Jamboree. His golden streak had continued into manhood. For this, he was eternally grateful to the powers that be.

The velvet Elvis rode shotgun so Rick could glance at it. It really was an ugly thing, but it would fit perfectly above the mantle in the Rock n' Roll room. Or should it go in the Motion Picture room? *Roustabout* was a dandy of a film. But no—the Rock room for sure, beside the genuine Beatles *Sergeant Pepper's Lonely Hearts Club Band* album cover—this signed by George Harrison himself. Perfect. He could hardly wait to get it home.

One of the benefits of driving to conferences was that one could stop and see the sights. Especially in this ornate pocket of country, where flea markets thrived and antique shops were king. There was one or the other every third mile and Rick took full advantage.

A sign loomed out of the trees around a bend in the highway.

Tuck's Treasures From Around the World! See the sights without leaving the state! Wonders your eyes have never beheld! Exit 22 toward Marengo! We'll be waiting for you.

Here was one now. The one Meryl had mentioned, in fact. Oh, this would be fun. This would be perfect. Rick drove two miles, then snapped on his turn signal when the sign pointing to the exit came into view.

A hand-painted sign with a chipped red arrow pointed down a gravel road that ran perpendicular to the main street. This one read simply: **Tuck's Treasures, This-A-Way!** Rick made the turn.

The store lay alone at the place where the gravel dead-ended into cornfield. Two cars sat in the lot, a maroon Saab and a green pickup. Rick wheeled between them and killed the engine. Sparrows fluttered overhead and somewhere a bullfrog lurched through a wet chorus. All else was silent.

This looks like something out of a horror flick, he thought, getting out. *House of Wax, maybe, or Wrong Turn.*

The facade of the building was red brick. Here and there it had been patched with cement. A rusted pump stood twenty feet from the west face, dripping into an equally rusted pail. Rick walked around the side of the building to where a green and cream awning stretched over the entrance. Its formal incongruity made him smile. He removed his sunglasses and pushed open the door.

A bell jingled, as he imagined it would. The smell of sawdust and incense was overpowering. From somewhere, a radio murmured out The Searchers' Love Potion Number 9. A man in a checked flannel shirt and straw hat sat behind the counter and Rick called hello.

The man didn't move and Rick frowned. Something was amiss. He considered the possibility again that he was walking into some sort of horror movie and almost turned around.

"Afternoon?" he called to the figure, but it remained motionless. It was only after a few heart-thudding moments that he understood it was a mannequin.

"Help ya?" a voice asked and Rick jumped. He turned to find a man—a real one—grinning at him from the curtained doorway to the back room where The Searchers had been replaced by none other than the King crooning *Love Me Tender*.

The proprietor stood an easy six feet tall with greasy hair growing wild beneath a cowboy hat. He reminded Rick of Michael Madsen in the *Kill Bill* movies.

"Jesus, you startled me," Rick laughed.

"Sorry 'bout that. Haven't had many customers today," the man said, looking over Rick's suit and sixty-dollar haircut. He approached and stuck out a hand. "Tuck Coleman, treasure hunter."

Rick took the hand. "Rick Enders, salesman and bargainer. Pleased to meet you."

"Bargainer, eh? Well, you come to the right place, friend. Have a look around and let me know if I can be of assistance. Eddie ain't much of a talker." He winked and cocked a thumb at the mannequin behind the counter.

"I noticed," Rick said.

"Fact, he's downright rude sometimes. He's definitely the bad cop. But what the hell do you expect? He works graveyard shift. Night watchman." Tuck's voice dropped. "Cuts down on having to pay for an alarm system."

"He must be working overtime today. I'll steer clear of him," Rick promised, then turned to examine a shelf of snow globes.

"Those're from Russia," Tuck said. "Found them at this tiny back alley antique shop in Leningrad couple or three years back. They predict the weather, you know."

"They're exquisite," Rick commented, though he thought they looked like cheap mass-produced knockoffs you could buy at Hallmark for $14.95 a piece. The tags on them were $19, but then, of course, the ones at Hallmark didn't predict the weather.

"Anything particular you're after?" Tuck asked. He plucked a pocketknife as if from thin air and began to trim his nails with it. Rick couldn't help but be impressed with the proprietor's sleight of hand and was on the verge of commenting on it, but was suddenly caught by something on the wall near the counter. His breath stopped short. "I just found it."

He hadn't known about the MTV television show named *My So-called Life* that had given Claire Danes her start until long after its cancellation. He had seen a couple of movies starring Claire, however, and had thought her excellent in *Brokedown Palace* and gloriously sexy in *Igby Goes Down*. But she had truly made him a fan with *Romeo and Juliet*. She'd filled the role with a grace and sorrow that broke his heart. Ever since, she was his leading lady. He'd purchased the wings she'd worn in the movie from an online auction site and they currently hung in a special place in his Motion Picture room, beside an authentic Oscar statue—the details behind acquiring this particular piece tickled Rick to no end; it had been a beautiful instance of his brilliance.

Now here she was again, wearing those wings and the smile that made her an angel. Here was not Juliet, but Claire. Beautiful, ethereal. Looking right at him. And…was it possible? Her signature scratched in blue marker beneath her breasts.

"That," Rick breathed, already reaching for his wallet. So much for bargaining. "That, that, that. How much for Claire?"

Tuck lit a cigarette with a Zippo he produced from somewhere, drew smoke, blew out. He shook his head. "Sorry. Claire ain't for sale. Display only."

What was with this cursed little corner of the world? How did people make their livings by refusing sales to paying customers? Rick felt his cheeks heat.

"Listen, Tucker," Rick began. He used people's first names when he wanted to make a point. He'd learned it as a domination technique—and the more formal, the better. "I've had a bad day. A very bitchy diner owner also refused to sell me something today and it pissed me off something fierce. So…"

"Yeah, I know. Meryl Gavin phoned me up."

"Why doesn't it surprise me you two know each other?" Rick said.

"Pardon me, but that was a pretty shitty thing to do to a nice woman," Tuck said. He picked a bit of tobacco leaf off his tongue and flicked it away.

"There was a price tag on that painting," Rick said, holding a shaking finger in the air. It was all he could do to restrain the tempest that wished to explode. He saw himself toppling display shelves and smashing Tuck's little bullshit Russian snow globes all over the floor. One of his hands crept out and snatched one up and began to shake it mechanically in an effort to quell the coming storm. Inside the world of the globe, a blizzard raged over a tiny Christmas village. Somewhere in the back of his mind, he realized this stopped being about commerce and started being a control issue.

"Doesn't matter much to me if there was a tag on the painting, *Ricky*," Tuck said. "If she didn't want to sell, she didn't have to. And you'll notice there's no price tag on Claire."

Rick looked around helplessly. Rows of kewpie dolls and teddy bears and marionettes stared back. A mounted swordfish watched with black, vacant eyes. A stuffed bison head with a $500 price tag dangling from one horn seemed to be grinning over this little to-do playing out beneath it. A mechanical clown mounted on a stationary bicycle giggled and waved while peddling off to nowhere.

"Okay, you win," Rick said. "I'm sure you don't mind if I look around. Business seems a little slow."

"Knock yourself out," Tuck said, smoking. "No one's been here all day, except Eddie. Not but three parking places outside any-how."

On a top shelf, Rick noticed jars of what appeared to be dead pigs in formaldehyde. He grimaced.

"Those're pickled pig fetuses from South America. Bolivia, to be exact. Supposed to bring the owner good luck, if you can believe the natives who jar 'em. Beneath you'll notice the vials of red feathers? Phoenix down…from India. Bring the dead to life." Tuck wiggled his fingers in the air and made ghostly noises.

"Well, this has certainly been an education," Rick said, eyeing a pair of crossed katanas above the door. "But unless you're going to sell me Claire, I should push on."

"Enjoy your day, mister," Tuck said, folding his pocketknife and studying his nail work.

"Can I just take it down and look at it?" Rick asked, desperately, spinning toward the proprietor. He hoped this move would work toward changing Tuck's mind. Sudden aggression worked wonders in sales, in Rick's experience.

"Can't allow it," Tuck replied without looking up. "Got something ugly behind it you wouldn't want to see. Spot of work that needs to be cleaned up."

Probably more patchwork in the rotten walls of this place, Rick thought. His mouth tasted hot and filmy.

He moved past the counter where Eddie sat watchful beneath his straw hat.

He parked behind a gas station facing Main Street after purchasing a flashlight and batteries at the local True Value. He paid with cash, something he carried in excess. His associates warned him of this habit, but Rick refused their advice. His avoidance of credit was the primary reason he attributed to his success. Debt will bury you quicker than an undertaker, was his motto. He carried platinum versions of both Visa and MasterCard, but used neither for purchases—ever. Anyway, he pitied the jerk who tried to rob him—another one of his accomplishments was a black belt in karate, which he'd earned two summers ago at the YMCA.

Rick waited for the dashboard clock to read half past eleven, then turned out onto the nameless gravel road toward Tuck's Treasures From Around the World.

A pickup was in the lot but the Saab was gone. The store stood dark. Apparently Tucker Coleman didn't believe in wasting money on night lights either. Leaving a dummy as sole means of security, the man was going to get burgled one of these days and Rick couldn't imagine a company that would insure this ramshackle business. Too bad for Tuck.

He didn't consider what he was about to do as burglary. Not at all. He fully intended to leave payment for his acquisition. Rick Enders was no thief. But he was also not a man to be refused. He removed his Visa from his billfold and approached the door. Hell, there wasn't even a deadbolt. A moment of jimmying with the credit card and the latch clicked back. Sweet singing Christ in a choir this was easy.

Flashlight in his fist, Rick entered. He played the beam along the counter. Eddie was absent. *Must be in the can*, Rick thought and laughed. From the back room, the radio whispered "Hey, Jude."

He took it as a matter of course; any man who would leave his store practically open to the world would undoubtedly not possess the presence of mind to shut off the damned radio at the end of the day. He stepped forward and stopped when he saw what he'd come for. Claire stared back with perfect petulant purity. His Juliet. His angel.

"Ready, babe?" he asked, raising his hands to remove the frame. What had Tuck said? He couldn't remove it from the wall because there'd be something behind it Rick wouldn't like? Work that needed to be cleaned up? What the hell was that supposed to…

The poster came away and Rick stared. The wall behind did not contain a hole in the drywall as he'd suspected. He was looking at himself. The wall behind the poster was a mirror. He saw his own hollow cheeks, his pitiless black eyes, his arrogant smirk. He stared, transfixed, heart thudding, at his image and wondered what the hell he was doing. He watched his mouth open to speak something—he had no idea what—and then he saw the blur that moved up behind him with the sickening speed of a demon. Someone loomed in a red-checkered shirt and straw hat, face pale as plaster. Lips the color of scar tissue, leering. Eyes the color of dead, wet earth.

Rick turned, dropping Claire, but he didn't hear the frame shatter. Nor did he hear himself scream.

"Afternoon, madam."

"Hello," the woman said. "I'm in love with your shop. I've been here five minutes and can already tell that."

"We have something for everybody," the proprietor said, stepping out from behind a backroom curtain. "Tuck Coleman, treasure hunter extraordinaire."

"Pleased to meet you," the woman said. She admired a shelf of chattering teeth, moved her gaze along to jars of magic powder. ***See Mystical Lands and Far-away Worlds!*** the label pronounced, then to a section of brass oil lamps. She didn't give the autographed poster of Claire Danes a second glance, nor the velvet Elvis painting beside it.

"Anything particular you're looking for?" Tuck asked.

The woman stopped on the area of flooring beneath the Claire Danes poster with a gasp. "This rug is lovely! How much is it?"

Tuck glanced down and sighed. "Sorry, ma'am, but that particular piece is not currently for sale."

"Why not?" she asked, dejection maiming her face.

"Sort of ashamed to say it, but it's covering something up. Don't think you'd much like to see it."

"A stain?"

"Sadly, yes. A bad stain. Come back in a week or so and maybe I'll have something else to cover it with and that rug'll be back on display."

"Oh, I suppose I could," the woman said, gazing at the carpet with a palm tucked beneath her chin.

"Bring your friends," Tuck said and tipped her a wink. "Not that we do a poor trade, mind you. Just that it can get awful lonesome out here with just me and him."

The woman turned and laughed at the mannequin in the suit and sharp haircut behind the counter. She dipped an awkward curtsey. "Pleased to meet you. Oh, he looks so real. How much is he?"

Tuck laughed. "Old Ricky's not for sale either. He's the night watchman."

THE NEW JUBILEE

ROBERT SPALDING

For as long as Michael Maloney could remember, he had been terrified by earth, the thought of being in it or under it to be more precise.

The notion was fixed in his mind that should he ever venture more than an arm's length into the ground then something, some dark and unimaginable thing, would come to claim him. To drag him down away from the sunlight into the bowels of the Earth where he would slowly suffocate.

He knew where the obsession came from; his very first memory was of being pulled from a hole. Pulled upwards to the light and crying, screaming for his family. The context of the moment was long lost, but the fear of being under the ground had always remained in him.

When he was a child, the local children had played a game they called Vietnam or Jungle Warriors. The game was simple: there were two sides and they would attempt to catch the other in a variety of jungle traps. The game was played on the large patch of wasteland behind the estate, overgrown with weeds and slim trees, little more than mud when it rained.

It was, of course, strongly frowned upon by the adults for the children to play there, which made the games just that little bit more satisfying.

On one occasion, one of the groups had contrived to spend the night before digging a pit trap and covering it with branches and leaves. The effort they had gone to was nothing unusual for them, but to the adults who later found out about it, the feat was a minor marvel. The pit was dug to a depth of five feet, nothing to an adult, but just deep enough to hold any unfortunate ten-year-old that might stumble upon it.

Michael was that unfortunate ten-year-old.

He had been running away from the opposition, unaware that they were driving him towards a trap, although he should have suspected, given the nature of the game. Ahead, he could see the open scrubland which his team had marked out as safe, and with legs pumping, he sprinted, until the ground beneath his feet collapsed and he was trapped.

It took Michael only a second to realize what had happened to him. There are few children who were ever so acutely aware of their depth in the earth.

In a mad panic, he tried to jump out, climb out, claw out. He bellowed and screamed for mercy, scrabbling furiously at the loose soil which betrayed him time and again to leave him in the pit. Above him Michael could hear the laughter of his captors, the celebration of a trap successfully sprung, but their voices were becoming dim to his ears. Instead, a steady thrum of vibration filled them. When he placed a flat palm on the wall of his prison, he could feel the earth vibrate beneath it, the sense of something coming for him and only for him. His legs felt like jelly and he found it harder and harder to remain standing. Something inside him wanted to lie down and have it done with, but his obstinate side, the ten-year-old who still wanted to see the new Star Wars film at the cinema, refused.

Instead he screamed again, the full fear and fury of his situation tearing at his throat.

Down in the pit, he produced noises such as the other children had never heard before and never would again. In a panic that he had hurt himself in some manner that would be impossible to hide from their parents, Michael's captors pulled him out. They had to grab his arms and drag him, commenting that for someone who was so desperate to get out of the hole, he wasn't helping much. They dumped him beside the pit and eyed him cautiously. He had stopped making the strange, animalistic howls he had scared them with and began to weep quietly. One of the older boys had to walk him home, reassuring the younger boy all the time that there had been nothing else in the pit, nothing clutching at his legs as they pulled him out. He did not think Michael ever fully believed him.

After that day the other children would not play Vietnam or any other game with Michael. He became a very lonely child for a time, as the story of his strange attack in the pit took on mythical proportions and followed him up to his next school. To avoid the questioning looks and whispers behind his back, Michael developed a love of numbers; physics and engineering became his playthings.

But from the day of the pit, Michael Maloney became obsessively careful about staying above-ground.

At the age of forty-two Michael had maintained a perfect record for thirty two years of never letting his feet go deeper than his knees into the ground, even that deep was enough to bring him out in a cold sweat and have him tossing and turning in sleepless nights for a week.

His perfect streak was about to come to an end however, and the foreknowledge of this had been keeping him awake for days on end and stretching his nerves to a breaking point. Finally his boss, Mr. Vinter, had insisted that he go to see a therapist; which was how he found himself sitting on a comfortable chair opposite Dr. Claire Stephenson for the eighth time in two weeks.

"So, tomorrow's the big day. Do you feel the work we've done has helped at all."

Michael smiled helplessly, he wanted to say yes, that he was cured, that she was a miracle worker and everything would be fine. He couldn't.

"I slept through most of last night. A whole five hours, that's four and a half more than before I started, so I guess that's something."

Dr. Stephenson nodded, flicking a stray strand of hair from her face, a motion that always fascinated Michael. "I would suggest that you don't go, but that's not an option. I can wish you had come to me a lot sooner, as soon as you knew you were going to have to face this, but I can't turn back time." She smiled disarmingly at him. "So we'll just have to go over your breathing and relaxation exercises again. We both know that tomorrow is going to be extremely hard, but if you keep your mind focused on your achievement and remember to breathe, I think we can get you out of there without too much screaming."

Michael nodded, Claire had actually been more help than he was letting on; he was even able to think about the next day's event without letting out any verbal screams or shrieks. They still rang in his head, but at least this way no one else would have to put up with them.

For the next hour, Claire ran him through his exercises, controlling his breathing, focusing his mind on open skies, slowing his heart by force of will. As their time came to an end, Michael used the techniques he had just been running through and asked Claire to be his 'plus one' to the next day's event.

For a heart-stopping moment she looked shocked and he wondered if her expression was going to turn into one of horror or disappointment. It did neither and a small smile opened her shock-compressed lips.

"I think that would be wonderful," she said.

Michael sighed with joyous relief.

"You did mean in a purely professional capacity to overcome your fears, didn't you?" she asked.

The joy crumbled, but he managed to keep the hurt from his voice. "Of course I did."

"Then I'll meet you tomorrow. Where shall I wait?"

"Meet me at the entrance to Westminster station. We're having the ceremony on the Jubilee platform." He suppressed a shudder and marveled at his ability to do so. To think about heading to the deepest point in all of London without needing to vomit or scream aloud was his proudest moment of the day.

Claire noticed it, too, and gave him a small smile.

"What time should I be there?"

"Eleven should do it. You may want to dress up. The mayor is coming to the ceremony."

"Oh," Claire said with a cheeky grin. "That's fancy."

Michael's fear of the earth had led to his loneliness, which had in turn led to his love of engineering and a career in that field. It was then, to him, the most horrific irony that the love which had grown from his fear was now forcing him into the most terrifying situation he could envision.

The university had been a time of hard work for him, learning all the principles that would lead him into a career. Michael's focus had always been on his work, leaving little time for socializing, but he had come away with a small group of acquaintances.

It hadn't taken long for him to acquire a job at Ramsen Design and from there it was his dedication to his work which had landed him the role for which he had been forced into therapy.

The project had been Mr. Vinter's baby, a redesign of the tube trains for London. He had been convinced that using the existing infrastructure, the trains could be made to run more efficiently. The job of achieving this aim had been Michael's. It had taken six long years of design, testing, building and more testing, but now the first of these trains was due to make its maiden voyage. They were going to have a ceremony at Westminster station, closing down that part of the station for two hours. The disruption to the rest of the system didn't really bear thinking about, indeed Michael did not, as it wasn't his responsibility. The new Mayor had made acquiring these trains a major part of his campaign and he was going to milk them for all he could; if one Sunday was a little disrupted, the publicity of the new trains and his part in them would more than make up for it.

This was why Michael found himself pacing outside the tube station in front of an amused policeman, wishing for a cigarette—or ten—and waiting for Claire to arrive. An angry crowd of disrupted commuters and disrupting antagonizers were behind barriers, all yelling obscenities at the people filing into the station. Why they didn't just use another station or line for right this moment, Michael didn't know. It couldn't be that hard to walk to another station, maybe a bit of exercise would flush some of their anger away.

Then Claire made her way towards him, waving her pass at the officers to let her through. Michael felt a great weight lift from the center of his chest, a weight he hadn't even realized was pressing on him.

"I made it." She smiled at him, her perfect teeth gleaming from the cherry red of her lipstick. Michael felt his heart skip and his breath catch in his throat. Luckily, Claire mistook the reaction for fear and laid a reassuring hand on his arm.

"I'm here. You can do this."

He nodded, not daring to speak lest his voice betray his pleasure at seeing her. If she thought his feelings towards her were anything but professional then she might leave, might not be willing to go down into the earth at his side. Right now Michael couldn't decide what would be worse, going into the earth, or going into the earth without Claire. Before the terror had always been the same, no matter the circumstances. For one person to have made this much difference to him, well, that was a breakthrough, wasn't it?

With a soft smile, Claire turned to him so that he was facing the entrance to the station. Now the fear hit him like a wave, the underground, *under the ground*, the very name usually gave him palpitations. But Claire's hand was upon his, acting as a wave breaker that streamed his fear into manageable rivulets.

"I can do this," he whispered.

"Say it louder," Claire encouraged him.

"I can do this!" he yelled, prompting a response of jeers from the other side of the barriers.

His left foot lifted and moved forward. His right repeated the action and he was walking into the station. The air was cool, refreshing against his face, and for the first time Michael believed he could do it.

The nearness of Claire, the warmth of her hand on his arm, was distracting him from the unconscious knowledge that very soon he would start to descend. They came to the first set of escalators and the knowledge was no longer unconscious.

Sweat beaded his brow and he could feel his armpits becoming damp with a speed that was terrifying for a man trying to impress the pretty woman touching his arm. His life-long fear had ruled over him with a free reign for so long that the intrusion of another emotion into its domain came as a shock.

He could feel his terror trying to force him to run, yet being prevented by his pride and feelings for Claire. Had he finally found his key? His guide to living as other people did without a thought?

Claire must have felt some of the struggle inside him manifest physically, a tremor or tremble in his muscles perhaps. Whatever it was she squeezed his arm at just the right moment and whispered into his ear, "I believe in you."

With a surge, his terror was forced back and control of his body became fully his. With an almost arrogant swagger in his mind, he placed his feet onto the escalator and began to descend.

Claire gripped his arm tightly for support, but as soon as the top of his head dropped below the first step of the escalator, Michael's terror rushed back. Much of his brain was now taken up with an incoherent scream of horror.

A promise of death and terrible things if he didn't turn back now.

Mental blows that felt nearly physical brought about the start of one of his headaches. His skull felt like it was warping from the blows and he longed to scream, to turn and run back up the steps, back into the daylight, to be above ground once more.

"Michael, look at me."

He turned to stare into Claire's green eyes.

"You can do this. Everything you feel, everything you fear, it's just in your head. It isn't real. I know this is scary for you, but I'm here and I promise, nothing is going to hurt you."

The pain subsided slowly at her words. His fear slunk back into the reaches of his mind, muttering darkly that this wasn't over.

When they reached the bottom of the escalator he could admire, for the first time, the feat of engineering that had gone into designing and building the station. It was a cathedral, a work of art, a huge space held open and up by human ingenuity. It was beautiful and the realization of this, even more so than Claire's tender touch upon his arm, calmed him.

They came to the next escalator and started down it. Still the fear didn't return although his headache would not go away. Michael wondered if he might be experiencing some sort of pressure headache, his body being so unused to being under the ground.

As they went deeper, Michael found himself trying to calculate the weight of the earth above their heads, from a purely engineering standpoint. All of his calculations were a trick Claire had suggested back in her office and it was working. His head was full of equations and calculations that he was ignoring; the pressure building behind his eyes and the fear that still coiled like a sleeping cobra around his spine.

Then he heard the noises.

A deep rumbling that was amplified by the curvature and openness of the tunnels and walkways around them.

"Do you hear that? There's something in the walls, something in the ground." The hysteria he had held at bay for so long crept into his voice.

"It's okay, Michael. That's the sound of the trains. They rumble and rattle. The sound carries through the tunnels around us. Especially with no one in the station to absorb the sound. Come on, you know this."

He did know it, should have known it. Yet his brain insisted that there was more to these noises than that. Something sinister, something that had waited for him for so long and now growled and shook with anticipation.

This time Claire had to actually tug on his sleeve to get him moving again. It was the sound of the trains, the old trains, the noisy trains that his design would soon replace. Michael repeated the facts over and over again, a mantra to calm himself.

As they descended the last escalator, they caught up with the other people heading down to the ceremony. Among an increased number of people, Michael felt his fear begin to ebb once more. He felt safe in the crowd, hidden from whatever might search for him down below. Claire's constant presence, her closeness and warmth made him feel as safe as he could have ever hoped to be in a situation such as this.

The rumbling sounds that surrounded them before moving on were becoming an acceptable background noise to him now. He still felt his skin electrify each time the first distant notes of it reached his ears, but he no longer felt a desperate need to hold back a scream.

As the group stepped on to the platform to see the mayor already in position, television cameras pointed at him as he waited to begin his speech, Michael thought that he might just about get through this with enough dignity left that asking Claire on an actual date might not be too embarrassing.

The mayor spoke for twenty full minutes, waxing lyrically on the effect the new trains would have. How their energy consumption levels would save millions in cost, their efficiency and build quality would reduce stoppages. Everything that Michael had been tasked to make happen, this oaf was taking vicarious credit for. This idiot who had taken a month of long explanations, and carefully boiled down the reports with no words longer than two syllables, so he could even understand what it was Michael and his team were proposing. Now the man smiled and preened for the cameras as though he had always been the driving force and not the driven dunce.

"You're grinding your teeth." Claire elbowed him in the ribs with a touch that was more familiar than professional.

"I hadn't noticed." He actually hadn't. His body had been performing some independent actions all the way through the speech. His legs were twitching and hitting him with mini-cramps, and his arms felt like useless jelly. His entire body was reacting as it sometimes did after a particularly strenuous session at the gym. He supposed that all of his terrified energy, all that fear and adrenaline which had pumped through him as he made his way down, had taken its toll.

Now the mayor was finally ending his speech and Mr. Vinter was making his way forward to address the cameras and the crowd.

For the first time in days, Michael could feel his excitement starting to build. Mr. Vinter was there to offer a few more platitudes and then call forth the new train. This was it; this moment was the start of what he'd been working towards for all those months.

His thoughts of being buried, being taken, everything that had frightened him for so long had vanished in one shining moment of anticipation. He gripped Claire's hand in a way that was definitely meant as more than something purely professional, and he smiled as she squeezed his in return.

"Ladies and gentlemen, it gives me enormous personal and professional pride to announce the arrival of the new Jubilee line trains. The Azmarti." Mr. Vinter's voice carried the notes of pride and joy that Michael could feel swelling in his own breast.

Now he could hear the familiar rumbling coming from the tunnel. The crowd pressed against the security glass that divided the platform from the track at each Jubilee station.

"This is wonderful, Michael. You must feel so proud." Claire snuggled in close to him and hugged his arm.

It was perfect, everything was as it should be. Then he listened to the rumble of his approaching train more clearly. There was no *click-clack* of wheels, no mechanical power echoing through the tunnel. He felt his heart speed up.

"I say, you're the designer chap, aren't you?" It was the mayor. "I must say, these Azmarti trains are certainly a lot quieter than I expected. We'll have to make sure the press includes that too, eh?"

Michael mumbled some platitude to the idiot, ignoring Claire's confused look, and stared intently down into the darkness of the tunnel.

The rumbling drew closer.

"So then, where does the name Azmarti come from? Vinter tells me you were quite insistent on it."

Had he been? He couldn't remember. "It's the name of a very old God who burrowed through this area. I found it in a folk tale or myth from some London book."

Michael's headache was coming back, a pain that broke in perfect rhythm with his heartbeat. His head felt like an ice cream in the sun, drooping and falling as it melted. The pain was becoming unbearable and he could barely see the mayor's stupid, puzzled face or Claire's worried expression through it.

Then the first Azmarti rolled into the station.

A brilliant white, the nose and tail were pointed, like a worm, to increase air flow. It was rounder, more suited to fit into the tunnels without the attendant disruption in the air. It was his finest piece of work and he couldn't enjoy it because of a stupid headache.

When the first scream came, Michael was thoroughly shocked to find that it hadn't come from him. He was leaning against the back wall of the platform, trying to gather what little thoughts he had into something cohesive, when someone else screamed in terror. Looking towards the glass partition, he saw something that brought every night terror, every waking horror into sharp relief.

The train that had arrived was not a train at all; instead it was a giant, writhing, white worm. Its segmented skin undulated and pulsated, pressing against the glass to leave smears of ichor and slime.

The crowd was trying to simultaneously get away from the sight and find a better vantage point to see what was going on. Claire was pressed against him in the crush, and for the first time Michael could find nothing exciting or comforting about it. They were real, the creatures he had been afraid of for so long had come to claim him.

He wanted to weep, to scream out in terror in his last moments before he died, but his mouth wouldn't work, his vocal cords were on fire and unresponsive. A high-pitched keening filled his ears, but whether he was the one making it or if it came from the creature on the tracks, he couldn't tell.

He was unable to tear his eyes away from the beast, even when Claire screamed at him to move and said she would leave without him.

The pulsating skin was coalescing into small lumps and then the lumps were developing motion of their own. As he watched, Michael saw hundreds form and then detach themselves from the large creature, becoming roving miniature versions of it. Then they started to press against the glass even as the television cameramen continued to film the award-worthy sight.

Finally, the glass could take no more, and it exploded along the length of the platform and an army of small white maggot-worms raced into the crowd. Now the screams began in earnest.

The smaller worms slid across the platform and into the crowd. They burrowed into any exposed flesh they could touch. What just minutes ago had been a peaceful crowd awaiting a new innovation became a crazed, dancing, swirling mass of screaming humanity as people tried to pull the slippery invaders from under their skin.

Michael watched with a horrified detachment as the crowd became a screaming mob, desperately tearing chunks from their own flesh to get the alien beings out.

The freshly cleaned white tiles of the platform began to change color, the blood that dripped from a hundred open wounds staining the platform beneath the panicking crowd red.

He found he could track the progress of the worms from the bulge they made on a person's skin when they were burrowing close to the surface. He watched as a man in a business suit scratched desperately at his face with manicured nails too smooth to do any helpful damage, until with an almost amusing *pop* his right eye shot from its socket and dangled like an obscene conker from the optic nerve.

Michael couldn't help it; he let out a short bark of laughter. He wanted to show Claire, but she was gone, along with several others, back into the station. Running for daylight and safety no doubt. Michael wanted to follow them; everything in his mind wanted to get out, get up and away from the cruel and devouring beasts, but his body wouldn't work. Even now his legs were becoming rubbery, unable or unwilling to keep supporting his weight. He managed to slide himself across to one of the benches and sit down.

The crowd became noticeably quieter, namely because there were fewer people alive to scream. He saw Mr. Vinter's body standing awkwardly while three of the worms writhed in his neck stump, his head having been forced off.

The mayor danced and slapped at himself until his fingers burst and he found that both of his hands now ended in five wriggling beasts. He started to laugh hysterically and then began smashing his face repeatedly into the platform. At last Michael found he could have some sympathy for him.

Only now, as everyone else was either dead or dying, did Michael realize that not one of the worms had come near him.

He found he was in a clear space where the bodies of the poor, doomed souls that had descended into this hell had never fallen; perhaps guided by the white monstrosities that had burrowed into them.

With a burst of gore as the last woman alive ceased screaming, the burrowing worms exited their temporary homes and began to flow up the stairs, chasing those who had tried to escape, including Claire.

Michael knew he should be worried for her, should want to save her, but found he couldn't care less what happened to her. Instead, he was transfixed by the sight of the large worm that still lay on the tracks.

He could tell that the keening he'd heard earlier was coming from the beast, and yet now it was soothing to him, a comforting song like the lullabies his mother had sung to him as a baby.

From up the stairs he heard the screams of the people who hadn't outrun the wave of Azmarti which had followed them. As he watched the giant Azmarti, the shape of a man began to form on its side. It pushed and bulged until a perfect replica of Mr. Vinter was suspended upon the creature's skin.

"Do you remember?" The skin-Vinter asked. "We have called you for so long. Do you remember?"

Michael tried to shake his head but found there was nothing he could do except twitch the upper half of his body.

"You should, but you were taken so young. You will remember, I will sing and you will remember."

The skin-Vinter was reabsorbed into the Azmarti and the soft keening began again.

This time Michael could make out the melodies, the hundreds of notes that human ears could not detect.

The sound flowed through him like an orgasm…and then he remembered.

He was in a hole, and hands were reaching down for him as he screamed that he wanted to go back to his family.

He was in the hole because he was experimenting. He was practicing his changes; he was looking like a human boy.

He was… speaking? Shouting perhaps, and they had found him. They found the boy in the hole and pulled him out. Saved him, as they thought, not torn him away from his family. Locked him in that place; that orphanage high above the ground for a month.

Now he remembered; now he knew. He knew that through their careless kindness the humans had trapped him in this imperfect form, kept him from his family for so long.

That was over now, that was all over.

"I remember it all."

The Azmarti shook in joyous appreciation. "My Prince, my Prince!"

As Michael's brain slid down from his head to its natural position in his torso, he allowed his human mouth to form one last smile before it was gone.

He was home.

GREENHORNS

DAVID JAMES KEATON

The six new recruits staggered up the ramp, heads down, feet dragging, gear slung over slumped shoulders, mouths pulsing in exhaustion. The job hadn't started yet, but they were already sluggish from the night before, an informal orientation at the bar where the captain selected a new crew for the beginning of King Crab season.

Jake had competed for a spot on a crab boat before, playing games like Mumblety-Peg, Knifey-Spoony, or the dreaded Record Races, where you supposedly ran relays with vinyl LPs in the crack of your ass or whatever the hell else a deck boss thought up to make you dance for your dinner. But he'd never auditioned that hard.

All night long, the captain had them bounce from table to table to enlist in every possible drinking and eating competition known to man, stuffing bellies with vast amounts of burger, elk, bear, beer, cod, beer, and more beer. Jake vaguely remembered passing out after some arm-wrestling turned thumb-wrestling, where the girth of the victor's biceps were logged and recorded for posterity. They weren't his.

There was a lot of measuring going on that night, now that he thought about it. It reminded him of his first day of kindergarten, when his mom drew a crayon outline of him on the wall to show Jake how much he would grow.

The outline never got much bigger. And eventually his brother traced it with masking tape and X'd out his eyes to call it a crime scene.

"Hurry the fuck up, greenhorns," came a voice from the deck. It was weary, disengaged, seemingly uninterested in whether the owner was heard or not, kind of like someone telling their dog about their day.

Jake squinted through his headache and the rest of his shang-haied brothers to scan the length of his new home, and he couldn't help but smile when he saw the nuclear-waste logo on the bow.

It was the *Gone Fission*, the biggest in the fleet. It took its name from a baseless rumor that it was actually a converted mine-sweeper. He remembered the boat from the show *Crab Masters*, the most popular television program on the planet. His brother even had their original logo stitched on a baseball cap. A crab flipping the bird. It made even less sense than the one they'd painted on with their Hollywood money.

Greenhorns.

Jake always hated the terms. Swabby, nugget, squid, pollywog, fumblefuck. They all meant the same thing to him: "Half pay."

"Naw, *'greenhorn'* is the worst, man," a deckhand told him once. "You know what that shit means? It means a freshly slaughtered calf, so young the horns pop off in your hands like cucumbers."

Once aboard and one lap around the stern, the six of them were divided into pairs. The deck boss, Randy (just coffee breath and a beard peeking out of a rubber orange hood like the rest of them, maybe a bit more smiley), said they'd be working shifts two at a time to prove themselves.

Competition didn't end at the bar apparently.

"Two by two!" he barked. "And we'll pick the best two. Just like Noah's ark!"

"How is that like Noah's ark?" Jake couldn't help but ask.

"They took two of *everything*."

The beard twitched, happy someone took the bait.

"Not everything, boy! Read your fuckin' Bible. Unicorns didn't cut it. And guess what color that horn was?"

Before anyone could answer, another hooded beard was pulling them along and explaining they'd be on bait duty. He said it so quiet they barely heard him.

Then all six of them spent the rest of the night chopping up crabs. King Crabs. Jake couldn't believe it. As he popped the legs and cored the meat out of a Red Alaskan the size of a medium pizza, he looked around for an orange slicker to ask more questions. A crewman scurried by to drop off a hammer for the ice, and Jake tapped him on the shoulder with a broken claw in his hand.

"Hey, man. You don't use crabs to catch crabs, do you? This fucker's probably worth fifty bucks."

He didn't answer. No one did, not even his fellow recruits. Jake looked around at the other five hangovers, dutifully cracking shells. He was amazed at the number of greenhorns they'd gathered for one trip, confused how a crab boat, even one as big as the *Gone Fission*, could ever sustain that kind of crew. What were the numbers? Half of a half of a half of a share? The math made his nose bleed. After a while, a big man with an even bigger beard showed them their bunks, then peeled off two of the recruits to drag back out into the night and tie down the pots. Jake climbed into his bed and peeked out a portal, watching them throw the ropes off the dock and head out.

"I can't believe we're leaving on a Friday," the greenhorn below Jake said, pulling his hat over his eyes. "I thought that shit was bad luck."

"Bad luck for someone is good luck for someone else," Jake said, and closed his eyes.

He laid there, listening to their stomachs bubbling and still trying to process all the food and drink from their night in Dutch

Harbor. He waited for the first stomach to empty, and sure enough, it splashed against the wall about an hour later. Jake had been hung over before, but he'd never gotten seasick—ever. He slept like a baby and dreamed of his brother drawing lines around his body, as if he was shrinking.

The next morning, one team of greenhorns was gone, and they were down to four.

In the galley, as they carb-loaded piles of eggs and doughnuts and chugged all the coffee they could handle, someone finally asked what happened to this guy and that guy. But crew members were suiting up and moving through too fast to throw anything back at them but stock answers.

"Couldn't hack it."

"Weak."

"No heart."

"Pussies."

"We dropped them off."

"You dropped them off?" Jake asked. "Where exactly?"

"Dogtooth Island," someone muttered.

Jake couldn't believe it. For one thing, he'd never heard of any Dogtooth Island, and more importantly, one of the two newbies that was missing was Bobby 'Stack' Hillstack. Stack was the biggest guy in Dutch, biggest guy by far at the bar the night before. He looked strong as hell, and was tough as shit. Jake even remembered his and another captain from a different boat measuring Dutch's legs, they were so long.

"What does that even mean, 'No heart'?" Jake scoffed.

Out on deck, Jake helped shuffle the swaying metropolis of massive cages, or 'pots' as they called them. The pots were a wall of iron, pulling the aft end of the boat so low that the waves hit their faces as often as the hull. Jake noticed the pots themselves had changed a bit since he'd been on a crab boat. As he steered the crane over to the stack, he kicked up something like a dog door on the end of one pot and then let it drop back down. It could only swing one way. It was more like a raccoon trap than a dog door, he decided. *But dog door sounds better.*

"Is this even necessary?" Jake asked. "They ain't *that* smart are they? You just need a hole, don't you?"

"You're about five questions past your limit today, pal, but I'll tell you this," Randy the deck boss said. "There's been a lot of debate about that lately. How smart they're getting. Shit, to save metal, we considered just making 'em totally open-ended, like a tube."

"No joke?"

Randy pulled back his hood a bit to let in the sun and let out a smile. "No joke."

Jake pondered this as he kicked at a pile of fish against the base of the crane. He noticed tooth marks in a tuna, small half-circles the size of a football mouth guard running all along its side.

"Did they come up like that?" Jake asked. "What fish has a mouth like that? How the hell…"

There was a squelch of static on the intercom, and the deck boss flinched and looked around, beard twitching guiltily. His hood came back up fast.

"Skipper wants to see you. Go on up."

Jake shuddered. When a captain wanted to see you, up always felt like down.

But when he reached the wheelhouse, the captain didn't let him come all the way up. He made Jake stand on the stairs while he lectured him about asking stupid questions, tucking in his gloves, and talking when he should be listening. The usual crap Jake had heard all his life.

But even though he was on the stairs, Jake could still read the radar over the captain's shoulder. On the screen was a thermal outline of a huge red biomass. Excited, Jake pointed at it.

"Sir, aren't we steaming right past a ton of crab?"

The captain smiled, and Jake braced for an ass-chewing. The captain was a big, Kenny Rogers looking guy, and Jake figured this lulled his crew into a false sense of comfort. But the smile didn't slip. He did shake his head sadly though, clearly worried that nothing he'd said had impressed Jake in the slightest.

The captain reached back and flipped a switch. Suddenly, the red blob turned blue and the blue one turned red.

"*That's* where we're going." A big smile on his lips.

"Isn't it too warm for King Crab there? I thought we were headed for…"

"We'll be on them all tomorrow. Go get some sleep." The captain was positively giddy now.

Don't say it, Jake thought. *Don't say it.*

But of course the captain said it. "You'll need it."

That night in his cabin, Jake heard the crabs moving in the hold. Tapping, tapping, tapping. The echoes sounded big and heavy. Too heavy. He figured there must be a pile of them tangled up, moving as one. They didn't act normal when their claws were tied. That's all it was, he told himself. He'd seen it before.

Jake tried rolling on his side in the rotting bunk to get comfortable, using his tried-and-true tactic of focusing on a broken nail to keep the spins at bay. A couple of seasons back, he used to stare at a dog-eared Polaroid of his ex, Jennifer, until he lost it. Lost her, too. She didn't have a picture of him, but she did have a prized collection of cigarette lighters adorned with all the late captains' faces from the canceled show.

Then he sat up, for the first time noticing the slew of abandoned electronics all around him. There was a camera mounted in each corner of the room, plastic bags over half of them, wires hanging from everything, even pairs of corroded batteries rolling across the floor with the dip of each wave.

Remnants of the show, he realized, a bit awestruck. *Crab Masters*. The much-revered reality-based program that had turned out to be the last of its kind. It dominated television right up until the final season, when every boat except this one suspiciously capsized in the finale.

In a way, that turned out to be the final season for everything, now that Jake thought about it. Reality TV suddenly became a poor substitute for the sorry state of the world outside everyone's windows.

He kicked over a bag hanging by his feet and heard his bunkmate grunt as it spilled an intestinal coil of cable and rolls of masking tape across the metal floor. Someone had stenciled 'gaffer' across the side, a word that made Jake smile. The gaffer on a TV show and a fishing vessel were two very different creatures, but Jake thought they would probably compliment each other quite well. The gaff could stab a beast and haul it on board, while the gaffer taped up an outline of where it landed. Just like his brother.

Jake reached behind his head to discover his pillow was actually a backpack, complete with official *Crab Masters* stickers all over it. He dumped it out and found a tightly-wound stack of pastel-colored index cards detailing the scripted reality of the show. He pulled three cards from the bottom of the pile and read the final episode titles:

"Last Boat Standing," "Gone Fishing," and "Apocalypse Not!"

Jake smirked and put the bag back behind his head to be comfortable for his flashback. He remembered the theme song of the original crab show where it all started, the granddaddy of them all, some hair-metal power ballad that had given young men like Jake a new lease on life by pairing rock music with slow-motion shots of frosty breath and manual labor. He remembered waiting for that promo as a kid, right before the final 'crab count' of each episode. They stole the crab count from the other show, the fake one. Jake hated that promo, and his brother swore it was really saying, "Next time, U*ndeadliest Catch*," instead.

Always bad at math, Jake loved that crab count.

Later, as the waves and scratching and thumping in the hold rocked him to sleep, a red light blinked on, on the top of the camera at the foot of his and the other men's bunks, and tiny motors hummed as the electronic eyes bounced back and forth between the remaining faces.

The next day, Jake was off bait, and he finally had the opportunity to haul real gear with the crew. He was so excited to prove his worth that he didn't notice they were down to just two greenhorns now, Jake and Josh. Josh was a lanky kid who'd earned his ticket at the bar by keeping up pound for pound with the captain's Salted Cod Chowdown and amazingly *not* puking after the infamous Milk Gallon Challenge. Jake made the mistake of trying that challenge once.

Once was enough.

Josh was on the bailer, coiling the rope that was coming out of the roiling ocean, and Jake was at the rail, ready to swing the cage once it came up. There were hooded beards everywhere now, movements suddenly sharp in the flurry of activity. Jake noticed they all carried huge Bowie knives on their hips and wondered when he would get his.

"You'll get yours," Randy promised.

Then everyone froze.

The pot was coming up.

Jake could hear by the strain of the line that it was full. He could tell by the creak of the cage that it was packed with squirming cash money, a massive, wiggling, rich reward. He couldn't quite see through the crowd and spray, but the veteran eyes of a crew member to his right quickly assessed the bounty it held, and he turned to silently signal the wheelhouse. He held his arms high, then opened and closed both fists over and over: Five, five, five, five, five.

There was a rousing cheer from the crew, and Jake frowned. Only twenty King Crab? That's it? It didn't seem like much to get excited about. He was still doing the math when the cage finally swung over the boat and banged into the rail.

Then he saw what they'd really been hauling out of the Bering Sea, and his eyes went wide.

The crew parted to reveal the cage, and Jake forgot all the math he'd ever learned.

Flopping, fighting, squirming and elbowing for the door were dozens of human beings that had been pulled from the ocean. Black water emptied from cracked mouths and noses, foam trickled from pitted holes picked to the bone by sea life, and deviled-egg eyeballs squinted at a sun they'd long forgotten. Jake recognized them from TV, sci-fi and reality shows alike, of course. It didn't matter whether they were choking and coughing up water or just moaning like they were supposed to.

They were the living dead, and that's what they'd been fishing for all along.

In shock, Josh stopped coiling and looked to Jake for help. Jake gave him a *let's get to work* shrug, and grabbed a corner of the cage to steer it to a sorting table the size of a concert stage. Josh got ready to pop the dog door, and the crew was suddenly all around them and all business, their hands on the butts of their knives, their long-hooked gaffs thrust out like gladiators.

The gaffs, Jake laughed to himself, thinking about the roll of masking tape in the cabin. He remembered his brother taping his outline on the wall and wished he could climb inside it at that moment.

Then the door was open and Jake wasn't thinking about anything except how to steer the slippery, snapping abominations to the drain in the floor.

The crew herded them to the open manhole with the skills of Animal Control, popping the gray skin of their necks with the tips of their hooks, stabbing and scruffing them like puppies. First up and away from the mob, then stuffing down, down into the hole, leaving just a bit of meat and scalp behind. One gaff hooked in too deep behind a lolling head, and its vertebrae popped out and dangled like a busted gas cap. The corpse lost motor control and started a break-dance seizure at their feet, hands squeaking for a grip on a rubber raincoat.

"Fuck! That's a thousand bucks you just flushed, asshole!" Randy the deck boss yelled.

Whoa, whoa, whoa. A thousand bucks?

Jake tried calculating again, while the deck boss pulled his Bowie knife and started sawing under the dead man's chin. Tiny crabs and crustaceans rode the flood of pink water out of the corpse's throat as its moans turned to hisses, then gargles.

"Snuggle…gurgle…snort," it seemed to sing.

That's when Jake saw Josh slip on the deck.

Sliding with the roll of the boat, he tumbled into the writhing gauntlet of bodies the crew had corralled with their hooks, and suddenly every dead eye rolled toward him like marbles. The hooded beards pulled back and offered no help at all. Randy actually stood up straight, sheathing his knife and snapping it secure with a sigh.

Jake started to move in to help, and a crewman slapped him in the chest with a huge gloved hand.

"Don't move, kid."

Before Jake could protest, ten or so corpses fell on Josh to disassemble him like a piñata that had just hit the floor at a birthday party. Purple hands scratched until they found a tiny hole in Josh's raincoat, then they made it bigger. Soon, they found his mouth and made that bigger, too. They stretched it so wide that Jake was convinced they were going to turn Josh's head inside out, lips and jaw first, before anything ever broke. Josh screamed protests through it all, his tongue rolling back into the deep crater that used to be his face as his struggles began to waver. That's when the dead found the ripe melon of his stomach, and punched, pulled and dug until volcanoes of beer-foamed gore and big chunks of salted cod were spread out on the deck right next to everything else that had been gutted and used for bait.

Jesus Christ, Jake realized. *No wonder Josh won the eating contest. He was barely chewing.*

Jake watched in silence, up until one corpse punched deeply into Josh and a white bomb of milk exploded from his innards, proof of his victory at the Gallon Challenge, and painting the deck gleaming white.

At the time, Jake couldn't believe he'd kept all that milk down, and had even accused Josh of cheating. He'd read somewhere that drinking a gallon of milk was impossible.

And they were right, he thought wildly. *You adjust the time limit to the next day and everything comes up after all.*

He watched dead men with milk moustaches angling for a drink, thought about a billboard reading, "Got Dead?" Then he laughed and puked at the same time. First time he'd *ever* done that at sea.

Josh's tongue was pulled free, and the screaming stopped completely, and Jake couldn't believe tongues had always been that long and hidden inside people's heads.

Gaff indeed, Jake snickered inwardly, his sanity slipping. He remembered half a conversation he'd had with a recruit two days prior. *Now there's a third definition for that word. Meaning 'fuck up.'*

Once they'd eaten, the mewling undead crowd was considerably slower, and Jake stood back to watch the crew run them into the hold like cattle. When they were all inside, Jake carefully crept over to the hole and looked down, watching them mill around in the water-filled hold and making no attempt to surface. Sluggish with their bellies full and the weight of their own hazy stew, they bumped lazily into the walls, hands probing for seams and bolts, feeling for exits, bouncing around in drunken circles like old people doing water aerobics. The dead moved slow enough *without* being submerged, and Jake found that watching them down there was as soothing. He was hypnotized.

He finally snapped out of it when the crew upended what was left of Josh into the hole, and the black water below turned blacker as the underwater dance sped up along with Jake's brain.

He grabbed Randy by the collar, but didn't even get his question out.

"It's worth it, kid," Randy said. "It's hard work, but it's fuckin' worth it."

"Nothing's worth this," Jake snarled.

"Bullshit. If we didn't do it, someone else would."

"But how did they get down there? I mean, how are they…"

"You remember when all that shit went down? Back when they were, you know, everywhere?"

"No," Jake said sarcastically. "I missed all that while I was living under a rock. Tell me all about it, will you please?"

Randy ignored Jake's snide remarks and said, "Well, we were fucked. Then suddenly we weren't. Didn't you wonder why?"

"Yeah, I mean, it was the Army. They took care of it," Jake said.

"Are you fucking kidding? There ain't enough bullets in the world for all the dead. Ain't you ever heard the story of the Marching Chinese?"

"Yeah, but…"

"But nothing. They're all down there. Down too far for anyone to cash in except us professionals. To the military, they're worth ten times as much as the biggest King Crab. Sometimes more."

"Shit, that's almost worth as much as a real person," Jake said, still sarcastic.

"Almost," the captain's voice came from behind him.

"They walk. It's as simple as that," the captain explained. "That's the one thing they do. All day, even when it rains. And if you walk long enough on this planet, you're gonna hit fuckin' water. So that's where they all went. They cover the ocean floors like a living carpet. Thicker than Tanners, thicker than Opies in the off-season."

"And they follow warm currents, don't they?"

"Yep. Which is good for them. Keeps them away from the crab, mostly. But you can see by their faces that the critters down there will eventually pick 'em away to nothing someday. But for now, they'll just keep walking, walking where it's warm."

Suddenly, Randy was on Jake's other shoulder with a heavy hand squeezing so affectionately that Jake thought it was squeezing his lungs. He held his breath until it stopped.

"If you want to make good money, kid, consider staying with us," the deck boss said.

Jake considered it so hard his nose began bleeding. They were making sense.

"Full share?" he asked.

They nodded. Then someone slapped a Viking helmet on Jake's head with two horns painted bright green.

"It ain't easy, but you made it!" the captain shouted, all teeth. "We needed a bait boy. Just one. And you're it, goddamn it."

Then they yanked off the Viking helmet and replaced it with a baseball cap. Jake pulled it off to get a good look. Across the brim, it read, **Gone Fission, Mom!**

He shook his head, almost sniffling at the gravity of the ceremony. He'd always wanted one. He couldn't lie.

"I always wanted one," he said.

There were pats on the back, more affectionate squeezes, less creepy than before.

"I'll do it," Jake announced, even with the horrible sounds coming from below his feet.

He slept well that night, like all men do after hard work for good money.

The next day, Jake drank black coffee with the crew and couldn't believe he hadn't dreamed of his brother.

He looked around. He was the last of the greenhorns, of course. Five young men gone. He didn't dwell on this. He'd never been good at math.

But today, they treated him different. Not cruel, like at the bar, but not like one of the crew either; it was with a crushing indifference that felt worse.

He'd watched every episode of the show, both shows, even the fake one, long before the world turned to shit, so he assumed this was just the typical shunning of a new crew member—a hazing.

"Come on, Jake," someone slapped him on the back. "Get the fuck out there. You're on bait."

Out in the brutal wind, Jake checked the bin, but only saw a pile of snow and ice.

"What bait?" he asked, but there was suddenly no one around to answer.

He walked around the deck to find the deck boss alone, standing near a cage that was primed to go over the rail.

"Are we out of crab already?" Randy asked without looking at Jake. "Check the hook in the pot. There might still be enough for one more soak."

Jake opened the dog door and leaned in to check the hook. There was a chunk of something red hanging, and he tugged to see if it was enough to set the trap.

His nostrils flared in alarm as he took a closer look. It certainly wasn't crab, but he thought it might be a piece of a *skate* fish. 'Hoped' was more like it.

He hopped right up until he saw the fingers.

He felt a work boot kick him hard in his spine and he went forward, hitting his head on the back end of the cage. The door slammed closed and he found himself facedown in the metal cage.

Three of the crew stomped on the bottom of the dog door to trap him inside, then, as a final insult, a gloved hand reached in to snatch the baseball cap off his head.

"Motherfucker," Jake hissed, his teeth clenched so hard that a molar fractured. The crane started to whine, and he gripped the bars to get ready for his ride.

The bearded men watched him go over the rail in silence, and down he went. Down to the bottom, his hatred keeping him warm.

Jake's brother told him once that you could only live three minutes in water so close to the North Pole, but Jake discovered it was more like nine when you were as angry as he was.

He made it all the way to the bottom.

It was dark, but he could see. He saw more of them down there than he ever suspected. Thousands, millions even, a lurching parade of green skin, pale hands, and teeth, all eyes locking on him, as tattered arms spiraled in toward his cell like the first swirl of soup in a bowl.

Pushing through the door, they surged into the cage with him, finding the warmth of his body quickly, cracking his bones easily, as if they were green, young vegetables, biting over and over and finding all the holes in his body where it was the warmest.

Then they began to make their own holes. Their fingers and tongues wormed into these new spaces like the slick, hairless heads of buzzards.

And right before the red of his anger turned to black, Jake saw one of them lift the dog door and hold it high above its head to let the rest of them in as efficient as any crew.

They knew what to do.

They knew the drill.

They knew where they were going.

With the last of his strength, Jake tried to protect his mouth and let them ruin the rest.

He hoped he had some teeth left when the crew hauled him back up.

ABOUT THE WRITERS

David Bernstein is a member of the HWA, and is the author of over 50 published short stories. Some of his work appears, or will be appearing in, "Best New Werewolf Tales from Books of the Dead Press," "Big Foot Among Us" from Coscom Entertainment, and "Don't Blink" from Cruentus Libri Press. He is currently working on his fourth novel, with the first three being looked at by publishers. He lives in the NYC, and hates car horns. You can visit him at davidbernsteinauthor.blogspot.com and email him at dbern77@hotmail.com

Vincenzo Bilof is an educator from Detroit, Michigan. Publication credits include six horror stories published with SNM Magazine in 2011, with appearances in three anthologies, including: "Book of the Dead 6" (Living Dead Press), "Zombie Buffet" and "Dead Christmas" (Open Casket Press). Poetry credits include Nuvein Magazine, The Detroiter, SNM Magazine, and Miller's Pond. He is currently finishing the post-apocalyptic novel, "Under a Red Sun."

Nickolas Cook lives in the beautiful Southwestern desert with his wife and four pugs. His short stories, articles and reviews have appeared in many and varied print and online sources Editor-In-Chief: The Black Glove Magazine (http://the-black-glove.blogspot.com/), free monthly horror culture and entertainment e-zine. Novels: THE BLACK BEAST OF ALGERNON WOOD (Dailey Swan Press) BALEFUL EYE (Stonegarden.net Publishing) ALICE IN ZOMBIELAND (Sourcebooks) Short story collections: 'ROUND MIDNIGHT AND OTHER TALES OF LOST SOULS (Damnation Books). Contact: Email: Nickolasecook@aol.com and he's on Facebook

Anthony Giangregorio is the editor of the book you now hold and the author of 38 novels, almost all of them about zombies, and has edited over 40 anthologies and books.

His work has appeared in Dead Science by Coscomentertainment, Dead Worlds: Undead Stories Volumes 1-7, and Wolves of War by Library of the Living Dead Press. He also has stories in End of Days: An Apocalyptic Anthology Vol. 1-5, the Book of the Dead series Vol. 1-6 by LDP, Zombie Zoology by Severed Press, and two anthologies with Pill Hill Press. He is also the creator of the popular action/zombie series titled Deadwater and his action/ horror novel Dead Rage is being optioned for a movie.

Check out his website at www.undeadpress.com and on Facebook.

Sarah E. Glenn a product of the suburbs, has a B.S. in Journalism, which is redundant if you think about it. By day, she works for the University of Kentucky. By night, she battles banality by writing weird stories. Several have appeared in mystery and paranormal anthologies, including G.W. Thomas' "Ghostbreakers" series, Futures Mysterious Anthology Magazine, and Fish Tales: The Guppy Anthology. All This and Family, Too, a vampire comedy, is her first novel.

Aaron Gudmunson was born in Belize while his parents volunteered for the Peace Corps. He lives and writes in the Chicago area. He has had fiction and essays published in numerous outlets including Apex Horror and Science Fiction, Doorways Magazine, Withersin, and Theatre of Decay. He has been writing since able to hold a pen.

Samuel J. Guss lives in Birmingham, AL with his wife, kids, dogs and cats and works primarily as a photographer. His first short story "Believe" was published by Living Dead Press in 2009. A non-fiction writer for almost three decades, he has a passion for apocalyptic fiction and speculative fiction in general. Sam maintains a blog at http://samuelguss.com

Elise Hattersley lives in England and writes full-time. In a creative capacity, she focuses primarily on horror and science-fiction, and she is currently working on "World's Collider," an alt-history shared-world anthology centered on the Large Hadron Collider and "Empire of London," an alt-history steampunk anthology situated in the UK. A short story by Elise, "A Jury of Your Peers," was published in Hirst Books' "Showcase" in late 2010. In her spare times, she reads and reviews books for Bookgeeks.co.uk.

Matt Kurtz loves all things horror. His twisted tales can be found in anthologies from Pill Hill Press, Open Casket Press, Evil Jester Press, Blood Bound Books, Comet Press and "Necrotic Tissue" Magazine.

David James Keaton's fiction has recently appeared in "Needle, Crime Factory," and "Pulp Modern," among others, as well as in horror anthologies such as The Death Panel, Deadcore, and "Dark Highlands." His story about killing coaches in "Plots With Guns #10" was named a Notable Story of 2010 by "storySouth," He's also the editor of "Flywheel Magazine" and spent five long years of his life close-captioning reality television, mostly shows where creatures are pulled reluctantly from the sea.

Mark M. Johnson is a horror and sci/fi fanatic, known on-line as, The Black Empty. Amongst other things he'd rather leave to your imagination, he enjoys writing as a hobby. His short fiction has appeared in many anthologies found on his Amazon.com author's page. He currently resides in Warren MI with his wife Cindy, one high school graduate son, one crazy dog, two cats, and a ferret.

Kevin Lewis' short stories have been published in Blood Moon Rising Magazine, MicroHorror, Sonor4 Science Fiction and Horror Ezine, and Open Casket Press. A graduate of Emerson College, Kevin works for Hachette Book Group. He is a member of New England Horror Writers (NEHW) and resides in Massachusetts.

Christopher Nadeau is the author of "Dreamers at Infinity's Core" through COM Publishing as well as over a dozen published short stories in such august publications as The Horror Zine, Sci-Fi Short Story Magazine, Ghostlight Magazine and many anthologies. He collaborated on two "machinima" films with UK animator Celestial Elf called "The Gift," and "The Deerhunter's Tale," both on YouTube. His novel "Echoes of Infinity's Core" is slated for a 2011 release. An active member of the Great Lakes Association of Horror Writers, Chris Resides in Southeastern Michigan.

Mark Rivett grew up in Frankenmuth Michigan— home of the world's largest Christmas store. At the age of eighteen, he moved to Pennsylvania to pursue several degrees in art and technology. His professional career has included four years as a multimedia instructor, six years as a web developer, and he currently works as an interface designer in downtown Pittsburgh. Mark is fascinated by the macabre and his writing is inspired by the horror and suspense genre. In addition to writing, he paints, builds models, plays poker, and continues to further his education.

Mike Shea is a published poet and freelance writer. He lives in Massachusetts with his wife and two cats.

Robert Spalding has written for a few places in his time; horror for the small press site "Whispers of Wickedness," comics for the crew at "FutureQuake Press," and recently a story for "The Nautilus Engine." He has a flash fiction piece appearing in the anthology "Out of Place, Out of Time" and regularly posts flash fiction and other short stories for free on his blog: robspalding.wordpress.com

Jonathan Templar lives in Cheshire, England. His recent published and soon to be published work includes short stories in Open Casket Press's collection "Dead Christmas" ('Secret Santa'), the shared world anthology "World's Collider" ('Basher'), Smart Rhino's collection "Zippered Flesh" ('Marvin's Angry Angel'), and in Wicked East Press' "Bedtime Stories for Girls," but nobody believes him when he mentions that.
Contact him at www. jonathantemplar.com

NEW HORROR FICTION FROM OPEN CASKET PRESS!

HEADSHOTS ONLY: A ZOMBIE ANTHOLOGY
Edited by Anthony Giangregorio

The walking dead cannot be stopped!
They never tire, never give up, and will come for you again and again!
Only one thing can put them down for good!
Grab your gun, take aim, and make sure it's a head shot!
One to the brain pan is the only way to save yourself from certain death!
So keep your weapon loaded, stay sharp, and remember…*Headshots Only!*

HOLLOW POINT: A ZOMBIE NOVEL
By Mark Christopher

Something horrible is happening in the small, bayou town of Cypress Pass. The dead are walking.
Caught in the middle of the undead uprising is Sheriff John Boudreaux; a retired Army Ranger, who still struggles daily with the emotional and physical pain of his time in the Iraq war.
Now he finds himself fighting an enemy that cannot be stopped, an enemy that shows no fear and wants nothing more than to eat his flesh. He's tasked with a mission that will define his life. He must save his friends and fight off the living dead that are overrunning his town. But how do you kill what is already dead?

CREATURE FEATURE: A MONSTER ANTHOLOGY
Edited by Anthony Giangregorio

Giant squirrels, massive zombies, killer trees and marauding severed heads are just a few of the twisted tales of creatures you will find inside this anthology.
So let your imagination free and embrace what isn't real.
For perhaps monsters are real, and it is you that does not truly exist.

ZOMBIE BUFFET: AN UNDEAD ANTHOLOGY
Edited by Anthony Giangregorio

If you're hungry for zombie stories, look no further than this anthology.
There's enough rotting meat to satisfy even the most discerning connoisseur, and our all-you-can-eat buffet is sure to please.
Rotting intestines, severed heads and exploding spleens are just some of the courses waiting for you within this book of undead mastication.
So grab a knife and fork, slap on a napkin, 'cause you're gonna get dirty, and prepare yourself for the Zombie Buffet.
A zombie feast of epic proportions.

DEAD CHRISTMAS: A ZOMBIE ANTHOLOGY
Edited by Anthony Giangregorio

Share the most special time of the year with someone you love, or better yet, with an animated corpse!
The living dead love Christmas. Whether they're hanging their entrails like garland, using severed heads like stockings, or hanging body parts like ornaments, even zombies enjoy the most wonderful time of the year.
Santa Claus isn't immune to the walking dead, either.
Zombie elves, killer reindeer and undead hordes, all seek to share in the joy of the holiday . . . and tear Santa apart and feed on his flesh.
So when you grab last year's fruitcake to re-gift to Aunt Martha, just make sure to bring a shotgun, too. Because for all you know, your aunt has turned into an undead flesh-eater, and if the shotgun won't kill her, the fruitcake most assuredly will.

RATS
By Anthony Giangregorio

Killer black rats the size of dogs are roaming the streets and no one is aware of their existence.
Wild dogs, the authorities warn. Stay indoors and all will be fine.
Domenic Salvatore soon finds himself in the middle of a cover-up of epic proportions; where no one will believe the truth.
And why would they? After all, he's just a kid.
What no one knows is that the rats have taken on a taste for human meat, a particular kind of meat actually…young flesh…the flesh of children.
As the kids are hunted one by one, killed and dragged off into the night to be devoured, Domenic realizes that it's only a matter of time before he's next.
Something evil stalks the town of Wakefield, Mass…and it's hungry.

CLAN OF THE BIGFOOT

ANTHONY GIANGREGORIO

ZOMBIES, MONSTERS, CREATURES OF THE NIGHT
OPEN CASKET PRESS
OPEN CASKET PRESS.COM
THE NEW NAME IN HORROR

THE PLACE TO GO FOR ZOMBIE AND APOCALYPTIC FICTION

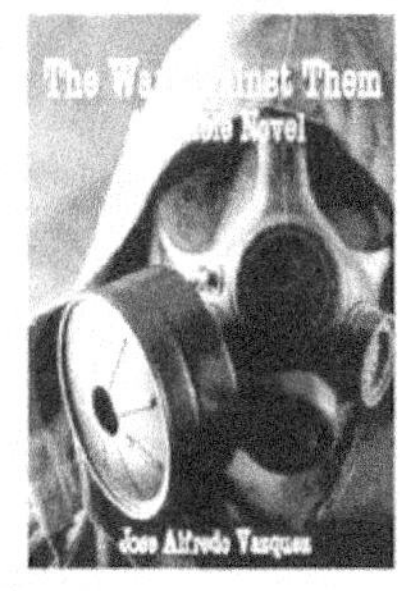

LIVING DEAD PRESS

WHERE THE DEAD WALK

www.livingdeadpress.com

CHECK US OUT ON FACEBOOK
GNOMBIES
Re-animated for your displeasure!!
Guaranteed undead!!
WWW.THEGNOMBIES.COM

www.ingramcontent.com/pod-product-compliance
Lightning Source LLC
Chambersburg PA
CBHW070452120726
47910CB00003B/1018